RESISTANCE

Kayla Howarth

DEDICATION

For Troy. I'm glad I chose you as my first husband.

Thanks for believing in me.

I may have to keep you.

ACKNOWLEDGMENTS

Sarah. I still love you, but I also still hate your red pen.

My betas, Theresa and Erin. It means a lot to have other authors comment and encourage me through this process, and I know that my writing is better because of you.

To the many friends and family who have supported me throughout this whole adventure, especially those of you who read this book and gave me feedback along the way: Mum, Aroha, Hannah, Lisa-maree, Kristen, Anna, Danielle, Carlye, Lana, Danii, Tina, you're all awesome.

To my husband—just for being you (although, would it kill you to wash a dish every now and then?).

And finally to Ben. I acknowledge that Ben is a butthead.

PRAISE FOR THE INSTITUE SERIES

Thanks for the great ride. I loved every minute of this series. Looking forward to reading more of this author's work. 5 out of 5 shiny stars!—Michelle Bryan, author of Strain of Resistance and The New Bloods Trilogy.

If you haven't read the series yet, I strongly suggest you start. The author is very talented, and I look forward to her future works—Kimberly Readnour, author of The Mystical Encounters Series.

Allira is a strong, courageous girl that anyone can look up to. I was drawn into the original storyline, realistic characters, and suspenseful plot—Bethany Wicker, author of the Aluna Series.

Love, love, love this series!!! It is so awesome to read about all the different super abilities and how they all work together. Definitely one of my favorite set of books I've ever read!—Amazon Customer.

CHAPTER ONE

"Today's the big day," Drew says excitedly, standing at the entrance to my bedroom and holding a cup of coffee.

"Yeah, it is," I mutter.

Living with my ex-boyfriend was weird in the beginning, but I've become accustomed to having him wake me each day in a similar manner. He brings me a cup of coffee, and I don't berate him. It seems to work. I'm still getting used to pretending to be married to him, though.

I sit up in bed, reaching for the coffee.

"It's your first arrest. You should be excited," he says, walking towards me to pass me the cup.

I can't help but roll my eyes. How he finds arresting people—for a defect that he also has—exciting is beyond me. I do it because I have to, not because I want to.

We've been investigating our target, a sixteen-year-old girl named Licia, for three months. We lost her and her parents when we started in Rockford, but it only took us a few weeks to track the Johns family to the next town over. They weren't exactly the most resourceful when it came to fleeing.

I got a job as a waitress where Licia works after school and on weekends as a way of getting close to her. I fought with Drew about me being the one to take point on the investigation, but as he so eloquently put it: becoming friends with her would be much less hurtful than him hitting on her, ultimately breaking her heart when she is arrested. That's a scenario I'm all too familiar with; it's how he was able to arrest me almost six months ago.

It's amazing that it has only been six months. I've been on the outside for the same amount of time as I was imprisoned by the Institute, but I feel as if I've lived three lifetimes since being arrested. The naïve schoolgirl I once was is long gone. No longer do I trust so easily, nor will I ever again. As it turns out, Drew isn't the only one I shouldn't have trusted.

"We've got time for a run, if you're up for it?" Drew asks.

"Sounds good," I say as I reach the bottom of my coffee cup, disappointed there's nothing left.

Drew leaves as I drag myself out of bed. I like running with Drew, but I'll never admit that to him. He's so competitive that it always pushes me hard. I don't even care that he always wins.

I get dressed, lace up my shoes, and grab my hooded jacket on the way out. It's spring but the breeze still has bite to it. My face stings as it hits the fresh air outside. I love the feeling of just setting out on our own and not having to think about suspects, leads, or blowing our cover. We only have one thing to focus on, and that's the sound of our feet beating against the pavement. We run five kilometres from our house down to the harbour and then turn back. By the time I reach the harbour, my mind is clear, and I feel refreshed and ready for the day. I can do this.

The sun warms my back while the chilling breeze cools my front. My lungs sting as I start to tire, and I feel as if I'm gasping for air. I lick my cracked lips, and my dry, scratchy throat craves water. But I push myself to keep going, breathing heavier and heavier with each footstep. I push through the pain. I want to defeat it.

I get an extra energy boost when we're almost home, and I actually think I might beat Drew for once. He nudges me out of the way with his elbow when I try to cut him off. I stick my foot in front of his, tripping him. He grabs my ankle as he falls, and we both crash to the grass on the lawn in front of our house. That isn't going to stop me though. Scrambling to my hands and knees, I crawl towards the front door. I'm going to win. He crawls after me and drags me backwards by my leg. Laughter escapes my throat as I try to grab onto the grass, but it's no use, and I just keep grabbing fistfuls of it.

"I was beginning to worry about you two," a stern voice says. Startled, we look up at our house to find out our fun has been interrupted by Lynch. "I thought I was going to have to track you. Hurry up and get inside. We have to get started."

Just like that, my feelings of calm and readiness turn to panic and worry. No—this is what I've been training for. This is what I have to do to protect my brother, Shilah. I can do it. This has been my mantra for at least three months, whenever doubt starts to cloud my thoughts. When that hasn't worked,

I've focussed on knowing that once Licia is arrested, I get to go back to the Institute and see my brother again. I *can* do this.

After a quick shower, I get dressed into my waitress uniform—tight black pants and a black collared shirt. I don't know how I'm going to make an arrest in this; it's not the most flexible of materials and constricts my movements. Drew is at the dining table eating breakfast when I walk into the kitchen to get another cup of coffee.

"Where's Lynch?" I ask.

"She went to meet up with the others in the arrest team. I told her we'd be right behind her so you better drink up, fast."

"I'm surprised to see her here. I didn't realise she was an agent. I didn't even think she was Defective."

Drew looks up at me from his plate. "She's not Defective. She's one of the few normal agents. You didn't think every agent was Defective, did you?"

"Well, yeah, I kind of did."

"Brookfield wouldn't allow a Defective person in such a high position. All of our supervisors, commanding officers like Lynch, they're all normals, but none of them work in the field. Lynch is in charge of arrests—it's really the only action she sees."

"So she was there for my arrest?"

Drew ignores my question. "You know what you have to do today, yeah?"

I sigh. "Yes, I know what to do. Get Licia out of the restaurant where you and the rest of the team will be waiting."

"Here, take this," he says, passing me a knife. "You don't have anything to protect you other than your hand-to-hand combat training. I've taken that class. I know how thorough they are. Or aren't, I should say."

It's true, the self-defence classes they run at the Institute are pretty poor. I spent most of my time trying to avoid getting beaten by a fifteen-year-old girl—my assigned sparring partner. I was just lucky to have met Chad, a fellow agent-in-training. He showed me how to *really* defend myself.

Come to think of it, none of the classes I took at the Institute helped me prepare for living as an agent in the real world. I guess they run the classes to boost everyone's confidence, make them feel important. But I know now. We're not important. We're expendable.

I take the knife and place it in the back pocket of my pants. I hope I remember it's there. I can just see myself sitting down and accidentally stabbing myself in the butt. I realise that's probably physically impossible, but if anyone could manage it, it would be me.

We walk to our rendezvous point, a van parked a few streets away from the restaurant where Licia and I work. Besides Lynch, Eugene's here and so is a guy with glasses who I don't know. Eugene is the guy Chad and I referred to as Jack during our time at the Institute because of how much of a jackass he is. I don't know the guy with the glasses, but I recognise him from my first interrogation and my field test. There are also two others I haven't met before, a small-built woman with long black hair that's braided down her back and a towering, lanky man with slightly greying hair. The five of them are wearing black uniforms with protective vests.

"Okay, let's get started," Lynch says. "Drew and Allira, you already know Eugene and Leo," she says, pointing to Jack and the guy with the glasses. "And this is Bek and Costello." We nod hello to each other, but no words are spoken. "So, are we ready?" The peppiness in her voice is meant to motivate us, I'm guessing. No one actually answers her, but she continues to talk anyway. "Allira, it's your job to get our target out the back. That's where we'll take her out. Eugene, Drew, and Leo, you'll approach from the front. Bek and I will each take a side. Costello will remain with the van, ready for us when we get her."

I'm fitted with a microphone, which transmits audio to the team's earpieces, so they'll be able to hear when I've managed to get Licia outside. Drew starts gearing up, putting on a protective vest and arming himself with a gun, matching the others. I don't get a gun or a vest as I'm going to lure Licia out. I suddenly wish Chad was here with me so I could borrow his protective force field ability if this arrest goes awry.

Thanks to months of training with Chad in between the classes the Institute ran, I've gotten a good hold on my abilities—both of them. When I touch Drew, I am able to amplify his ability, almost to the point of him becoming a Telepath instead of an Empath. He can't hear word for word, but he can pick up on key words and work from that. I'm able to borrow that power too, so I can hear what Drew hears and what he thinks. The good thing about that is: Drew doesn't know that I'm able to borrow his ability, and, thanks to Chad,

I'm able to block Drew from listening in on me.

"You'll be fine," Drew says, putting his arm around my shoulders. I pull away from him, annoyed. Even though I have learnt to keep most of my feelings from him, he can still pick up on some things—like right now, he can sense I'm freaking out about this arrest.

I'm worried about how it will go, I'm worried about it failing, but I think I'm more worried about it being successful. Forcing Licia to endure the kind of torture I experienced when I was arrested is not something I want for her. She's a nice girl, and I would actually consider her a friend. At least we know what Licia can do, so maybe it won't be as bad for her as it was for me when I was first arrested.

Discovering her ability was kind of a fluke. I was tailing her home one day after spending weeks profiling her actions, and she disappeared into thin air. At first, I thought she could teleport or something, but according to my Institute training, her personality didn't match that kind of profile. I spent the next few days doing the same thing, just following her and watching from afar. I got pretty good at getting close to her without her being aware of me.

Then came the day Drew almost blew his cover. I was at work with Licia, and he was supposed to be at her house gathering evidence. He burst through the restaurant entrance looking as if he'd just run a marathon.

"Hi sweetheart," he said in between gasping breaths.

"What's wrong?" I asked, getting him a glass of water.

"Problem. At the house," he replied vaguely.

"At your house?" Licia asked.

He nodded subtly but gave me a look that said that's not what he meant.

I turned to Licia. "Cover for me?"

"Of course."

Drew dragged me outside, and suddenly we were running. Running away from the direction of our house and towards Licia's. Drew didn't slow down until we got to her street.

"Stay low," he instructed.

We scurried our way to her living room window, and there, asleep on the couch, was Licia.

"What the f—"

"She can project a secondary physical form of herself," Drew whispered. "The girl at the restaurant isn't the real her. I'm just lucky I got out of there before she woke up."

"You were inside? You didn't check the place out first before breaking in?" I hissed.

"It's not the first time I've screwed up on an investigation," he said, raising an eyebrow at me, probably referring to my arrest. "But that doesn't matter. I got out, and she didn't wake up. It's okay."

The exertion from running and the adrenaline from finding out Drew was nearly discovered slowly subsided, and I could finally let the revelation about her ability sink in.

I couldn't think of anything else to say other than "Holy

crap."

Every day from then on, while I was at work with her, Drew would scope out her house. He discovered she was only projecting to and from work on specific days. She could clearly do it well; she could spend hours, whole shifts, in her projected state. She had her limits though, and after logging her activity for almost three weeks, we concluded she was unable to do it on the days she was rostered for a full eight-hour shift. That's how we were able to orchestrate this arrest date, knowing she would be here herself and not her projection.

The arrest team has checked their equipment and the plan twice already, but Lynch still hasn't given us the green light. It's getting close to lunchtime, and I can't stand this waiting around anymore. I've stretched out my legs and back so much, I'm surprised I'm not taller by now.

"Okay, let's get this over with," I say, trying to hurry things along, ignoring Lynch's command chain. Before hearing her response, I walk in the direction of the restaurant. Fear and nerves course through me.

You will get to see Shilah, you will get to see Shilah, I keep telling myself.

I reach the entrance to the restaurant, and I pause for a moment, taking a deep breath before opening the door. The nerves inside me are building, making their way from my stomach and into my throat, trying to find an escape. My heart tries to fight Leo, who is just outside the restaurant, forcing it to maintain a slow rate. All it wants to do is thunder in my chest, but he's forcing me to calm down. That's his ability—

controlling peoples' heart rates. He did it to me while they were interrogating me. I also borrowed his ability to help me pass the field test before I became an agent.

I walk into the restaurant filled with anticipation and nerves. I make my way into the kitchen, ready to lure Licia out the back of the restaurant.

"Well, this is a little anti-climactic," I say when I realise Licia is nowhere to be found. One of the chefs is near the walk-in fridge. Maybe she knows where she is. "Hey, Jo, have you seen Licia?" I ask casually.

"She's called in sick. Her and one of the dishies. You're going to have a pretty busy shift," Jo scoffs, clearly pissed that we're understaffed.

She's going to be even angrier in a minute, when I tell her I can't stay either. I would feel bad, but it's not like this is my actual job or that I even get paid. As a field agent, we aren't allowed to keep the money we earn. Everything we need is provided, and any wages earned from undercover jobs goes straight to the Institute. I guess they figure if we're given the chance to financially support ourselves, we might be inclined to try to leave. Just another way to make sure we don't try to escape.

I don't know how to tell Jo I'm going to have to leave, too. Should I start faking a coughing fit? Tell her I'm leaving? Should I just walk out?

"Hey, honey," Drew's voice comes from behind me. I still shudder at the notion that we're married—according to everyone in this town anyway. That was the brilliant cover story our bosses at the Institute came up with. I turn to see

Drew rushing towards me without his protective gear, seeming panicked. "There's been a horrible accident. You need to come to the hospital with me, right now. It's your father."

Dad? My eyes widen in a brief moment of fear, before narrowing in confusion. That can't be true; we don't know where Dad is. The Institute lost track of him after I was arrested and ... Oh. Duh, this is my out. Drew heard Licia isn't here in his earpiece and is giving me an excuse to leave. It's a horrible excuse, usually one that's saved for terrible dates. I remember having to do it for my friend Ebbodine—a couple of times, actually.

"I'm so sorry, Jo, I have to leave," I say, matching Drew's panicked tone. We don't wait for Jo to respond before we leave the restaurant and head back to where we met up with the team a few streets over.

"You're welcome," Drew says.

"I'm sorry, am I meant to thank you? I was about to tell her I was sick so I could leave. I didn't need you."

"Oh, please, you and I both know you would've stayed out of guilt from leaving them understaffed. You're too nice."

"I am not." He's actually probably right, but I'm not going to admit that and give him the satisfaction.

We get back to Costello and the van and climb in the back. "So, I'm guessing the arrest didn't go well then?" Costello asks as he starts up the engine.

"No, it didn't go at all," Lynch replies, crossing her arms over her chest.

"So that's it?" I ask. "What do we do now?"

"We'll have to get her from her home," Lynch answers. "The same plan will work. You can use some story about hearing she was sick and you wanted to see if she was all right."

I try to protest, but Drew beats me to it. "You want to send in an unarmed, unprotected newbie, by herself? No. I won't allow that—it's too dangerous."

I really want to yell at him for standing up for me—I don't *need* him to do that—I can do it myself. But I agree with him, and if I dispute that, I may end up unwittingly volunteering to go in.

"Well, you aren't the one in charge, are you, Jacobs? She'll be fine. It's not like the target has an aggressive ability," Lynch replies.

"There has to be another way," Drew argues.

"We can take them by surprise," Bek chimes in. "We surround the house, Eugene can break down the front door, forcing the target and her parents to take the only escape route out the back where the rest of us will be waiting."

Lynch thinks about it for a moment. "Okay. Leo, Allira, and Eugene, you take the front, the rest of us will wait out the back. Allira, we can give you a protection vest, but you haven't had any special weapons training, so we can't give you a gun. You'll just have to stay behind Leo and follow his lead."

I'm fitted into a vest as we pull up just short of Licia's street.

This all seems to be happening so fast. *Why do I even have to go in at all?*

"Are we ready?" Costello asks. Lynch looks to all of us and takes our silence as agreement.

"Let's do this," she replies. "Move silently and move quickly."

The van takes off again slowly and continues to creep along the street until coming to a stop in front of Licia's neighbour's house. We file out, and Lynch, Bek, and Drew run swiftly with light footing; it's almost elegant to watch. They disappear around the back of the house while Jack, Leo, and I cautiously approach the stoop to the front porch.

Jack takes out the door with one swift kick. He raises his gun and checks the first room, before moving onto the second, as Leo and I enter and double-check the first room. It's awkward; I'm pushed up against his back, kind of using him as a human shield. I hope he doesn't know that's my intention.

Jack clears the living room and then moves onto the bedrooms. We follow, double-checking all of them, moving on to the bathrooms, the laundry, and finally the kitchen. There's no one here. They've left—in a hurry too by the look of it. Nearly everything is still here, and an untrained eye would simply think they're out for the day. Not us—we're trained to notice things like the missing family photos.

There's no doubt that they've fled again, and I have to remind myself that smiling would be a really inappropriate thing to do right now.

* * *

We spend the remainder of the afternoon and most of the evening asking around the neighbourhood about the Johns' last known whereabouts and searching their house for any indication of where they might be headed. By the time Drew and I are back home in our shared house, I'm exhausted and starving.

At least this house has two separate bedrooms unlike the first one they gave us, which had one bedroom and one bathroom. I feel as if I have my own space here, and I need that.

"So we're not going back to the Institute anytime soon, are we?" I ask Drew as we sit at the dining table for a late dinner.

"I never thought I'd see the day where you were hoping to go back to that place."

"You know why I want to go back."

Drew nods. "Yeah. I do. We'll be back soon enough."

"We both know that's not true. We have no idea when this assignment will end."

We continue eating in silence. I don't have anything to say, and I can sense he doesn't know what to say.

I haven't seen Shilah in three months. I don't know if he's still in the training program. I don't even know if he's okay.

While I couldn't help smirking at the fact our targets fled, it means we won't be returning to the Institute. I'll have to continue to wonder about Shilah until we finally catch Licia or are called back for a new assignment.

"So, where do we go from here?" I ask Drew.

"We start again. We ask those who knew them and try to find out if they had anywhere to go."

"The last time they tried to evade us, they moved to a town only thirty minutes away before they thought they would be safe. Maybe they're still close?" I speculate.

"Maybe. Or maybe they've learnt from their last attempt."

I sigh. "I think I'm going to go to bed." Even though no arrest ended up happening today, it was still an exhausting day, physically and mentally draining. I'd love nothing more than to go to my room, climb into bed, and close my eyes. But that's not why I'm going to bed.

Closing my bedroom door behind me, I get the wooden chair that sits in the corner and place the backrest under my door handle, preventing Drew from being able to open it. I go to my bed, lift the fitted sheet, and slide my fingers into the hidden slot that I cut into my mattress. It's where I keep my key, the key that was given to me by Paxton, the head of the agent training department of the Institute. I unlock my Institute-issued tracking bracelet and place it under my pillow. Slipping my feet into my boots and making my way over to the window, I slide it open as silently as possible and grab my jacket before climbing outside and sneaking away into the night.

I half-walk and half-jog the few blocks to where I need to go. My breath puffs in white clouds in the crisp air, and I put my hands in my pockets to keep them warm.

As I walk past an old children's playground behind an abandoned apartment block, the neglected swing set and broken monkey bars catch my eye. I think back to a time when I used to be able to play carefree. Then we discovered Shilah was Defective, and we never visited a playground again.

My thoughts are disrupted by the rustling of leaves behind me. I'm quick to turn around, but with my hands in my pockets, I'm not quick enough to react, and I'm knocked to the ground by someone. Trying to break my fall with my hands, I fail, and my head smacks the pavement. *That's going to hurt later.* I'm fast to get back up on my feet though, fast to stand poised, and ready to face my attacker.

My heart starts racing, and I take in a deep breath, telling myself to concentrate on him, on the way he moves. He raises an eyebrow cockily before making his move. I block his hit, punch back, and push my way forwards, all the while dodging his hits and blocking him from advancing on me. He's ready for my punches, though, and evades every one of them. I keep lunging forwards, attacking with my fists, making him retreat backwards. I don't give him a chance to come at me. A look of realisation and defeat crosses his face when I corner him against an old oak tree. He can't go back any farther; he can only come at me or go sideways. He's mine. From here, I can take him out no matter which direction he goes.

I grin, relaxing my stance. "Oh, Chad. I'm so disappointed in you."

"Not as disappointed as I am in you," he says.

"What? What did I do wrong this time?"

"You weren't ready for me. I should never have been able to get you on the ground. You're lucky I didn't knock you unconscious." He steps forward, touching his hand to the back of my head where it slammed onto the ground. "How's the head?" he says with a slight smile on his lips.

I sigh and move away from him. He's right. I wasn't ready for him. I was too distracted by the playground, reminiscing about my childhood, and unarmed myself by putting my hands in my pockets. My head hurts from my fall, but I'm not going to admit that.

"I still had you." I smirk.

"You got lucky," Chad replies in his serious "I am your trainer" voice. "So how did today go anyway?"

"Funny thing happened. The Johns family have seemed to have disappeared."

"Well, that's a shame. I wonder what could've happened to them," Chad says, a knowing smirk crossing his face.

CHAPTER TWO

"So, they arrived safely?" I ask.

"Setting up house at the compound, as we speak," Chad replies with a triumphant smile.

I can't help but return it. I saved them; we saved them. "I wish I could've taken a photo of everyone's faces when they realised Licia and her family were gone." I laugh.

"I would've paid to see that."

"Well, it's not like you didn't have the opportunity. You could have, had you stayed working as an agent for the Institute," I say, trying to hide my annoyance with him.

"And leave you, with *him*? That wasn't going to happen," Chad says, sitting down at the base of the oak tree next to us. Anyone from the outside would misconstrue what Chad just said as jealousy. It's not. Anytime he's come close to admitting any sort of feelings for me, he covers it up by blaming it on his cousin. "I promised Tate I'd protect you." *Yup, right on cue.*

I don't want to have this conversation *again*. Chad decided to disappear from the Institute and is annoyed that I chose to stay.

When Chad turned himself over to them after Tate was arrested, his plan was to get Tate out. They were going to train as agents and then disappear together to the Resistance compound out west, but Tate wasn't okay with that plan. He decided to stay where he was. After all, he found me in The Crypt; maybe there would be others he could find. Others he could help escape.

From what I've learnt over the last three months, the Resistance is an activist group fighting for equal rights and the disbanding of the Institute. Chad and Tate were recruiters for them until Tate was arrested. Chad successfully recruited my best friend Ebbodine, not long before I was sent to the Institute. Everyone thought she was dead. She'd disappeared without a trace, and no one had any idea where she could've gone. I didn't know she was Defective. Then again, I didn't even know *I* was Defective. I've only seen her once since I joined the cause. Actually, I've only seen everyone who was there that night once, except Chad.

That whole night is still a bit of a blur, starting from when I first woke up on the hard ground in the middle of a forest.

Trees surrounded me, only giving partial view to the stars and sky above me. Cicadas chirped loudly in my ears.

My mother leaned down, gently brushing my cheek with her hand. She said ... something, but I couldn't make it out.

"What?" I croaked, my voice hoarse.

"Welcome to the Resistance," she said, her voice calm and soothing.

"The what?" I said, confused. I tried to stand, pushing my mother out of my way, but I was wobbly on my feet.

Chad was suddenly at my side. "Sorry about that. I didn't want to drug you, but we knew you'd put up a fight, scream, and probably wake up Drew," he said, wrapping his arm around my waist and holding me close.

"You drugged me?"

He winced. "Not my idea." He glared at Paxton.

My vision started to blur. "What is this?" I asked as Chad lowered me back down to the ground.

"There's so much to say," my mother said. My mother. I couldn't believe I was sitting just a few feet away from the woman who died eight years ago.

I was in too much shock to feel anything. Numbness took over my body, and it was as if I was slipping into a haze.

The only thing I could focus on was Paxton's tone of voice when he said, "We don't have enough time to explain everything." He was strictly business.

What is Paxton even doing here? *I thought.* He's one of them. He's the guy who "tested" my amplification ability by making *me blow up a car battery alongside another Institute resident. He's the one who deemed me good enough to be recommended for the agent program. He showed me around the training centre and inducted me into the program. He's one of them!*

Ignoring his words, I glared at my mother, wanting answers. "You've been alive this whole time? You walked out on us, abandoned us, for what?"

"It's not as simple as that, Lia." Her voice was small. "If you come with us, we'll have all the time in the world to discuss it."

"Go with you, where?"

They all started talking at me, cutting each other off, trying to explain what was happening. Whether it was the drugs or the lingering shock, I don't know, but my brain wasn't in comprehension mode. All I could gather was they wanted to take me somewhere, over the small mountain range that had been the backdrop of my horizon for my entire life. They were all expecting me to make this momentous decision on spur of the moment. To go with them or to stay? I sat there, watching the five of them talking and arguing over what would be best for me as if I wasn't even there.

It didn't help that Paxton kept saying, over and over again, "We don't have time for this. She needs to decide now before it's too late."

That's when I snapped.

"Everyone shut up," I yelled. They all turned to look at me, stunned at my outburst. "Stop talking about me like I'm not

here. I need to get this straight. You're saying the Resistance have a compound out west, close to the radiation perimeter, completely secure from the outside world. And you want me to go there?"

They all nodded.

"Okay, so what about Shilah? I can't just leave him at the Institute." I shake my head, my decision made. "No way. It's not going to happen. You don't think Brookfield will punish him if I go missing?" I turned to Chad. "How did you get away?" I looked down at my wrist, but my tracker was gone.

"It was always the plan to get out," Chad said with little emotion.

"Why didn't you tell me?"

He ran a hand through his hair. "I wanted to. Tate wouldn't let me."

"So Tate's in on it, too?"

"He's kind of our leader," Ebb added.

"Leader?"

"There's eight of us, actually," my mother said.

"Total?" I asked, which received a few chuckles.

"Eight leaders," Paxton clarified. "Tate, your mum, me, Chad's mother, and four others you'll meet when you come with us."

I shook my head. "No. I'm not leaving Shilah."

"He'll be safe, I'll make sure of it," Aunt Kenna said.

"How could you make sure of it?"

She came to sit beside me on the hard ground. When I turned to look at her, I was no longer looking at my aunt but at the doctor who treated me at the hospital when I hurt my ankle at the Institute.

"You!" I screamed.

"I wanted to tell you. So badly."

I reached over to touch her face, and she let out a small laugh. Her face contorted slightly, making my hand flinch away from her. When I looked back at her face, she was Aunt Kenna again.

"I can shape shift. But it's not all that impressive considering I only have the two faces to change into."

In the middle of a forest, surrounded by these people who were meant to be my family and friends, I realised I truly knew nothing about any of them.

"Is there anyone who hasn't lied to me?" I asked no one in particular.

"It was too risky to tell you, Lia," Aunt Kenna said. "I'm not Kenna to the Institute. They only know me as Kandice Randall. They don't know I'm your aunt. They don't know I'm Defective. I've been working for them for years, and they're none the wiser about my true identity. I couldn't risk exposing myself."

Ebb suddenly appeared at my other side. She didn't walk over

23

to me. It was as if she blinked and was suddenly there. I stared at her, wide-eyed. "I can teleport," she said nonchalantly, wrapping her arm around me.

With each new reveal, it was as if a wire in my tiny, naïve brain short-circuited. I furrowed my brows in confusion and pain.

"I know how you're feeling. I felt the same when Chad approached me to join them," Ebb said, as if it was meant to reassure me.

"I—"

"I'm really sorry, Allira. You need to make a decision," Paxton cut in.

"What happens if I say no?"

"You won't remember this ever happened," Paxton replied.

"How?"

Paxton gestured to my mother.

"I tamper with memories," she simply stated.

"What if I don't want to forget? If what you're offering me is real, I want it. I want it more than almost anything. Almost. *But Shilah's safety comes first."*

Chad asked for a moment alone.

"Two minutes," Paxton said, gesturing for the others to leave us.

Chad took Ebb's spot next to me. "I wanted to tell you."

I didn't respond. I didn't know how to.

"Come with me."

"Just like that? Leave and don't worry about the consequences? You're not scared about what will happen to Tate with you gone?"

"He told me to leave. He also told me to drag you with me— kicking and screaming." He took a piece of paper out of his pocket. "This is from him."

I was hesitant at first but reluctantly reached for it. Placing it on my lap, I stared at it, willing myself to build the courage to open it. It didn't come. "I want to. I want to go with you, be with you ... and my family," I added, suddenly aware of the words falling out of my mouth.

"Then come with me," he repeated. He reached over and tucked my hair behind my ear. With that one simple gesture, I was so close to saying yes.

"Get Shilah out, and I will," I whispered as a lump formed in my throat.

That was it. I'd made up my mind.

After that, there was little discussion. The others came back, and I stated what I wanted. Paxton reluctantly agreed to leave my memory intact, assigned Chad as my handler, and I was home and tucked up in bed at my Institute house just before sunrise.

* * *

As creepy as it is—knowing I have Chad watching me a lot of the day—it also gives me slight comfort that if I ever need him, he's there. He's made it pretty clear that he isn't exactly pleased that I'm still connected to the Institute and to my ex-boyfriend, Drew.

My head really begins to pound from where I hit the pavement during our scuffle earlier. Chad and I are silent, not looking at one another, as tension fills the air. He's fidgeting, and I'm standing unnaturally still. It has been pretty awkward between us lately. More so than usual. Chad and I have always had a bit of an odd friendship. We went from practically despising each other to tolerating each other for the sake of our mutual relationship with Tate to almost kissing during a training session one day to what we are now … which I don't exactly know what that is.

"Maybe we should just stick to business talk tonight," I say as I sit down next to him, leaning up against the tree. "I don't know where they're going to take the investigation from here. Licia's gone and she's untraceable, but they don't know that. They know she's left, but I think they'll send us on a wild goose chase for a few more months before reassigning us."

"Maybe that's not such a bad thing," Chad replies.

"Yeah, well, you're not the one who has to put up with Drew twenty-four hours a day. I want to get reassigned. I want a new partner. Actually, if I'm demanding things, I want Shilah to be out of there so I don't have to work for them anymore."

"You know you don't have to now, right? Paxton and your aunt said they'll get Shilah out," Chad asserts.

"Yeah, well, you'll have to excuse my lack of trust in people these days," I retort.

He sighs. "Do we really need to have this conversation again? You said you understood."

"I do understand, but that doesn't mean I don't have the right to be angry about it. You lied to me. Tate lied to me. My whole family lied to me for most of my life. I understand why you all did it, but that doesn't make it any less hurtful."

We've had this conversation many times over the last three months, and I know I don't have the right to be angry. They lied to protect me. I get that. I just … I don't know. I feel betrayed. What they did is not much different from what Drew did to me except they gave me a choice to join them; Drew and the Institute gave me no such choice. I don't want to be upset by it, but for some reason, it still bugs me.

I'm not really angry at Chad though. He just has to bear the brunt of it because he's the only one I see.

"I'm sorr—"

I interrupt Chad before he gives me yet another apology. I'm sick of hearing them. "Don't apologise again. You don't need to. None of this was your fault. I know that."

"I think maybe you're right—we should just stick to business talk tonight."

"Fine," I say with a sigh. "Drew says we'll be staying where we are until we get a lead off someone who knows the Johns family, but they haven't been here all that long. I don't know if we'll be able to find anyone helpful."

"So I guess we won't need to meet up again for a while."

"I guess not."

"It's probably best. The less you sneak out, the less chance of *Drew* finding out." He practically spits Drew's name at me. It annoys me because it's not like that between Drew and me, not anymore.

"How's Ebbodine?" I ask, not even trying to hide the passive aggressiveness of my tone.

"I wouldn't know. Even if I was at the compound, I wouldn't know," he replies.

I just roll my eyes.

"It's not my fault you thought we were together."

Chad and Ebbodine were never together as he led me to believe. Chad merely recruited her, and that's the extent of their relationship. Or so he says.

"Letting someone believe something that's untrue to cover other lies is still lying," I state.

"I couldn't tell you how I knew her because I couldn't tell you about the Resistance," he says in frustration, picking strands of grass out of the ground repeatedly.

"So much for only talking business," I mutter.

I wish there were magic words that could fix everything between Chad and me. Most of our meetings have been fine, but we just seem to get on each other's nerves when the whole "Resistance versus Institute" thing comes up. I think he just assumed that I would leave and was shocked when I decided to stay.

For a moment—while they were all trying to convince me to leave and join the Resistance—I thought Chad was asking me to go to be *with him*. I sometimes think that when I chose Shilah, Chad thinks I actually chose Drew. Nothing has come of "us" ever since.

Any romantic feelings I had for Chad were shelved when I found out about the Resistance. Shelved but not thrown out. Butterflies still attack my stomach when he smirks at me or when we're training and our bodies are up against each other. I still blush when I think of our almost kiss at the Institute.

I wish I could just tell him how I feel, but no, my stupid mouth won't say the words I want it to. Too much time has gone by now to suddenly tell him I have feelings for him, that I've had feelings for him for months. So I remain silent, mentally kicking myself every time I walk away from him.

"So, do you have your question for today?" Chad asks, clearly trying to change the subject.

"I still have so many questions."

Chad has allowed me one question per meet-up. It saves him from being bombarded with a million questions in one night.

I've asked about the leaders or council, as Chad puts it. He told me they didn't want a singular leader. They wanted different people from different backgrounds—rich, poor, Defective, and surprisingly, non-Defective. Paxton is on the council, and he's not Defective. I think it's sad that my initial reaction to finding out Paxton is risking his life—his normal non-Defective life—for us was shock. It shouldn't be shocking that people want to fight for us, but growing up in the world we do, it has been drilled into us from the beginning that Defective people are dangerous and shouldn't have any rights. The Resistance made sure the council was diverse enough so their actions are fair and not promoting an individual agenda.

Even though I've been filled in on a lot of Resistance information, I still have so many questions about my mother. It creeps me out that all those times sitting in Tate's cell, talking to him about life, about family, and about my mother, he knew exactly who I was talking about and had actually spent time with her. I think this is why I'm still angry with him.

I also have questions about Dad. Where did he go? Why can't they find him?

Chad doesn't have the answer to any of these questions even though I've repeatedly asked him such things. He always replies with, "You'll have to ask them that."

So tonight, I decide to ask him something he'll know.

"Why were you reported missing? You say your dad knew about the Resistance because of your mum's involvement and that he knew you were working for them. Then why did he report you missing when you turned yourself over to the Institute? And why were you still living with him and working for the Resistance? Isn't that a rule? Leave everyone and everything behind?"

Chad sighs. "Mum wanted to take me with her when she joined the Resistance years ago. I was eleven and Dad said no. Dad made the argument that I would be safer with him. So they made a deal that I was allowed to finish school, and when I was eighteen, I could make up my own mind. Of course, I left as soon as I could. I would've left earlier if Dad had let me.

"Tate had already been with the Resistance for a few years, and when Aunt Jene died—Tate's mum—I felt I had to do something. I ended up joining the Resistance just before my eighteenth birthday, but I already had enough credits to graduate, so technically, it didn't break Mum and Dad's original deal.

"Tate, even though he'd just been given a chair on the council, took me in and trained with me. That's when we started working together. It was about a year later that we came back to Eminent Falls. We were there for recruitment, and that's when we got Hall and Ebbodine. Seeing as Dad knew everything about us, I was allowed to go back and stay with him. I hadn't been gone all that long, so we just told everyone I went to university in the city and was back to become a teacher, just like Dad.

"It would've been completely different with your mum. Your mum was a missing person; she was assumed dead by everyone, even the police. She couldn't have just come back."

I guess it wasn't too hard for Chad to decipher why I really wanted to know the answer to that question. It makes sense.

Mum was presumed dead.

"But that still doesn't explain why you ended up being reported missing? I saw your missing persons report," I say.

"Dad did that after he found out I turned myself into the Institute. Mum suggested he do it so not to bring suspicion on himself about knowing what I was capable of," he replies.

"Sounds like your dad and my dad would get along." That's the kind of thing Dad would always think and talk about when the hypothetical scenarios about getting caught were discussed. "So your mum and dad still talk?"

"Sometimes," he says but doesn't elaborate.

"How come—"

"Don't ask me how it is that they can still keep contact but your parents couldn't. You'll have to ask them that."

The worst thing about having so many questions with no sufficient answer is I feel like I don't have any control over the situation. I'm at a loss for how to feel. If I just stop thinking for a moment and look at the positives, that Mum's alive, I'm alive, Shilah's safe, and I'm working at making the world a better place, I can accept that. It's when my brain wants to analyse every little detail that things get fuzzy and frustrating.

"I guess that's it for tonight then," I state coolly. "It's getting a bit late."

We've been trying to keep our meetings down to a minimum. Even though I barricaded the door when I snuck out the window earlier tonight, if Drew tries to get in there and succeeds and I'm not there? I don't even want to think of the consequences.

Chad stands and reaches out a hand to help me up off the ground. I know it's just a simple gesture, but just like when Drew helped me earlier by getting me out of my shift at the restaurant, it annoys me. I just want to say "I can do it myself," but I don't. Deep down, I know I'm being petty and immature. Accepting his hand, I let him pull me up. He leaves his hand lingering on mine a little longer than one would expect. I don't retract mine either, and for a split second, I start to wonder what he is doing, what *we're* doing.

I don't want to keep arguing, but I don't know how to fix it. The frustration is building inside of me. It's sitting in my chest, urging me to yell or scream or just do something.

Without thinking, I take a step closer to him. He looks down at me but doesn't move away. Our hands are still together, and I'm surprised when he intertwines his fingers with mine. My eyes are locked on his, but neither one of us makes another move.

A voice startles me from the left. "Well, I can see not much has changed with you two."

"Shilah?" I ask in disbelief, dropping Chad's hand. "What are you doing here?"

"Gee, missed you too, sis. What kind of greeting is that?"

CHAPTER THREE

My arms wrap around Shilah, and I vow to never let go.

"Is this real?" I ask.

He slaps me on the back of my head as he pulls away from my embrace. "Well, you aren't dreaming."

Paxton appears from a car parked on the street. It takes me a moment to recognise him in his civilian clothes. I'm used to seeing him in a suit. He actually looks younger than I remember. "It's a good thing we caught you two," he says, interrupting our little reunion.

"Paxton? What's going on?" I ask.

"Well, Shilah graduated," he replies, patting Shilah on the back. "We were able to get him out. So now, you can get out too. That was the deal, right?"

"Seriously? This is really happening?"

"You want me to slap you again to be sure?" Shilah asks. I shake my head. I don't, I really don't. He managed to hit my head right where I smacked it earlier when Chad attacked me. I rub the back of my head where an egg is forming.

"Nah, I'm all good. Thanks."

"So let's go," Paxton interjects.

"I have to go back to the house first," I say.

"We need to get out west before anyone discovers you're gone," Paxton says.

"If they search my room, they'll find the key." They will also find other incriminating things I should have gotten rid of a long time ago.

Paxton sighs. "Okay, you go back and get the key, and we'll wait for you in the car. We'll park a few houses up. You've got three minutes, okay?"

"That's plenty of time," I say as I start running towards the direction of the house.

I run faster and harder than I ever have before. It's happening. It's finally happening. I'm free. Shilah is free. My heart is beating fast, but I don't know if it's because of the exertion from the running or because of how liberated I feel.

When I arrive at the house, all the lights are out, so I'm assuming Drew has gone to bed already. Silently approaching my bedroom window, I slip back into the house. I rush over to the bed, pulling out the key to my tracking bracelet and the note from Tate, which I kept in the same spot. It really should've been destroyed right after I read it, but it has brought me so much comfort over the last three months, I just couldn't bring myself to get rid of it. I would find myself reading over it, time and time again. It reminded me of what I'm fighting for, what I'm trying to save. And besides, I figured if they found the key, I was going to be screwed anyway, so I kept the note and the key together knowing I would do anything to keep them hidden.

I place them in my jeans pocket and quickly glance around the room for anything else to grab on my way out.

"Going back out?" Drew asks casually as I practically jump out of my skin. I've been so distracted by getting the key and the letter, I didn't even realise he was in the room.

The chair I pushed up against the door lies broken on the floor. I swear at myself for not being more careful. I freeze in panic. Even though it's dark in here, I can feel Drew's eyes burning into me as I frantically try to think of a way out of this.

"I just went for a run," I say as innocently as possible.

Drew scoffs, "Yeah, like I'm going to believe that." He gets up and starts walking towards me. I prepare myself for a fight, but he stops a few feet away from me when he senses I'm ready to attack. "I'm not going to fight you. I just want to know where you were."

"I just wanted to get out."

"Don't lie to me, Allira. Unless you want to go straight back to the Institute and The Crypt," he threatens. "What's in your pocket?"

"I don't have to answer to you," I say, still frozen next to my bed. "You're not my boss, we're partners."

"It doesn't seem that way. Partners trust each other."

Now it's my turn to scoff. "That's rich, coming from you."

"I'm not going to ask again. Where did you go?" Drew asks sternly.

Words escape me. I can't tell him the truth, but I can't lie.

Chad appears at the window. "Allira, hurry up, we don't have time …" He stops short when he sees Drew's in the room.

"You're alive?" Drew asks as Chad reluctantly climbs through the window.

"You thought he was dead?" I ask.

"You knew he wasn't? Just how long have you been sneaking off with him. How have they not alerted me to your late-night activities?" Drew reaches for my wrist. "Where is your—what happened to your bracelet?"

Shit. "What do we do?" I whisper to Chad, but it's pointless. Of course, Drew can hear me. Chad looks as lost as I feel. We're screwed.

"Fuck! We'll have to take him with us," Chad says.

I'm taken aback. Chad is rattled; he's usually quite composed. I can feel the frustration coming from him.

"I'm not going anywhere with you," Drew responds before

turning to me. "What does he mean? Where are you going? What's going on, Allira?"

"I'm so sorry," I say to Drew, before punching him out cold. I'm thankful for Chad teaching me how to knock someone out by hitting a certain pressure point in the side of their neck.

"Ugh, what did you do that for? Now we're going to have to carry him to the car," Chad complains. "Don't get me wrong, I'm not saying I didn't enjoy seeing that, but I'm sure we could've forced him to walk to the car."

"Get Paxton to bring the car closer," I say. Chad sticks his head out of the window and signals to Paxton, who's idling the car two houses away. "I'll grab his legs."

"Oh, sure, now you get the lightest body part to carry?" Chad says sarcastically but upbeat. I think he's just as excited as I am, if not more. We're getting out of here. He's getting to go home. In a way, I feel as if I'm going home too. I've never been to the compound before, but I'll be with Shilah and my mother. The only thing missing is Dad. It's as close to a home as I will ever have.

I'm reminded that Drew still has his tracking bracelet on. Taking the key out of my pocket, I bend down and unlock it, tossing it behind me before grabbing Drew's legs.

"Out the window?" I ask. "The street is closer to my bedroom window than the front door, so it's less distance to carry the body. Wow, there's something I never thought I'd have to consider."

Chad laughs a little. "Yeah, we'll have to hurry up though. He could wake up any minute now."

We manage to get Drew out the window and over to the car before Paxton opens the driver's side door and gets out, one foot still in the car.

"What happened?" he asks.

"Drew was in my room when I got back. He realised I've been sneaking out."

Paxton runs his hand over the back of his neck, just like Chad does when he's nervous. "And you thought the best thing to do would be to bring him along? We should just leave him here."

"He also saw me," Chad explains.

"And that I was no longer wearing my tracking bracelet," I add.

"Yeah, okay. Put him in the back," Paxton concedes. "And hurry up before someone sees you."

We half-push and half-throw Drew into the car and prop him up in the passenger seat, his head flopping against the window. We then climb in the back seat with him. It doesn't feel overly awkward until I realise I'm sitting in between Drew and Chad. The tiny hatchback car doesn't have a lot of room, and both of my legs are brushing up against theirs. *Nope, not awkward at all,* I keep telling myself.

As we drive off, Drew starts coming to.

"Ugh, what ... What happened?" he asks hazily before opening his eyes. "Where are you taking me?" He frantically tries to open the car door, but Paxton must've engaged the child lock. There's no way he's getting out.

"Consider yourself lucky, Agent Jacobs," Paxton says while looking at Drew in his rear view mirror.

"Paxton?" Drew asks, surprised.

"You were never part of the plan, but I guess you've been thrown into it now," Paxton replies.

"He's going to kill us all, you know that, don't you?" Drew says, panicking.

"Brookfield?" Paxton asks. "He doesn't have the capability. To come after you, he will have to tell numerous agents that you've escaped. He can't let them know that it's possible to do that. It will give them ideas. Why else do you think you were told Chad was dead? Killed in action, wasn't it?"

"Hold up," I say, looking to Drew. "You were told that Chad was dead, and you didn't think I would've wanted to know that?"

"Like it matters anyway. You've been sneaking out to see him. You knew he wasn't dead."

"That's not the point. Weren't you saying only ten minutes ago that we're partners and meant to trust each other? One of my friends dies, and you don't tell me anything?"

Chad shifts in his seat.

"I didn't want to be the one to tell you," Drew says sheepishly.

I shake my head. "Typical Drew."

"Can you two have this lovers' tiff sometime else, please?"

Paxton says seriously. I should object to his insinuation, but I don't have the energy.

"How long will it take us to get there?" Shilah asks from the front seat.

"From here? About two hours, maybe three. It's basically the same distance to the compound as it is to the Institute, just further northwest. I'm only taking you halfway. I need to get back as soon as possible."

Suddenly, I don't care about Drew, or Chad, or the awkwardness that fills the cabin of the car. I lean forwards. "I can't believe you're really here," I say to Shilah, playfully punching him in the shoulder.

"I kind of can't believe it myself," he replies. "So, we're going to see Mum?" he asks.

"You know about her?"

"Ever since I saw that police report you brought home about her probably being out there somewhere, I figured she was alive. It didn't really occur to me that she would be part of all this though."

"What *is* this?" Drew asks behind me. "Can someone please give me some answers?"

I can't help giggling. "Hmm, sucks to be on that end of it, doesn't it?" I spent the first few weeks at the Institute trying to find out what exactly was happening to me with no real response from anyone but Tate. Chad has been silent since we got in the car, but even he laughs at that a little.

"There's no point in explaining it to you right now," Paxton says with a tone of impatience and authority.

I sit back as the car fills with silence. It seems Paxton might appreciate the quiet. I'm used to seeing him so collected and politically correct.

Chad is the one to finally break the silence. "So how did Shilah get out so soon? We were given the impression that he wouldn't be out for a long while. Allira was told that he'd be placed with her once he graduated."

"To be fair, Allira was set up to go out on assignment with Shilah in a few days, but Licia's unsuccessful arrest today caused Brookfield to bring forward his start date and gave him a new partner. And I may or may not have given Shilah the answers to the agent test," Paxton says, smiling.

"But the obstacle course?" I ask. "That was really hard."

"Maybe for you." Shilah laughs.

I guess in my happy stupor, I've neglected to notice how fit Shilah is. He looks healthy. It brings a smile to my face to know that even though he was stuck in that place for months, he doesn't seem too damaged by it.

"So you turn seventeen and suddenly become some buff, tough guy, hey?"

Shilah lifts his arm, flexing his toned bicep. "Yup." His smile is infectious.

How can things change so drastically in only three months?
"I'm sorry I missed your birthday."

He shrugs it off.

"How's Tate going?" Chad asks. I look to Paxton for an answer, but it's actually Shilah who responds.

"He's the same. He'd want to know you're not really dead though. He still thinks you are," he says.

"Why didn't you tell him, Paxton?" I ask.

"I can't go down to The Crypt. It would bring too much suspicion on me and on Tate. He's not Defective to them, remember? It was easy getting messages to him while Chad was there, but since you left, I haven't been able to fill him in on anything," Paxton replies.

"I always knew that guy was Defective," Drew says arrogantly.

I forgot he was even here for a moment. "Don't get too self-confident. You may have known he was Defective, but you're an Empath who couldn't even tell that Tate was gay," I snigger at him. Chad and Shilah laugh. "Who told Tate that Chad was dead?" I ask.

"Sorry, that was my fault," Shilah says. "They told everyone in training that he died on his assignment. It was only a few days after you left. I thought Tate deserved to know."

"You weren't to know it wasn't true," Chad reassures Shilah.

"Can't you get the message to him somehow?" I ask Paxton. "You don't even need to go see him to tell him. I'm sure if you walked by the entrance to The Crypt, he'd hear you think it from that distance."

"So *that's* why we couldn't work out what his ability was," Drew mumbles. I ignore him.

"I'll see what I can do when I get back," Paxton says. "But he's the one who chose to leave his position to stay there. He knew there was a chance Chad could've died trying to escape. He's probably dealt with it by now."

It's surreal how casual Paxton is about death—as if it's just an everyday fact of life. I get a sudden pain in the pit of my stomach, and I begin to get nervous about what I'm getting myself into—myself and Shilah. This is the world he's taking us to—where death is nothing but an occupational hazard.

"I can tell you for a fact that he hasn't got over it," Shilah says.

"How do you know that?" I ask.

"He blames himself for Chad's death. I've been visiting him, like you asked me to."

The car goes silent again. I feel for Tate. He thinks Chad's been dead for months. I know what that's like. I thought my mother was dead for eight years.

I turn to Chad, but he's staring out the window, refusing to look at me. He's angry; I can sense it. Is he angry because he knows Tate is suffering and it's his fault?

"Do you think they'll tell everyone that Shilah, Drew, and I are dead, too?" I ask Paxton.

"I'd say so. I don't know how they're going to handle the three of you disappearing. Maybe they'll tell everyone you and Drew have run off together as an act of love, not insurgency." I try not to vomit in my mouth. "Maybe they'll tell them you all died on assignment, like Chad. I really don't know. If it was just one of you, they could tell everyone you were killed in action. Two of you is suspicious, but three? It's going to be hard to cover this one up."

"Then send me back," Drew says.

"Yeah, that's not going to happen," Paxton replies. "We can't trust *you*—Mr. Brookfield's lackey—to not tell him everything you know."

"That's funny coming from you. Up until an hour ago, I would've said *you* were Brookfield's lackey, not me. So you're just going to hold me hostage for the rest of my life?"

"Well, that's no different than what you've done to every person you arrested while working for the Institute," I retort. "Although it is a little different, because I can guarantee that they won't torture you where we're taking you."

I can't actually guarantee that; after all, I've never been there before. But I can assume that a group of people wanting better things for us would not be interested in harming other Defectives.

"She has a point there," Paxton says. "I think you should be thanking us, not looking at us like we're doing wrong by you."

Drew has nothing to say to that.

By the time Paxton says "We're here," my eyes feel heavy, my butt is numb from sitting, and I'm so ready for bed.

"We're in the middle of nowhere," Drew complains as we all file out of the car.

I take the opportunity to stretch and try to wake up.

"This is halfway. Cyrus should be here any minute to take you farther," Paxton says.

"Who's Cyrus?" I ask.

"He's on the council," Chad says.

"He's very dedicated to the cause," Paxton adds. "I would be too if I had his abilities."

My mouth suddenly dry, I almost choke. "Abilities?" I cough. "Plural?"

Paxton gives me a look, one I am unable to read. "He's the only one I've ever known to have a double ability. Apparently, there have been a couple at the Institute, but they didn't last long. I've never met one in my time there." He finally breaks his gaze with me. "Cyrus is a little weird around the edges, but you get used to him."

Another double ability, just like mine? Chad never told me there was someone else like me at the Resistance. When I look at him, he shakes his head slightly, and I can sense he's nervous. Tate has been adamant from the moment we found out about me that no one should ever know I have a double ability. He told me if the Institute was to find out, I would spend the rest of my life being experimented on. They would then kill me when they got all they needed from me. I feel myself start to panic a bit before I force myself to squash it down so Drew can't sense it.

But they don't seem to be like that at the Resistance. After all, this Cyrus guy is a council member. They have promoted him to a leader, I assume *because* of his double ability, not in spite of it. They have embraced it. Then why has Chad become so uptight since Cyrus was mentioned?

"I thought double abilities were a myth?" Drew asks.

"No, not a myth. Just rare," Chad says, kicking the dirt and avoiding eye contact with me.

Headlights appear on the road, lighting up our surroundings. Thick-forested hills surround us, and I realise where we are. We're at the base of the mountain range Chad told me about. The compound is on the other side of it. It was hard to see in the dark, but we've driven through the outer city suburbs, the sub-rural areas, and the deserted farmlands that stand between where we are now and the city.

"Should we hide?" I say, regarding the car that is about to pass us.

"No need. This will be Cyrus now," Paxton says. "We're the only ones who use this road. The radiation barrier fence is just up ahead, so generally no one ventures past it. Well, except us."

"Radiation barrier? You expect us to live in there?" Drew asks, worried.

"We have the necessary safety precautions in place, don't you worry about that. Radiation gauges, escape routes, we have all of it, and since my time with the Resistance, we've never come close to needing to evacuate. We think the government just wanted to close off this part of the countryside so they didn't have to man it."

The car, a giant four-wheel drive, pulls up across the road. Cyrus gets out of the car and walks over to us. Actually, it's more like swaggering. He looks around Paxton's age. I'd say he's around thirty, maybe thirty-five. He's wearing a brimmed hat, even though it's night time. His black jeans are tighter than any pair I've ever worn, and his white collared shirt is unbuttoned down to his chest, revealing a hint of dark chest hair. He has topped off his look with a thin scarf that's clearly there for decoration and not warmth. I think Paxton may have underestimated the weird factor.

"Ah, Paxton," Cyrus says, reaching a hand out for Paxton to shake. "Good to see you, brother."

Brother?

"He's your brother?" Drew asks.

"Everyone is my brother," Cyrus responds. "Sorry I'm a bit late, one of the kids was refusing their bedtime," he says, rolling his eyes.

"Which one?" Chad laughs as he steps forwards to also shake Cyrus's hand.

"I dunno. The young one." Cyrus laughs back. Hmm, it must be an inside joke, I guess. "So unless my eyes are playing tricks on me, there are more than expected? I was told there would only be three."

"Yeah, that's a bit of a story. I'll let Chad fill the council in on that one. I have to get back. Good luck and I'll see you all soon," Paxton says, swiftly getting back into his car and driving off. We all stand there, watching him leave.

Cyrus looks at us when Paxton's car is no longer in view. "So, who do we have here?" he asks, walking over to Drew.

"That's Drew," Chad responds. "He's no one."

"Nice," Drew says sarcastically.

Cyrus doesn't even question it and moves on to Shilah, "So you must be Shilah," he says, shaking Shilah's hand. "It's good to meet you. Your mum and I are great friends. I bet you're excited to see her." He walks over to me before Shilah has a chance to answer him or greet him properly. "So that means you are Allira," he says, taking my hand in his. "Whoa. I was not expecting that," he says, gripping my hand tighter.

"Expecting what?" I ask.

"Oh, sorry. You just … you look so much like your mother," he replies. "Okay, let's go." Cyrus walks across the street and back over to the car.

The four of us start heading to the car when Drew comes beside me. "Your mother's alive?" he asks.

"Yeah. I was surprised too."

"You want to ride up front?" Cyrus asks me.

"I guess so," I say, even though I'd really love to sit with Shilah in the back. I climb into the front seat, and it really is a climb; this vehicle is huge.

Cyrus starts the car, does a U-turn, and we're on our way. I get an all-round sense of awkwardness flowing in from the back. Shilah was at least smart enough to sit on the passenger side, but that also means that Chad and Drew are sitting next to each other.

I also get a sense of … what is it? I can't pinpoint the emotion one hundred percent. Intrigue? Suspicion? All I know is it's coming from Cyrus.

"So, Allira," he says. "You're able to borrow abilities?"

My face goes dead straight. I tell myself not to turn to Chad and not to freak out. My heart starts trying to thump its way out of my chest.

"Actually, I can amplify others' abilities," I respond as calmly as possible, but I just know it has come out shaky.

"Oh, sorry. I just assumed you …" He takes his eyes off the road and studies my face. "Sorry, my mistake," he says, returning his gaze to the windy, climbing path we're following. I let out a quiet sigh of relief.

I turn as casually as I can and look at Chad. He again shakes his head ever so slightly, just as he did earlier when the whole double ability thing came up with Paxton. It's taking all of my strength not to yell at him. I don't have Tate here; I have no idea what he's trying to tell me. I just look back to the front of the car and remain silent.

The road over the mountain seems to go on forever. We start climbing the hill, only to start going back down and then back up again. Who designed these roads? Granted, they've been neglected and abandoned for years—evidenced by lack of upkeep—but it's still the same road that was used by many, a long time ago.

"So, Chad"—Cyrus looks in his rear view mirror—"you're

back to stay this time? Where have you been holding up lately, still in Brendale?"

"Yeah, we were there for a few months while I've been going back and forth. Most nights I just crashed in one of the abandoned apartment blocks."

"So squatting is still happening out there? I bet you're happy to be going home then. Brendale isn't the safest of neighbourhoods, is it?"

"It's not so bad," Chad replies. "It was quite handy though—that area is perfect for squatting."

Squatting—while completely unnecessary due to the low population and plentiful accommodation—is still common with those who don't want the government to keep track of their whereabouts. If you don't have the money to buy or rent your own place, the government leases available housing to you for little money. But there are still some out there who can't afford it or don't want to be tied down to one place. Not to mention the government housing isn't in the most desirable neighbourhoods anyway. So they squat. From what I have been told, the rules of squatting are simple: If it's vacant and completely empty, it's available. Any form of furniture or permanent fixture means it's occupied.

The car fills with silence again, and the air feels stale and tense.

"So what's your deal, Drew?" Cyrus asks.

"I don't have a deal," Drew responds.

"Right. Okay," Cyrus replies, confused.

"He's … a hiccup," I explain. "He caught us trying to make a break for it."

"Ah. So he's an Institute man," Cyrus says. Drew doesn't respond. "We can fix that."

Fix? I think Cyrus should just try to give up on the whole small talk thing. There are clearly more issues in this car than in a melodrama.

"Well, we'll be there soon. I bet you two are anxious to get to your mother," Cyrus says to Shilah and me. I guess he's not picking up on the fact that none of us really want to chat right now.

"I guess," Shilah replies.

I just nod my head and try to smile politely. The truth is I *am* anxious about seeing my mother. So anxious I feel sick to my stomach. I don't know what to say to her. Scenarios run through my head about how tonight will go as I stare out my window. Will she greet us warmly? Will she still be mad at me for choosing to stay with the Institute for the last three months?

"Would you like a peppermint?" Cyrus asks. As I turn my head to look at him, I'm faced with a floating packet of breath mints.

I'm taken aback. This is not exactly something you see every day.

"Uh, no thanks," I respond. I actually wouldn't mind one, but I feel weird taking it from something that's hovering mid-air.

"Okay." Cyrus shrugs and the peppermints float their way

back to the centre console.

"Telekinesis," Chad says from the back seat. "One of Cyrus's abilities."

I wonder what his other ability is.

It's about another twenty minutes of awkward silence and small talk after we reach the other side of the mountain.

But everyone goes silent when we pull into a gravel driveway in between two fields of long grass. We keep going until there's nothing but trees in front of us. For a moment, I think we're going to drive straight through them, but Cyrus turns at the last minute and starts heading left, following the tree line to the end, and then around the group of trees. A large, elevated double-storey farmhouse appears as we get around the back. The porch light is on, but I can't see anybody. The dashboard clock says it's 2:31 a.m. No wonder no one is out here.

Cyrus stops the car and takes the keys out of the ignition.

"Well, this is it," he says, getting out of the car.

I hesitate for a second. The liberation I felt when Paxton turned up with Shilah has left me. This is it; this is my freedom. I should be more excited, but the anticipation of this moment happening has been building up for so long, I don't know if I can truly believe it.

I open the car door and slide out, joining Shilah, Chad, and Drew who are all standing, watching shadowy figures make their way down from the house.

As the two figures emerge, I suddenly feel as if we've walked into a trap. Two officers in military uniform are approaching, and my first thought is to flee. But when the headlights of the car illuminate their faces, elation crosses mine. Not only am I met by my mother, who I was expecting to see anyway, but standing next to her is a face I've been longing to see ever since I was arrested. Tears of happiness fall down my cheeks as I take him in my arms.

"Dad!" I scream.

CHAPTER FOUR

"What the hell is *he* doing here?" Dad asks pointing at Drew. My brief euphoria comes crashing down.

"It's a long story," I respond.

Dad looks at me, confusion crossing his face. "Please don't tell me you two are still—"

"No! God, no. It's not like that," I say.

"I'll take Drew up to the house," Chad says, leaving us.

"I'll move on," Cyrus says, getting back into the car.

The surreal feeling I had when I arrived is nothing compared to what I'm feeling right now. Mum, Dad, Shilah, and me all together.

"I promised myself I wouldn't cry," Mum blubbers, bringing

Shilah and me in for a hug. Great, now my tears start again as well.

Dad just shakes his head as he joins in on the group hug. "Women. Right, Shilah?" he jokes.

Shilah tries to sneakily wipe tears from his eyes. "Yeah. Women," he says with a croaky voice, making us all laugh.

"Come on," Mum says. "We'll take you two up to the house. We'll sleep here tonight and move into our own quarters tomorrow."

We walk up the small hill to the double-storey weatherboard house. It smells of pine and a little stale, as if the house has been closed up for a while. Chad and Drew came in here just moments ago, but they aren't in the main areas. I can't see them anywhere. Mum and Dad lead us to a living area with a fireplace and leather-bound couches. Shilah and I sit down across from Mum and Dad. Seeing them together is just weird. It's really odd to see them being affectionate towards one another. They aren't being completely obvious about it, but it's the little things like Dad placing his hand on her lower back as she walks by, both of them sitting that little bit closer to each other than necessary, and the quick looks they give one another. It's nice but weird.

"I guess I should start," Dad says. "I'm sorry I ever agreed to that harebrained idea about the woods. I knew I shouldn't have let you go, Shilah. I'm so sorry."

"Dad, it wasn't your fault. It was mine. I brought Drew into our lives," I say.

"Neither of you were to know that boy was working for the

Institute. For all you knew, he was just another Defective person looking for refuge from the same fate," Mum interjects.

"What do you know about it?" I ask a little more hastily than intended.

"Only what Chad and your father have told us," she replies.

Okay, now I'm weirded out for another reason—Chad talking to my mother about my totally messed-up relationship with Drew. I actually let out a little laugh at the idea of it.

Taking in a deep breath, I look at my mother as I build up the courage to ask something I've wanted to know the answer to for three months, ever since I found out about the Resistance and her still being alive.

"Why didn't you come for Shilah?" I ask her, but it comes out so quietly I don't know if she heard me.

"There's something you have to understand, Allira," Dad answers. "I wouldn't have allowed it."

"You knew? You knew Mum was alive this whole time?" I ask.

"Allira, don't," Shilah says, his voice pleading with me not to get into it.

"He was doing the right thing," Mum says. "As a parent, you only ever want the best for your child. A life on the run can be lonely, stressful, and dangerous. I wanted better for you two. I wanted Shilah to have a normal life. If we had known that it was both of you that needed protection, I would've brought you both with me." Mum grabs a hold of Dad's hand. "I would've brought all of you with me."

"But how was running away with Drew different to running away with you?" I press.

"Drew was offering a life of solitude," Dad answers. "You can't become a part of an organisation like this without sacrifice. There will always be an element of danger living here, more so than just running away to the woods to hide. You're responsible for not only your safety but the safety of others. At the time, I chose what I thought was the better option. But I was wrong, and I'm going to have to live with that decision for the rest of my life. You were both locked away because of me, and I couldn't be sorrier."

"But—"

"Allira, enough," Shilah interrupts me.

"I just want answers, Shilah."

"And you will get them," Mum says. "But emotions are running a bit high tonight. We're all tired, it's been a long day. We should all get some sleep."

"I'll be fine here for the night," I say, looking at the fireplace. "The fire is thawing me out."

"Me too," Shilah says.

"I'll go get you some blankets," Mum tells us.

Mum leaves the room, and I can't hold back my questions. I just need to know.

"Where did you go?" I ask Dad.

"What do you mean?"

"Drew said the Institute lost track of you after I was arrested. Whenever Chad gave me updates about the Resistance, he never mentioned that you were here. So where were you?"

"I originally set off to find the cabin in Boyce Forest where Drew said he would be with Shilah. It took me a while to work out it didn't exist. I think deep down I knew as soon as I started looking that it wasn't real, but I didn't want to accept the truth. I finally went to your aunt. I wasn't entirely sure she was a part of all this, but she was the only hope I had. She led me here, back to your mother." He pauses, holding my gaze. "The reason Chad didn't tell you was because I asked him not to. I didn't want you to jeopardise your plan to get Shilah out by trying to get to me."

He knows me too well. I had been tempted, so close to leaving Shilah. If I knew Dad was here too, I may have done it.

Mum comes back in with some blankets and a pillow each for us before I get a chance to respond to Dad's words.

"Get some sleep," she says, kissing Shilah and me on the forehead. It's almost as if the last eight years didn't happen. She's fallen straight back into the mother role. But it's not as easy for me to fall back into daughter mode with her. Dad follows her out, and Shilah gets up and moves to the opposite couch.

"You don't think they are … you know … sharing a room?" Shilah asks.

I shiver in disgust. "Eww, I hope not." We laugh briefly but a small smile lingers. I wonder if this is what it feels like to be a normal teenager—being totally grossed out by your parents. I've never had that, not that I can remember anyway.

Shilah and I are silent as we stare at the yellow and red embers flickering over the fireplace. Lying down, I bring the blanket up to my face.

"Can't sleep?" Shilah asks after a while.

I shake my head. "I think I'm too wired." I turn to face him. "I'm just trying to take it all in."

"Same here. But I think that may take a while," he replies. "Apart from all of that, are you okay?"

I shrug. "I guess I'm just in shock. I've been thinking about this moment for three months. It just doesn't feel real."

"Things will be good here. It will be different. It won't be like the Institute," he says.

"I know," I reply. I really do want to believe that. "How are you doing with the whole Mum 'Hey kids, I'm alive' shock?"

"It's weird but strangely normal. I don't know how to describe it."

"It's just straight out weird for me," I say. "I don't want it to be, but it is."

"Speaking of weird—what's the deal with you and Chad?" he asks.

"Really? You're already asking me about that?"

"Well … you called him your friend back in the car. I thought you would've sorted your shit out by now. Especially after seeing what I saw when I arrived tonight," he says, smiling.

"I don't know what's going on there."

"What do you *want* to happen with him?"

"I don't know. I can't stop getting angry at him for lying to me."

"Lying seems to be a way of life," Shilah says flatly.

"What do you mean?"

"You're angry about everyone lying to you, but it's not like you've never lied, right? In this world, lies are a necessity for survival. Especially for people like us."

"How are you handling this so well? How are you not as angry as I am?"

"You really need to let go of your anger," he says.

"Oh, okay then, Zen Master. Just how do I do that?"

Shilah shrugs. "The way I see it, I've just been handed a gift. The gift of never being trapped inside a dark, windowless world for the rest of my life. I'm not angry at anyone for lying, I'm not angry about finding out Mum is alive, I'm happy. Happy that everything I've ever wanted is right here … well, almost everything."

"Almost?" I ask, one eyebrow raised.

"Yeah. Almost," he says, blushing.

"Okay, I so need the details of *that*. You're seeing someone?"

"I was. Well, sort of. I'll explain another time. It kinda hurts to think about it too much with them still being back at the Institute."

I nod. No—I need more. "Sorry, you have to tell me."

Shilah smiles. "Tomorrow," he says. "I'm going to try and get some sleep."

I hear footsteps coming into the room. Sitting up, I see Chad walking towards us. I pull my legs up and make room on the couch for him to sit.

"There's a room at the end of the hall that's free if you want to take that, Shilah," he says.

Shilah smirks. "Sure." He gets up and leaves. and my heart starts beating a little faster.

"Hey," Chad says. I just nod my head. "How are you going? You doing okay?"

"Why does everybody keep asking me that as if I might crack at any moment? I'm fine." It comes out a little less than fine, but I can't help my tone.

"Yeah. Sounds like it," he mutters.

"So, where's Drew? Not escaping, is he?"

"We wouldn't want that. now would we," Chad replies sarcastically, slouching down on the couch farther as if he's pissed off. "He'd be stupid to try. We're a day, day and a half's, walk away from anywhere in every direction. Even if he was to get out, we'd get him before he'd even reach the Institute or civilisation of any kind." He laughs. "And I locked him in his room." He still seems annoyed, but at least the arrogant smirk that I know so well is present.

"Are we ever going to be able to have a conversation without an angry undertone ever again?" I ask, looking at the fire and not him.

"I hope so. I suppose you're angry now because I kept your dad from you?"

"Well, I'm not any *angrier* at you, but yeah, still kind of angry."

"What if I promise that from this moment on, I will completely tell you the truth? About anything," he says.

"Complete truth?" I turn to face him.

"There's no reason for secrets anymore. I've got what I wanted."

"And what's that?"

"You, me, here," he says, reaching for my hand.

Our hands find each other in the dark as a small smile crosses my lips.

"And Tate?" I ask, glancing back towards the fireplace.

"What about Tate?"

"Aren't you going to cover yourself now by saying it's what Tate always wanted?"

"Did you mean what you said in the car before?" Chad asks, ignoring my accusation.

"I said a lot of things in the car. You might need to be more specific."

"When you found out Drew thought I was dead. You said I was just your friend. Is that what you want?"

I hang my head. He chooses *now* to have this conversation? At 3:45 a.m.?

"I didn't think calling you my friend was all that shocking, but I guess it was, considering Shilah brought it up and now you. What else was I meant to call you? That's what we are, aren't we? *Friends?* Or do you just see me as some kind of assignment?"

He lets out a sigh, throwing his head back to rest on the couch. "I've never seen you as an assignment."

"Then how do you see me?" *Damn my shaky voice.*

He sits up and moves his head closer to mine. My heart skips a beat as he cradles my head and pulls me in close. His eyes pierce mine, and my breath catches in my throat. Bringing his mouth down, he presses his lips gently and briefly against mine.

"Does that answer your question?" he asks, breaking away just an inch. He doesn't give me a chance to respond before he takes my mouth with his again.

Is this actually happening? Yes, I'm definitely kissing Chad. His tender touch becomes firmer when I start kissing him back. I kiss him harder, and he holds me tighter. My heart races, and I wonder if he can feel it too. Months of avoiding taking this step has led to this—pawing at each other in hopes of squashing any residual sexual tension between us. Pulling myself onto his lap without breaking our lips apart, I wrap myself around him. His hands slide down the middle of my back and rest firmly on my hips. All I can think is, *Why haven't we been doing this the whole time? I want more.*

He pulls his mouth away from mine and starts tracing kisses down my neck. I arch my back, pushing myself into him harder.

"So beautiful," he murmurs against my skin.

"Your room?" I ask, trying to be confident, but it comes out nervous and a little desperate.

"I would love that, I really would. I don't think you realise how much."

"Uh, actually," I say, looking down at myself sitting in his lap. "I have a pretty good inkling."

He lets out a groan. "If only I didn't just give my room to your brother."

"Damn it," I say, touching my forehead to his.

We sit there for a moment, just trying to catch our breaths. Climbing off him, I sit down next to him, but his arm still lingers around me. "So I guess I can't call you 'just a friend' anymore."

"You better not," he says jokingly, but then his face goes straight and he gets flustered. "I just realised how possessive that came out. I didn't mean it like that. You can tell people we're just friends if you want. I ..." He's getting tongue tied, which is weird for Chad—he's usually good with words. I smile. "I didn't mean—"

"Chad," I say. "Stop talking." And I kiss him again.

* * *

Sitting next to the fireplace, I take in its warmth. Chad stayed with me in the living room last night, but sharing one couch and one blanket between the two of us got uncomfortable really quick. Plus, Chad snores. It sucks. It's not like how I imagined sharing a bed with someone. The romantic fantasy of falling asleep in each other's arms, waking up refreshed, and not at all with a crick in your neck was dashed when, after an hour of trying, I just couldn't fall asleep.

The pile of logs next to the fireplace is getting smaller, but the orange light of dawn is starting to peer through the window. Pulling out the letter that Tate wrote me those many months ago, I read it for the zillionth time.

Wipe that stupid look off your face, Allira. Nice way to start a heartfelt goodbye letter, right?

I know everything is hard to understand right now, and I know you have no idea what is going on. All I really need you to know is that I am sorry for having kept a big part of me a secret. I had to. I had to do it so I could get you out of here.

You can't get angry at me (I won't allow it) for the lies

between us. I know on some level you are comparing what Chad and I have done to what Drew did to you. But I'm telling you now that there is one big difference between us. He did everything to save his own skin. We did everything to save yours. In fact, the only thing I get from this is I lose my best friend. So your argument is invalid.

Now, before you get all teenagery on me and claim our whole friendship was a lie and blah, blah, blah, let me explain this— I had no idea who you were when I befriended you. I didn't realise you were Persephone's daughter. I didn't know until I met Shilah. On my last assignment before I was arrested, we were under strict instructions not to approach him because of who he was. Your mum did not want Shilah to live the life of a fugitive. Finding out who you are had no impact on the way I feel about you because you were my friend first. I'd already fallen for you (in the platonic sense, of course, because as we have already established, you are not a dude).

Also, don't punish Chad for obeying my orders. Outranking him really does come in quite handy when I want favours. He was doing it to save you just as much as I was. I told you he was on the right side. He's on your side.

As much as I would have loved this letter to be well-written and inspirational, even a bit philosophical, I have little time and am taking a big risk by even doing this at all. I can't say anything more other than, I'm sorry. I'm sorry I hurt you. I am not sorry that I did it. I would do it again if it meant you got to live the life you deserve; a life of choices, a life of freedom and hopefully one day—a life of equality.

If you ever doubt yourself, just remember: YOU'VE GOT THIS. You're one of the strongest people I know, even if you don't feel it sometimes.

And with that, I say goodbye. I love you.

He didn't sign his name.

I look at the words, written out in front of me. Tate knew exactly how I was going to feel, exactly what I was going to be thinking when I found out about the Resistance, right down to the look of astonishment that resided on my face.

I hate that he's still there. I hate that he refused to come with us. He's probably right though—if they knew what he could do, he'd most likely not be allowed out of their sight. He would be trapped forever, as he is now, but also doing unspeakable and inhumane things to others.

I miss talking to him. I miss *not* talking to him. Our telepathic conversations, while often rambling and nonsensical, were some of the closest and meaningful conversations I've ever had with anyone. I often find myself wondering if the whole concept of a soul mate was true. I had found mine in Tate. Not in the romantic way, of course. I always thought the soul mate fantasy an unrealistic view of the world—it should have nothing to do with sex and everything to do with friendship. A soul mate is someone you spend your entire life knowing. You grow with them; you become a part of who they are and vice versa until there is a point where you don't know where they end and you begin.

Looking down at the letter, I reread over and over that Chad was just obeying orders. It makes me wonder if it came down to making a choice between the Resistance and me, which one would he make? Would he be able to put his unambiguous determination aside and pick me over the cause? Not that I think he will ever have to, but I worry I'll always come second with him. Looking up at him still snoring on the couch, I want to believe he's on my side. In this moment, I decide to.

Carefully and quietly, I gently climb back onto the couch next to him. Letting the warmth of his blanketed body cover me, I freeze when he stirs for a moment, but he is back to sleep within seconds. I didn't realise how cold it was until I felt how warm he is. With my head in the nook of his shoulder and my hand on his chest, I think I might actually fall asleep even with the snoring.

CHAPTER FIVE

"This looks cosy." Ebbodine's voice wakes me. I look to the couch opposite us where she sits. Has she been there a while? I didn't even hear her come in. Then again, she can teleport, so she probably only just got here.

Jumping off the couch, I forget about any desire I *should* have not to disturb Chad. I tackle Ebb on the opposite couch.

"Whoa. I don't know if you know this, but I'm not into girls," she says, laughing. She always says this whenever I show her any form of affection, whether it be a mere compliment or any form of physical contact. "Plus, I'm not into sloppy seconds," she says, gesturing to Chad.

Chad sits up, rubbing his face trying to wake up. "I'm so glad you considered my request to stop popping in whenever you wanted seriously, Ebb."

"Yeah, sorry. I couldn't really help it when I found out Allira was finally here," she says, wrapping her arm around me.

"What time is it?" I ask as I hear banging and clattering of pots and pans coming from what is presumably the kitchen.

"Eight," Ebbodine replies.

"Wow, and you're out of bed?" I ask her sarcastically. The Ebb I know struggled to get out of bed in time for school to start at nine.

"Yeah. Don't get much of a sleep-in here; too much to do," she says with a sigh. "Come on, let's get some breakfast."

Mum is putting food on the dining table where Dad, Shilah, and Drew are already seated when we walk out of the living room. Dad at least seems a bit friendlier towards Drew this morning. And by friendly, I mean not yelling at him.

Mum and Dad are both still wearing military uniforms though. I meant to ask why last night, but there were more important things to discuss.

"So what's with the uniforms?" I ask, taking a seat at the table.

"Oh, this is kind of a welcoming house. We usually only put people in here for the first day or two until we can get them settled into their own accommodations. It's pretty run-down, and we don't tend to it often as it's too close to the road to set up here permanently," Mum starts to explain. "Because of its proximity to the road, when someone stays here, we put on these uniforms for anyone passing through. We don't get many people stumbling upon us, usually just teenagers on dares, snooping their way through. The uniforms scare them off pretty quickly, and we tell them it's too dangerous out here and that they're past the radiation barrier. It's lucky we only get the occasional interested teenager or member of the public. These uniforms aren't standard, and if an official was to come out and find us, they'd see right through the charade. It's just a safety precaution."

I nod, accepting her explanation, and then glance at the food. There isn't really anything I would like to eat. There's scrambled eggs, a platter of fruit, and plate of greens to choose from.

"Coffee?" I ask.

My parents just stare blankly at me.

"Sorry, darling, we don't have any coffee. We don't grow the beans in our crops," Mum replies. "We have tea?"

"Oh shit," Drew says, smiling at me. "I do not want to be around you this afternoon."

"No, that's okay," I reply politely to Mum while kicking Drew under the table. He knows what I'm like when I don't have my morning coffee. I shake my head. *No coffee? What kind of hell is this?*

"So what's the plan for today?" I ask, while shovelling food in my mouth. I didn't have much of an appetite to begin with, but tasting the eggs reminded me of what I'd been missing out on while at the Institute, where everything was laboratory grown. Even the restaurant I was working at used synthetic foods. I can't get the fresh food in fast enough; it tastes amazing and reminds me of my past life—meals at home with

Dad and Shilah. I take a break from stuffing my face to take in this moment. My family, my friends, all together at one table … and Drew. But it's easy to ignore him when I'm this happy.

"I'll show you around the compound today, introduce you to a few people," Mum says. "Then we'll organise some housing for us now that there will be the four of us."

"Four?" Shilah asks. "You and Dad … are … you know?"

"I don't know if I want the answer to that question," I joke.

My parents look at each other, smiling like lovesick teenagers. "We didn't separate when I left. Well, we did, but not because we didn't love each other," Mum replies.

Shilah makes a pretend puking noise, making me laugh.

"I was thinking, Mrs. Daniels," Ebbodine says, "I could really do with a roommate. There's enough room at my place for another bed, and I wouldn't mind the company if you would allow Allira to stay with me."

Mum and Dad look at each other again, and it almost seems as if they can talk telepathically to each other. I guess when you've been a couple for as long as they have, even after an eight-year gap, you still have that kind of connection.

"You're eighteen, Allira, so it's not up to us," Dad says.

"I wouldn't mind sharing with Ebb. If you guys are okay with it."

I do want to stay with my family, but the thought of going back into a cramped living space like our old farmhouse with

73

not only Dad and Shilah but with Mum as well? I really got used to having my own space and my own area while living at the Institute. Living with Drew took some getting used to, but eventually that felt natural too. I'm sure living with Ebb will be easier than living with three other people.

"Whatever you'd like, sweetie," Mum responds.

I glance sideways at Ebbodine in excitement. She mouths something to me. I think it's "you're welcome." I don't know what she exactly means by that, but I shrug it off.

Chad reaches over, his hand finding my thigh under the table. I look at him, smiling, but he just casually keeps eating as if nothing's going on—as if this transition from friends to … more than friends isn't a big deal.

"We'll be leaving soon," Mum says. "So if you wanted to shower and maybe get a change of clothes, I'd go now. Your dad managed to save most of what was in your wardrobe from home, and some of the others here at the compound have donated some of their old clothes. Drew, would you like to go first?"

"Umm. Sure, I guess," Drew replies, getting up from the table.

"Just down the hall, on the right. There's a pile of clothes in there you can pick from. Towels are in the bathroom," Mum tells him.

As soon as Drew leaves and we can hear the water running, Mum's expression turns serious.

"So what actually happened last night?" she asks. "How did

Drew end up coming with you? Do you think we can trust him?"

"He caught her sneaking out," Chad answers. "I wouldn't trust him as far as I could throw him. Actually, I reckon I could throw him pretty far, so I take that back." He smiles. "I don't trust him, but we had no choice."

"So what are we going to do with him?" she asks.

"Can you do your thing and send him back?" I ask her, referring to her memory tampering skills.

"That's not such a great idea. My ability is somewhat unstable. To make sure we got all the right memories, I'd have to erase the last twenty-four hours. And even then, he may still remember what happened but assume it was a dream. That happens sometimes. When the Institute question him and they realise a whole day is missing, they'll know someone like me is out there. We've been fairly good at flying under the radar so far, we don't really want to give too much of us away."

"So you guys aren't with the same rebellion group protesting all over the city? I saw them once," I say, remembering the day not long before I was arrested when Drew and I were practically jumped on by a fiery redhead protesting to get Defective people released from the Institute.

Mum scoffs, "No. We have nothing to do with them. I know they're trying to help our cause, but I think they're just going to end up getting their very own cell at the Institute."

"So what does that mean for Drew?" I ask. "We can't erase his memory. We can't trust him. What do we do?"

I'm surprised when Shilah answers. "We do to him what the Institute does to everyone else. We train him up, teach him to think like us. We still don't have to trust him. We just need to keep him here, keep him busy, and not tell him too much."

"It could work," Dad says.

"I don't know about that," I say. "He's been with the Institute a long time. They've completely brainwashed him into thinking he was doing the right thing."

"We can show him what the *actual* right thing is," Shilah suggests.

The shower stops running, and we all go back to eating. I actually stop eating because I've shoved the food in so fast, I'm starting to feel sick.

Drew comes out of the bathroom, clean and wearing jeans and a baggy T-shirt. "So what's the verdict?" he asks, sitting back down at the dining table.

"Verdict?" I ask.

"What are you going to do with me?" Oh. He knows we only sent him to the shower so we could talk about him.

"You'll stay and be a part of our community," Mum says. "But you have to understand that we can't let you be on your own yet. I'll set you up with one of the families living here— with Allira living with Ebb, maybe you could stay with us."

"No!" Dad and Shilah say in unison.

"Whatever you think is best," Drew says without protest.

He's being remarkably calm about this whole thing. Last night he was trying to get away, resisting the whole time, but now he seems easy. Too easy. He has a long way to go before I can put any sort of trust in him.

"I'm going to go shower," I say, leaving the table.

Walking down the hallway, I find the room where the clothes are and search high and low for something I could wear. I find a pair of jeans and a long-sleeved black top with a plunging neckline. It must belong to Ebb—she must have donated it—and it's mixed in with all of my old clothes from the farm. I search for something to wear underneath it so my boobs are at least a little covered.

I jump in the shower, and as much as I'm enjoying the warm water washing over me, I know I need to hurry. Everyone is waiting for me. When I get out of the bathroom, Dad, Ebb, and Chad have left.

"Where did they go?" I ask.

"They had to start on their jobs," Mum replies. "Everyone works here, Lia." I just nod, but I smile at the fact she called me Lia. And even though she was kind of condescending, my smile appears anyway. It's a nickname only Mum and Aunt Kenna use for me. "Are we ready to go?" she asks.

"I might just grab a quick shower," Shilah says.

"Okay. While you do that, I'll go check that the car is charged and ready to go," Mum says.

Drew and I are left alone. I shift my gaze away from him.

"A bit ironic, don't you think?" he asks me.

"Ironic?"

"Well, yeah. Running from the Institute, hiding? Is this not the same plan we had for Shilah and me months ago?"

"Yes, but wasn't that plan actually fake?" I argue.

"I'm not going to get into another fight with you, Allira. The truth is that plan—while fake—was something that I often found myself thinking and dreaming about. I've always wondered what it would be like to live like this, to be free. So, thank you."

"For?"

"For bringing me here," he replies.

"I think you need to thank Chad, not me. If it was up to me, you never would've come with us last night."

Drew nods. "Fair enough. I'll remember to thank him later."

I doubt very much that Drew will actually do it.

"And I just want to say that you don't have to be all defensive towards me. I know we will not be getting back together. I thought that might have been a possibility because the last three months have been great. I even thought we were building some trust again. But now I realise it was just an act on your part. I hope we can put everything behind us and start fresh though. I hope we can be friends."

"I guess," I reluctantly agree. "But just because we're friends, that doesn't mean I have to trust you. And remember, my boyfriend will kick your ass if you do anything remotely close to screwing me over again." I play it off as if I'm half-joking, but I think we both know there's truth to my words.

"Oh, so he *is* your boyfriend now?" he asks. I don't answer him. I don't need to. I think my face—the horrid blushing—says it all. "To be honest," he says, "I'm actually more scared about you kicking my ass. I feel a bit sore today, in case you were wondering," he says, rubbing his neck.

I smile. "You can thank Chad for that too. He taught me how to knock someone out with a single punch."

"Okay, are we ready?" Mum interrupts, walking back in. She's changed out of her military costume and looks more like the mother I remembered. Her hair is neatly braided down her back, and a long maxi dress covers up her strong, fit body. I give her a smile.

"I am," Shilah says, coming down the hallway. Drew and I stand.

"Let's go," Mum says.

We follow her out to where a car is parked. Another old, beat-up hatchback. I guess the Resistance doesn't have access to fancy cars like the ones at the Institute.

"So as you can see," Mum starts as we all get into the car—Shilah in the front and Drew and I in the back. "We run everything on solar here," she says, pointing to the roof of the house where solar panels cover the roof tiles. "All of our properties are solar based. We have battery storage tanks that charge throughout the day to give us the electricity we need at night."

"What happens if one of the panels break?" Drew asks.

"Someone fixes them. If we don't know how, we learn from someone who can, or we fiddle with it until it works," Mum replies. "That rule applies to everything. If it's broken, fix it. If you can't fix it, find someone who can. We have handyman types, but their list of jobs is always ridiculously long, so we only ask them as a last resort."

We drive out of the gravel driveway and onto the road. I look back at the property, and while I can't really see much through the big group of trees hiding the house from the road, the smoke from the chimney and the pathway from the road are clearly outlined. I can see why that house definitely isn't the best hiding spot for a fugitive rebel group.

"How many of us are there?" Shilah asks.

"More than you would think," Mum replies but doesn't elaborate.

"Well, there can't be too many. There's roughly only six hundred Defective people countrywide," Drew says. "And of that six hundred, I think the Institute would have at least two hundred of them."

"While you are correct in saying we don't have that many here, definitely not four hundred, you're wrong in assuming that every statistic the Institute gives you is accurate," Mum says. "One in five thousand was a very broad guesstimate that was made many years ago and never updated. There's no telling how many of us are out there, but the statistics we have show that there's probably a lot more out there than the government expects or leads us to believe. We're finding Defective people in every city we go to for recruitment. How would that be possible if one in five thousand was correct?"

"Why wouldn't they tell us there's more?" Drew asks.

"What would the public do if they were to find out that, say, one in fifty were Defective? Finger pointing, accusations, vigilante executions, maybe? The government doesn't want to be responsible for that happening again. They can't afford more lives lost. They probably don't want us knowing that we are stronger in numbers than what they think either. Anything to avoid a war with us."

"Is it one in fifty?" I ask. That would mean there could be sixty thousand of us out there. That's a big jump from six hundred.

"We can't know for sure, but we are confident our numbers are in the thousands, even the tens of thousands," Mum replies.

Maybe this is one of those things we shouldn't really be discussing in front of Drew. Who knows what he might do with that kind of information. Although, I assume Mr. Brookfield would have the same stats, so maybe it's not so important to keep to ourselves. Drew suddenly pinches his head, right at the bridge of his nose as if he has a headache. "Sorry. Might have overshared a bit there," Mum says, smiling a little. She was thinking the exact thing I was.

"What happened?" Drew asks. "When did we get in the car?"

"That is so cool," Shilah says.

That *is* cool. I want to try it. But no one in this car knows I have the ability to do that, and if Mum can't really control it, I might make someone forget their whole life or something. That wouldn't be good. I'm under the impression this memory tweaking ability of hers can't be reversed.

We continue to drive west. Sugar cane, corn, and wheat crops slowly minimise the farther we get, and dry land begins to fill the area.

"So where are we going?" I ask.

"I figure we'll go to the most western point today. You'll hardly ever have to come out here, unless you're on food deliveries. We've taken over some old underground dwellings in the desert. Some people live out here full time: the ones who are too frail, young, or unable to do any of the hard work on the farms for any reason. It's also our last resort if someone comes looking. They're right on the border of the radiation barrier, so it's the safest place to hide. There's still a number of decades left before it will be safe to rebuild on the western side of the boundary."

"How long will it take to get there?" Shilah asks.

"About an hour," Mum replies.

An hour? Just how big is this compound? When Chad told me the Resistance was set up at a compound, I figured he meant a single property on maybe an acre of land. Not numerous properties on numerous acres of land.

"So there's really no military or anyone out here guarding the radiation zone?" I ask. "It seems pretty careless for the government to just let anyone wander into a radioactive wasteland."

"I think they are of the mind that no one would be stupid enough to risk their health by coming out here. They don't exactly have the funds or enough military for that kind of surveillance."

Mum and Shilah exchange small talk in the front as we continue to drive. She asks him about his ability training from the Institute and how strong his ability is now. It's really hard to hear them, even though I'm only two feet behind them in the back seat. I stop trying to listen after a while and just stare out the window, taking in the scenery of undiscovered land.

Mum pulls off to the side of the road, literally onto a dirt path covered in red sand. I haven't seen a tree for kilometres, and everything is flat and dry. The road is bumpy to say the least. The four-wheel drive we had last night would be much more accommodating right now. We drive for what feels like an eternity. Being told "We're almost there" numerous times is not helping. I think it's been easily twenty minutes since Mum first said it.

She finally stops the car in the middle of nowhere and says, "We're here" gleefully as she gets out of the car.

The sun hits me as I get out of the car, and my skin absorbs the heat immediately.

"Are you sure?" Shilah asks. There's nothing in sight. I know she said the housing is underground out here, but where's the entry? There's flat ground for as far as my eyes can see.

"Just follow me," Mum says.

We start heading north … or is it south? My sense of direction clearly hasn't improved over time.

It doesn't take long to feel as if I'm overheating. I know the desert is hot, but this is … I shake it off and tell myself to stop complaining—I'm outside. I remind myself, whenever I feel myself beginning to complain about anything, that it could be worse. I could still be stuck at the Institute where there are no windows and constant artificial light.

We get to a wide ramp leading down to expansive glass panel doors. No wonder we couldn't see anything when we got out of the car, the building is literally built *into* the ground.

"Pretty perfect hideout," Shilah says in awe.

"Wait until you see the rest of it," Mum says, leading us down. She takes out a key from her pocket, unlocks the door, and lets us in.

At first, I'm amazed at what I'm seeing. Typical household furniture and appliances are placed throughout the cavernous structure. They look out of place because the walls, the floors, and the roof are made of rock. There is nothing between us and the earth that surrounds us.

I get an all-too-familiar sense in here though. One of confinement, of imprisonment, of the artificial lighting I was just thinking about. I must remind myself when it comes to working at the compound—don't choose food deliveries or any other job that will send me out this way. As impressive as this bunker is, the architecture of it anyway, it won't make a suitable home for me. We only just got here, and the longer I stand here, the less cavernous it seems.

A familiar face and a few unfamiliar ones greet us when Cyrus walks in from a hallway that leads deeper into the cavern. Three kids are running circles around him, chasing each other and laughing. Strewn over Cyrus's shoulder is a pink cloth covered in white milky vomit, presumably coming from the bright-eyed, pudgy, and yet so adorable infant he's holding. He's not wearing the silly hat that he was last night, and even though there's pretty poor lighting in here, he looks remarkably younger without it. His clothes are still ridiculous though—the same tight pants and heeled boots—but today he's wearing a vest with no undershirt.

The baby is staring at me. Piercing blue eyes that look too big for her head bore into me, and I can't help but smile at her. Mum and Cyrus exchange pleasantries, but I'm distracted by the tiny human smiling at me while I pull funny faces.

"Would you like to hold her?" Cyrus asks. He startles me. I didn't realise he was watching me. "Here," he says, handing me the baby.

I hold her on my hip and start bouncing her around, quickly stopping after I recall the vomit-covered towel on Cyrus's shoulder. I continue to make funny faces at her and she reaches for my face, not taking her eyes off me for a second.

"You're a natural," Cyrus tells me. He looks over to my mother, "Ready to be a grandmother, Seph?"

"Not even slightly," Mum responds.

I hand the baby back to Cyrus. "I'm with her on this one," I say. Cyrus just laughs.

"We won't be here long," Mum says. "I'm just showing these three around today."

"Where are you off to next?" Cyrus asks. "Can I get a lift to the Fields?"

"Sure. I was going to show them the Fields this afternoon. Allira will be staying there with Ebbodine."

I interrupt. "Okay, I didn't know sleeping in a field was part of the deal. Is it too late to stay with you?" I ask Mum. Cyrus and Mum smile.

"That's just what we call that area." Mum replies. "It's the main farming area. Your Dad and I are staying there at the moment too, but we'll have to move to make room for Shilah. I don't think any of the housing there is big enough for us."

"Just let me know when you're leaving, and I'll come with you," Cyrus says.

"Will do," Mum says before leading us down the hallway in which Cyrus appeared from.

"What are all of these rooms for?" Shilah asks as we walk past numerous doors evenly spaced along the hallway.

"These are all apartments. We think this place used to be some sort of hotel or tourist attraction. We've made some renovations to the place since we discovered it fifteen years ago, but it was abandoned long before that."

"Fifteen years?" Drew asks. "Just how long have you all been here?"

Mum stops and turns to look at the three of us, unsure of what to say. I sense she doesn't want to give too much information in front of Drew.

"The Resistance didn't start out with the purpose it has now. It has always been a kind of refuge. It's what the Institute should have been, what they claim they are. Our founding members were an elderly couple. They weren't even Defective. They owned most of the land out here and had spent their entire lives farming it. When the Institute was built, they would get runaways from the city, from the surrounding suburbs, all looking for a place to lay low and hide. They knew that these runaways were Defective, but they didn't care. With young people around, they didn't have to work as hard. They were aging and the farm had seen better days. This was twenty-nine years ago—just one year after the Institute was founded. Eventually, when the rumours spread about how bad it really was at the Institute, the ones they had taken in started going back into society and recruiting more of us. From there, it led to where we are today." Mum leans in and whispers in my ear, "Do you think I gave away too much again?"

I give a little giggle and whisper back, "No. I think you're all good." As much as I'd love to see Drew all dazed and confused again, I think it'll be good for him to know that this whole operation was built by two non-Defectives just wanting to help people.

"Okay, let's keep moving," Mum says, turning and walking farther into the cavernous structure.

We finally get to the other side with more glass-panelled doors that lead to a large atrium. Light flows in from the roof to a paved courtyard with a single tree in the middle. It's out of place, we're in the middle of the desert, how is a tall green tree able to grow here? The roof is glass, and looking up, I realise just how far underground we are. It has to be at least twenty, if not thirty, metres down.

"If anything was to ever go wrong, if we were found out or if we were to be invaded, this is where we are to meet," Mum explains.

Shilah, looking at the tree just as dumbfounded as I am, asks, "How is this even possible?"

Mum just smiles. "Sunlight, water, the two essential things to keep trees alive," she says with slight sarcasm.

"But the glass roof," I say. "What if people come looking and discover it?"

"In the highly unlikely situation of that happening, we have Nina for that," Mum replies.

"Did someone just say my name?" a voice says. I turn around just in time to see her appear. Not from a doorway but from thin air.

"Another teleporter like Ebbodine?" I ask.

"Not quite," the woman replies before disappearing again. When she reappears, she's standing next to the tree. She reaches out with her left hand, and simultaneously, she and the tree disappear.

"She can cloak things," Mum says. "Plus, the only way to see the glass roof would be from an aerial point of view or if they stumbled across it by foot. And the odds of that happening are ridiculously small." The woman appears again, close to us. The tree remains invisible. "Nina, this is my daughter, Allira, my son, Shilah, and this is Drew."

Up close, I realise Nina is young. She can't be much older than me. She has tanned skin and long brown hair, braided to one side.

"Welcome," Nina says.

"I'm just showing them around today," Mum says. "But we're about to go, and I think Cyrus was going to come with us."

"I better go relieve him of child duty then, I suppose," Nina says, sighing and walking out. The tree reappears after she's gone.

"She's Cyrus's—"

"Wife," Mum cuts me off. I was going to say daughter, but okay.

"Wife? Really?" Drew asks.

"She looks a little young," Shilah adds.

"We better get going," Mum says, ignoring our comments and questions.

She leads us back through the corridor, out into the main living room and kitchen area of the cave where Cyrus is handing the baby over to Nina.

"Will you be back tonight?" Nina asks Cyrus.

"Maybe. I'll see how it goes. It might be easier for me to stay at the Fields tonight," he replies before leaning in and kissing her on the forehead gently. He kisses the baby on the forehead too and starts to walk out when one the children from earlier runs up to him, grasping Cyrus's leg tight.

"Don't leave, Daddy," the child pleads.

"Aww, sweetheart. I will be back. I promise," Cyrus says,

leaning down and hugging the young girl, who looks to be about four years old.

"Okay," the girl replies with clear disappointment in her voice. She walks away with her head down and dragging her feet. I can't help feeling sorry for the girl.

"We ready to move on then?" Cyrus asks. We nod in unison. "Then let's go."

CHAPTER SIX

After another gruelling long car trip, this time with me wedged between Shilah and Drew, we arrive at the Fields. We drive down a grassy path, the faint wheel imprints the only sign the path exists. After a few rocky and bumpy minutes, making our way down a bit of a slope, we come to a clearing. We're in the middle of nowhere, yet here we are, driving through what reminds me of the main street of Eminent Falls, where I used to live with Dad and Shilah. Houses line one side of the makeshift street, which is made of dirt and loose gravel. Colorbond steel sheds line the other side. At the end of the road, a cattle gate blocks off the street.

This is more what I was expecting when Chad told me about the compound. Maybe not the town-like feel, but definitely the proximity to everything. We drive about halfway down the street and stop outside one of the larger sheds.

"This is what we use as a town hall," Mum says. "All of our meetings are held here."

"It's really the only place big enough to fit us all," Cyrus adds. "But that's no fun—let's go meet everyone in the dining hall."

We get out of the car and walk to a different shed down the road. Cafeteria-style tables line the entire shed, and mismatched chairs of all different types and heights align with the tables.

Feeling a little overwhelmed by everyone lifting their heads to look at the new kids standing in the doorway, I sink back a little, shielding myself behind Shilah and Drew.

I spot Chad, Ebbodine, and Dad sitting at the end of the middle table. They're accompanied by a group of people still staring at us, while most sets of eyes have gone back to their plates.

Chad gets up and walks over to me, taking me off guard as he wraps his arm around me and kisses me, hard and passionately. Right here, in front of everyone. I'm taken aback and a little bit shocked, and even though I want more, I gently press against his shoulder to push him away. I wasn't expecting a big public "we're together" gesture. Chad doesn't seem like that kind of person either, so his actions are confusing.

When he pulls away, we're met by an array of different expressions and feelings coming from those around us. Chad remains close, runs his hand down my arm, and clasps my hand in his. I shiver at his touch—in a good way—and his lips curl up at the ends, enjoying my reaction to him.

Drew's strong feelings of hurt come from behind me. Ebbodine and Shilah's typical mocking attitude oozes from their expressions. I don't even need to use Drew's ability to know what they're thinking about. Mum has made her way over to Dad at the lunch table, and they are both surprised by our kiss, but there's a feeling of disgust—no, *disappointment* coming from that same general area. I can't tell who it's coming from until a woman stands from the table and approaches us. She has sandy blonde hair, just like Chad's, and similar hazel eyes. She doesn't need to introduce herself for me to know she's his mother. Chad, still holding my hand, squeezes it a little tighter.

"You'll have to excuse my son," the woman says. "He's always had a bit of flair for the dramatic."

I look at Chad.

"This is my mother, Belle. Mum, this is Allira," Chad says.

"I figured that, dear," she replies condescendingly. "Come, have some lunch with us," she says, addressing me. Fiddling nervously with the sleeve of my top, I make my way over to where they're sitting.

"Are you hungry?" Chad asks. "I'll go get you a plate."

"I'll come with you," I respond quickly. Chad's mum's eyes burn into me. I don't really want to be left with her without Chad.

We join the line where the food is. I'm too distracted by Chad's mum and the hostility she's feeling to focus on what I actually want to eat, so I just pile anything on my plate. I try to block her out, but I can't help it. I think because I've been around Drew so much the last three months, my connection to his ability is the strongest. Hopefully, with time, my subconscious will attach itself to a different ability, and soon. Knowing what people are feeling all the time can get exhausting, and it's not like Tate's ability where white noise can block it out; words are easy to ignore, but feelings are not.

We go back to the table, and I take a seat next to Ebb, and Chad sits down on the other side of me. I avoid eye contact with Belle as I sit across from her.

"So, you're working on a farm?" I turn to Ebb.

Ebb rolls her eyes. "Yeah, only when your aunt's not here. She's training me in medicine."

"You'd be really good at that."

Ebb has the nurturing, outgoing personality that medics need.

"The farming isn't as bad as I thought it would be," she says. "But I don't think I've ever been this exhausted."

"I'm kind of looking forward to it," I say.

"Yeah, you would." She laughs.

"Wanting to work on the farms, are you, Allira?" Chad's mum interrupts. I didn't realise she was eavesdropping.

I clear my throat. "It's probably what I would be best at. I've done it before."

"Well, the council will be the ones to decide what you would be best at."

I nod instead of responding. With that much animosity in her tone, it looks as if I'm already doing a great job at pissing off my boyfriend's mother, and I don't even know what I've done. It's not exactly how I imagined meeting her would go … not that I've actually given much thought to meeting her at all. I also didn't imagine her to be so intimidating.

Over at the table next to ours, Cyrus sits with a woman. With his arm around her, and their flirty nature between each other, I can't help but wonder who she is.

"Who's that?" I ask Chad quietly so his mother can't eavesdrop again.

"With Cyrus?" he asks, nodding in their direction. I nod back. "That's his wife."

I give Chad a confused look. "But, I just met Nina," I say. Nina has dark hair; this woman is blonde.

"Oh. Umm … yeah." Chad looks over at his mother, who is still staring at us from across the table. "I'll fill you in later," he whispers.

I nod, even though I really want to know now. Looking down at my tray, I notice that I filled it completely with rice, only rice and nothing else. Damn my distracted self. If I wasn't so focussed on Belle's feelings, maybe I would've at least put some sort of protein on my plate. I eat as much of the bland, dry food as I can before I have to give in and leave it.

Everyone else has finished, and they sit around chatting amongst themselves. I feel too self-conscious to talk above a whisper to anyone but Chad or Ebb.

Cyrus walks towards the table. "What have you got planned

for the rest of the afternoon?" he asks Mum.

"I was thinking of taking them to the training arena next," she replies.

"Oh, good," Cyrus says. "I was hoping to get a few training sessions in for the four newbies before the council meeting next week."

"Council meeting?" I ask.

"For your placements," Mum replies. "The council takes your preferences into account when they make their decision. But we have other factors to consider as well."

"I'll see you all out there this afternoon," Cyrus says before leaving.

I count Shilah, Drew, and myself. Who's the fourth newbie that Cyrus was talking about? It isn't until we get up to leave that I realise just who that fourth person is. It was only twenty-four hours ago that I was trying to arrest her. Licia sees me too and gets up out of her seat and rushes over to hug me.

"Thank you," she says. "Thank you so much, Allira."

I give a half-smile. "Don't mention it," I reply.

Drew comes in between us. "You?" he asks me. "You organised her escape?"

"Well, I had help," I gesture to Chad.

"But how ... when?" he asks, but I have a feeling it's rhetorical. "I really don't know you at all," he says, shaking his head.

"What's that supposed to mean?" I ask.

"I didn't mean it as a bad thing. I just didn't realise what you were capable of. You're not as innocent as you make out to be."

"Well, I guess I can't really argue with that. You really don't know me at all," I say as I walk away.

Licia follows me outside. "So you guys aren't really married then?" she asks.

"Not even close," I say and give a little laugh. "So how are you settling in? How long have you been here?"

"We only got here in the very early hours yesterday morning. We've really only had time to move into our new residence and kind of find our bearings. My dad has already been assigned to the farms, and Mum is going to be working here in the kitchen. I'm yet to get my work detail."

"Yeah, I think all of us will be assessed next week. According to council members anyway. I wonder why your parents aren't being assessed."

Licia looks down at her feet. "Neither of them are Defective," she says almost shamefully. "They asked them if they had any skillset, but Mum has only ever worked in the food industry, and Dad has just taken odd jobs here and there so has no real trade to work in."

So they only assess Defective people?

The others all walked out while I stopped to talk to Licia, and

Mum's voice cuts through from outside. "Allira, we have to go now. Licia, you can come with us if you like?"

Licia nods to her parents to let them know she's coming with us. We walk out to the car where Shilah has already taken Cyrus's spot in the front seat. I sigh and get into the back with Drew again. Licia climbs in after me.

"Where did Dad and the others go?" I ask, not wanting to say Chad's name after that very public kiss. I don't want that to be brought up right now. In fact, I'll be happy to avoid any conversation about that—now and in the future.

"They had to get back to work," Mum replies.

It feels like I've spent most of the day in this crazy small hatchback, squished in between someone or another. As we drive down the street, Mum points out where some of the residences are, not mine though. She said it was in this area but hasn't actually told me where yet. I wonder if someone is setting up where Mum, Dad, and Shilah will live. This morning they weren't sure where there would be room.

We get to the end of the street, and two people open up the cattle gate for us as we drive through. We drive farther down into the valley, in between where two mountains meet. Moving away from the small township, I see now that it kind of rests on a plateau, halfway down the mountain. It's well hidden from above and below. I'm relieved I'll be staying there and not at the Welcoming House where it's so open and exposed.

We drive past a group of farmers, making their way down the hill on foot. Scanning the crowd for Chad or Ebb, even Dad, we go past them too quickly for me to see anyone clearly.

"They walk up and down the hill every day?" I ask.

"Yes, Lia. They do," Mum replies, sighing.

I know I haven't seen Mum in years, and granted a lot of the childhood memories I have of her are the nice ones, but I can't shake the feeling that she thinks I have an entitlement ego. It's her little comments like *"Everyone works here, Lia"* in the same condescending tone Chad's mum used with him. Is it just every parent's job to use that tone or just council members?

I want to defend myself. I want to tell her that I have no problem with hard work; I've been doing it for years. She wouldn't know that. She wasn't there. But I bite my tongue. It's a cheap shot.

At the bottom of the valley, we reach the Fields. Wheat, sugar, and corn grow on one side, and fruit and vegetable beds are on the right. The two mountains have more distance between them than I first suspected. It's quite an optical illusion; it confuses your depth perception and hides the farming crops well.

We drive beyond the Fields that seem to go on forever and arrive at what is clearly the training arena, as Mum called it earlier.

I'm getting a bit of déjà vu. For a moment, I feel as if I'm back at the Institute. An obstacle course is to my right, very similar to the one I ran for my field test. I let out a little groan. I haven't done weights or anything since being on the outside of the Institute, only running with Drew.

Mum parks the car and we all get out. We start walking

towards the obstacle course, and I look to my left at Shilah and see him smiling. Ugh, he's excited about further fitness torture.

We walk past the obstacle course to a shooting range behind it. A row of targets shaped like people line bushland with markers placed around the range to shoot from. The markers are at random intervals allowing shooting from all angles.

"Want to have a go at shooting?" Mum asks us. Shilah's face has turned from a smile to a child-like grin. "I'll take that as a yes, Shilah?"

Shilah nods excitedly.

Mum walks us over to a large walk-in rectangular storage container. Inside there is a metal cabinet as wide as the container itself. She walks over, enters a combination in the safety lock, and opens the cabinet with one slide of the panel door.

Guns, guns, and more guns line the cabinet: rifles down the bottom, and pistols up the top on a shelf. Mum stands in front of the cabinet, looking at us with expectant eyes. "Well?" she says. "Come pick one."

Shilah is first to get over to her, of course. He picks one of the rifles, the biggest gun they have. I give a little sigh, go up, and collect one of the handguns from the top shelf.

"Are they loaded?" I ask. I'm scared I'll shoot myself in the foot just by carrying this thing. I never had any weapons training at the Institute, and I'm actually kind of glad of that fact. If I'm not using a weapon, the less chance there is of me hurting myself.

"Not yet. We'll load them once we're out there," Mum replies.

Okay, good. At least I don't have to worry about shooting myself until we're outside.

"We use blanks for practice anyway, if you're worried about hurting yourself," she says, smirking at me.

How does she know me so well when she hasn't been around me for so long?

Drew walks up next and also grabs one of the bigger guns, like Shilah. Licia follows my lead and selects a handgun. We walk back outside and over to the shooting range. There's a large table at the back of the range. Mum sets the ammunition down and tells us to put our weapons on the table, too.

"There's really only one rule, but it's an important one," Mum says. "If someone is in front of this table, no one is holding a weapon unless they're in the field. Do you understand?" We all nod in response. "We may be shooting blanks, but they can still cause injuries, even fatalities at close range. It's also best to practice safety at all times so it becomes a habit. We'll only load one gun at a time and will empty the round before loading another. Shilah, you want to go first?"

Now that it's time to actually use the gun, he has become nervous, and I can't help but giggle at him a little. Mum shows him how to load the weapon and how to aim and trigger it. She tells him to step back while she takes the first shot to demonstrate. Shilah walks over to where the rest of us are and watches intently. She stands at a forty-five-degree angle, her left shoulder facing the target. She raises the gun, the butt resting in her right shoulder, and her elbow is held high. She aims, breathes out, and pulls the trigger. I'm expecting a bang but hardly any noise comes out at all.

"Silencers?" Drew asks.

"We *are* in the middle of nowhere, but it's better to be safe than sorry. We don't want to be drawing any unnecessary attention to ourselves," Mum replies. The target sways gently. She hit the dummy target right in the middle of the chest. Perfect shot.

Shilah steps up. Mum places the gun in his hand and again shows him how to hold and aim it. "Are you ready?" she asks him. He nods and takes his place at the line.

He lifts his elbow high, imitating Mum's stance. I see him take a deep breath in and lower his head. He pulls the trigger. I look to the targets but can't see where he has hit. I guess he missed. Licia points to the very left edge of one of the targets. There, in the bottom corner, is the hole. He hit it but only just.

I've been so distracted by trying to see where he hit, I didn't notice Shilah holding his right shoulder with his left hand and the pained expression on his face.

"Are you okay?" I ask as I rush over to him.

"Sorry," Mum says. "I forgot to mention the kickback."

"Thanks," Shilah says sarcastically.

"Does it hurt badly?" she asks.

He slowly lifts his arm and does slow circular motions with it. "Nah, it's not too bad. I think it was just the shock from the jolt that got me." He stands to take aim again. This time when he shoots, he barely flinches.

He has become a lot stronger than the boy I lived with six months ago. I'm sure if this happened then, he would've been complaining for days, avoiding his chores and being an all-round pain in the ass.

"Allira, you want a turn?" Mum asks after Shilah empties the clip in his gun.

"Uh … maybe Drew can go first," I suggest.

Drew goes to join her. He picks up the gun he chose and puts his hand out for the ammo.

"Uh …" Mum hesitates.

Drew drops his head to the side. "Really? You think I'm going to turn it on you?" he asks lightly.

"Of course not," Mum says, but her eyes tell a different story.

"That wouldn't exactly end well for me, would it?"

Drew's smart. He knows doing something stupid would only result in a lose-lose situation.

"Do you know how?" Mum relents but not before a reassuring nod from Shilah—he must have caught a glimpse of what's going to happen. Mum hands Drew a cartridge.

"Yeah, I know how."

He takes the cartridge in his hand and swiftly and effortlessly loads the gun. He steps up to the mark, aims, shoots, and then shoots again, repetitively until he's out of bullets. I lose count around ten. He hits the target every time.

We all stand there, looking at him gobsmacked. "Institute trained me," he says, shrugging it off as if it's not a big deal.

"Licia, you go," I say. I know I'm procrastinating, but I think the more I watch, the better chance I'll have of not embarrassing myself when it's my turn. Licia steps up to the mark, and Mum starts showing her how to load the gun. Drew comes back and stands next to me. "That was pretty impressive," I admit to him.

"You could've been that good, had you turned up for any of the training," he says.

"What training?" I ask.

"After you became an agent. You spent every day of our last week at the Institute in The Crypt with that Tate guy."

"But they never offered me any further training?" I say.

"Yes, they did. Did you ever check your schedule? They weren't mandatory classes, so they never missed you, but they did offer you the opportunity."

I try to think back to three months ago, right after I became an agent. I don't remember seeing anything about further training, but I was also feeling sad and sorry for myself that Chad was gone and I didn't know when I was going to see him again. I remember spending my mornings with Drew going over our case and my afternoons with Shilah or Tate. I guess if they really did offer them to me, I wouldn't have taken them anyway.

"Right. Allira, you're up. No getting out of it now," Mum says, smiling. I didn't even see Licia have her go, but by the added holes in the target, I can see she's a natural at this.

I nervously make my way up to the marker. Mum passes me the handgun and shows me how to load it. My hands tremble, but I don't know if it's from nerves or excitement. I assume nerves, but there is something exhilarating about holding such a powerful weapon. Exhilarating, scary ... same thing, right?

She takes the gun off me and shows me the proper way to stand and the best way to aim. When she hands it back to me, she tells me to have a go. I turn sideways, holding the gun out with both hands. Lifting the gun to eye level, I look along the top of the gun to line it up with the target. Taking a deep breath in, I hold it while I squeeze the trigger. I was expecting a large kickback like Shilah had, but being a smaller gun, and prepared for it, it barely made me flinch. I aim again and shoot. I keep going until I'm out of ammo.

As I look at the target, all of my bullets hit, but they're not as precise as Drew's. They're pretty scattered considering I thought I was aiming at the same spot each time. I'm not disappointed, but I am competitive. I want another go.

"Okay. I'm going to go change over the targets to new ones," Mum says. "Rule number one applies. Allira, place the gun on the table and step back." I do as she says, and she heads out into the range to change over the paper targets.

"Not bad," Drew says. "For a beginner."

We spend the next few hours shooting. My nerves left me after the second round, and now I just want more. We try each other's guns and get a feel for the differences. I actually don't mind shooting the rifle that Drew picked, and Shilah has gotten really good at shooting my handgun. While none of us is as good as Drew, you can tell we all want to be. All four of us are getting competitive, and I think it's the most fun I've had in a really long time.

There have been moments of fun between Drew and me while we were on assignment—the running and the mucking around trying to beat one another. Most meetings with Chad were good too—our continued training and the moments I did actually beat him and caught him off guard when we sparred. It didn't happen often, but they were fun when they did. But those moments were nothing like this one.

A woman's voice interrupts us from behind. I know it's Aunt Kenna without even having to turn around. "Geez, Seph, getting them trained up already? They haven't even been here a full day yet."

As I turn, the bright afternoon sunlight shines on her long mahogany hair, giving her an angelic-like glow. My feet propel me forwards, running to her.

Even though I was livid for her betrayal, I've never stopped admiring her. She's Defective, and yet she risks getting caught every single day when she goes in to work for the Institute. That's the type of bravery I didn't know existed.

Any time I doubted myself while working for the Institute, I thought of Kenna and what she's doing for the cause.

All of the anger I had for her keeping secrets is gone with the simple action of an embrace. I don't know if it's because I'm truly free now or if it's because I'm finally here, but holding on to my anger just seems as if it's not worth it anymore. She was there for me when my mother wasn't. It'd be impossible to hold a grudge against her.

"What are you doing here?" I ask excitedly.

"I came as soon as my shift ended," she replies while moving away from me to hug Shilah. "I have to go back tonight, but I had medical supplies to come drop off, and I just couldn't resist seeing this for myself."

"Well, we best get in some quality family time while you're here," Mum says.

Cyrus arrives just as we're about to leave.

"Do you mind putting the weapons back in lockup?" Mum asks him.

"No worries," he says as he starts packing up the shooting range. We start back towards the car, but I pause when I see what's to the right of us.

The obstacle course and shooting range seem pretty standard for a training arena. What I wasn't expecting to see was an actual arena. It's large, about the size of a football field. Cement barricades are placed randomly throughout and are of different heights and shapes.

"What is this used for?" I ask. I can see by the look on the others' faces that they have no idea either. I look to Mum for an answer, but it's a voice behind us that answers.

"War games," Cyrus says with glee.

CHAPTER SEVEN

After spending the night back in the Welcoming House with Aunt Kenna, I'm awoken by a stomach full of nerves and excitement. Cyrus has called for a match of these so-called war games. Chad assures me that's just a scary name for what's essentially just more training.

It's just going to be a friendly match today—just for us newbies—but Cyrus made it clear that these matches are very popular with the residents and always draw a crowd. Most of the council members will be there, and they'll be very interested in seeing what we can do.

Aunt Kenna left just after dinner last night and informed us that she doesn't know when she will be able to come back. She finished her shift before word spread of our escape so she doesn't know how much the Institute knows and what they're going to do to rectify the situation. With four agents now missing—three of whom disappeared just the other night—she fears the place might go into lockdown. She told us not to expect to see her or Paxton anytime soon. So we hugged her tight and said our goodbyes, knowing that we would see her again, someday.

I walk out to the living area where Mum and Dad are both in the old military uniforms again. They're pottering around in the kitchen as Shilah and Drew get started on breakfast at the dining table. Joining them, I scoop a big pile of eggs and green beans on my plate.

"So what time do the games start?" Dad asks. "I was hoping to catch a glimpse of what you two can really do," he says with a hint of pride.

"We should head down after breakfast," Mum says. "So eat up, quickly."

I don't know how I'm going to go today. I'm coming down from a long, drawn-out coffee addiction, resulting in a fierce headache this morning.

"I don't suppose we have any painkillers here?" I ask.

"Are you okay?" Dad asks, concerned.

"Yeah, I'm fine. I just have a headache."

"The fresh air will do you good," Mum says.

She hasn't actually answered my question, and I suspect there are in fact pills here, but she just does not want to waste them on a headache.

"It's the caffeine withdrawal," Drew points out. "You should drink some tea. It has caffeine in it."

"Right now, I'll give anything a try," I say, holding the right side of my head.

Mum hands me a cup of tea, and I slowly sip. I tell myself to try to stomach some food. The thought of eating makes me want to puke, but as soon as the food touches my lips, I can't get enough.

We finish breakfast and make our way by car down to the Fields, but not before I grab a bag of my clothes to take with us, seeing as I will be staying down there from now on.

Cyrus was right about the games bringing in a crowd. When we arrive, there are people everywhere. They all crowd around the arena, and I quickly count at least fifty people just on this side. *How many people actually live out here?* I also don't see anyone who looks to be over the age of fifty. Everyone is young. There are a few in their thirties or forties, but most are in their teens and twenties, I'm guessing.

"Shouldn't everyone be working?" I ask Mum.

"We're pretty lenient when it comes to watching the games. It's really the only source of entertainment around here, and we don't get to play very often."

We make our way down to the arena, and like magic, the crowd parts for us, making a clear line to the entryway. I feel the stares, but they're not ones of judgement. They're stares of excitement and anticipation.

We make it into the arena where Chad, Cyrus, and Licia already await. Staring at Chad in his jeans and tight fitting T-shirt, his arrogant smirk plastered on his face, I have to resist the urge to rush over to him and throw myself at him publicly and ferociously like he did to me yesterday in the cafeteria. I didn't see him at all last night. I haven't seen him since that kiss, and I can't get it out of my mind.

"We should have an interesting game today," Cyrus says with a big voice, addressing everyone in the crowd. Cheers and screams echo from everyone around us, and the nerves kick up a notch while a smile spreads across my face. "I've asked Chad here to captain the other team, but seeing as I'm on the council, I will pick first." For a moment, I get excited at the thought of being on the same team as Chad—we work well together, and we could probably win. But my excitement is dashed when Cyrus speaks his next words. "My first pick is Allira." I feel my face drop in disappointment, but the screams and whistles from the crowd perk me back up as I go stand with Cyrus. My hopes of possibly winning this are fading fast. I certainly don't want to be against Chad; I know how good he is at this type of thing.

"I pick Shilah," Chad says confidently with a smile on his face.

"Interesting," Cyrus responds. "I guess I will take Licia. I'm sure the three of us could handle the boys. Don't you think, girls?" Licia nods excitedly as she comes to join me next to Cyrus. Chad rolls his eyes and sighs as Drew joins them. "Only one rule applies," Cyrus yells. "You can use your ability to help you through, but you cannot use your ability to harm others. Okay, to our corners!"

The two teams head to opposite ends of the field. The game is quite simple from what we've been told. The object of the game is to get to the other side of the field without being caught.

We get to our corner, and Cyrus throws me a vest and a gun. I jump out of the way of the flying handgun, and it hits the ground. *What the hell?* So much for all the gun safety crap Mum was going on about yesterday.

Cyrus laughs. "It's not a real gun," he explains, picking up his own and shooting a round into one of the cement barricades. The bullet explodes into a blob of coloured paint, sticking to the wall.

"Oh," I say in amazement. I hadn't noticed the small dots of paint all over the arena until now. They're obviously there, and they're bright, but it's one of those things you don't notice until it's pointed out. Now I can't focus on anything other than the fluorescent-coloured splotches everywhere. I pick up the gun and put on my vest.

"What are the vests for?" Licia asks.

"They may not be real guns, but they still sting like a bitch when the pellets hit you. It just prevents bruising," Cyrus explains. He hands us each a pair of protective sunglasses, which makes everything glow with an orange tinge in my vision, and then we're geared up, ready to go.

"So do you have a plan?" I ask Cyrus before we take to the field.

"Yes. Get to the other side," he says with a laugh.

"No strategies, teamwork, or former successful plays to go by?" I ask.

"If this was the annual comp, I'd suggest we come up with a plan, but today is really just for show," he replies with a shrug.

The nerves kick into overdrive as we wait for a bell to ring, indicating the game has begun. We all take our places behind barricades, me on the outer edge facing the crowd, Cyrus in the middle, and Licia on the far side of the arena. The crowd is still cheering and going nuts. I barely hear the bell ring signalling the start. We have thirty minutes to make it to the other side without getting shot.

I look down at my gun and shoot a paint pellet at the wall opposite me to check what it's like to shoot it. There's no kickback after pulling the trigger, and it doesn't feel like any of the guns I shot yesterday. It's light and flimsy.

I creep to the edge of my barricade and peek around the corner. Chad has already gained a lot of ground. Cyrus has moved too. Cyrus shoots at Chad, but Chad's force field ability protects him from the impact. It's going to be impossible to get him out. I can't see Licia or the two others anywhere.

Looking around the arena, I make sure I have a clear path to the next wall. Taking in a deep breath, I make a run for it, diving behind the wall and keeping low, squatting to cover myself. The crowd gives me a whistle and a shout of encouragement. I don't know if that's a good thing or not. Because I'm the one on the outer side, I'm the only one the audience can see. So their encouragement—while appreciated—is giving me away. The others will know whenever I make a move. I hear them shout again, and I realise there's another person on the other team who would've started on this side of the barricades as well. I know it's not Chad, so it has to be either Drew or Shilah.

I take in another breath and peer over the barricade. Drew's head is sticking out, all the way on the other side of the arena. He shoots at Cyrus who deflects the pellet with his telekinesis. I lift my gun and aim it at Drew, while still squatting behind the barricade. The only part of me that is exposed is my head and my arms. I double-check my aim and fire, but Drew ducks at the last second, and I miss him.

"Damn it," I say as I duck back down.

I hear footsteps running towards where I am. I can't tell where they are coming from, but they are coming fast. Panicking, I make a run for the next barricade. It's tall and could conceal me better. When I reach it, I see Chad is running my way. I stand poised, ready to shoot.

He sees me too and slows down but doesn't lower his gun. We both refuse to shoot.

"Just let me pass," he says, smiling. "You don't need to get shot."

Raising my eyebrow at him and smirking, I ask, "You want a free pass?"

"We can both have one," he negotiates.

I think about it for a second. "Okay," I respond. He goes to move, but I don't lower my gun. "But," I add, "you have to pay the toll first."

"What's that?" he says with wry smile.

"A kiss," I answer him. Hearing our negotiation tactics, the crowd standing closest to us wolf whistles and cheers.

He takes a step forward. "Done," he says. "Now lower your gun."

"You lower yours." Over Chad's shoulder, I see Shilah's head pop up from one of the outer barricades near the fence line, nearest to the audience. He's low to the ground and an easy shot. "Duck," I say to Chad, and he moves out of the way. I quickly aim my gun and shoot, but I miss him too. I'm not doing too well with aiming this gun. I'm quick to aim it back at Chad after Shilah ducks back down.

"Count of three?" he asks.

"One ..." I say.

"Two ..."

"Three ..." we say in unison and lower our guns.

We close the small gap between us. Placing my left hand around his neck as he wraps his arms around me and pulls me in close, I touch my lips to his, and the crowd goes wild.

I pull the trigger with my right hand. A paint pellet explodes on Chad's leg.

"Shit," Chad swears, breaking away from my lips. He drops his gun, putting both of his hands up in the air, yelling, "I'm out."

I see Cyrus lift his head from closer to our target and smile. "Wow. She's a sneaky one." He laughs at Chad. I don't know if he saw what happened or if I'm sneaky because I took out a key player. Drew appears on the other side of the field, one barricade away from Cyrus. He plants a paint pellet into Cyrus's arm. "Damn it. I'm out."

I look over to see Drew aiming at me and quickly duck back behind the cement barricade. The sound of the paint pellet exploding on the other side of me makes me flinch. Peering around the barricade, I can't see Drew, who has retreated again. The coast is clear for me to run to the next one. I'm making up ground, but I still don't know where Shilah or Licia are or if Drew has moved.

I miss where Drew pops up and hits Licia, but the next thing I hear is Cyrus say "Licia's been hit. She's … oh, wait … No, she hasn't! It was her projected state. She's on the outside, making a break for it. She's—" Shilah pops his head up two barricades away from me. He lifts his gun and fires at Licia, hitting her in the chest.

"I'm out," she yells, surrendering. I have to get to the other side now. I'm the only one left on our team.

Out of the corner of my eye, I see Drew making a run for it. I quickly turn, aim, and shoot—and just keep shooting. One of the pellets gets his leg, and I jump up in excitement, but then I remember Shilah is still out there and quickly hit the ground.

"I'm out," Drew says.

"And then there were two," Cyrus's voice booms through the air. "Brother against sister, Daniels against Daniels," he says, entertaining the crowd with his banter.

Breathing deep and heavy, I peek around the corner, but I can't see anything. I have no idea where he is. What do I do?

Do I rush it, or do I tactfully try to make my way to the middle and outrun him?

It's all in or nothing. I run. No, I try to run, but a foot comes out of nowhere, tripping me, making me face plant into the ground and my gun go flying. Shilah was waiting on the opposite side of my barricade. Quickly rolling on my back, I lift my foot and kick his gun out of his hand. Now it's an even playing field.

I flip myself up to my feet. This is going to be a long standoff. Whatever move I make, he will see before it happens. What he doesn't know is I can do the same. I shake my head at myself. Why have I only just realised that I could've been borrowing his ability this whole time? I can borrow Chad's for that matter, although that might be a little obvious, and I don't need every member of the Resistance finding out about my double ability right now. As tempting as it is, I remind myself it's just a game and not worth exposing myself.

Shilah goes for my gun that landed on the ground near his feet. My instinct is to run the other way, but I tackle him instead. Constantly changing my mind about what I plan to do could throw him off enough for me to win. Shilah must have been good at self-defence classes, because he manages to push me off him, and I wasn't expecting it.

We both get back on our feet, and I realise I'm going to have to concentrate just as hard as if this were a training session with Chad. I've been training with him for months; I should be good at this by now. I know Shilah has bulked up a bit since I last saw him, but how did he get this good this quickly?

I start walking slowly around Shilah, circling him like an animal stalking its prey. Smirking at him, I taunt, "Let's see what you've got."

He raises his eyebrows at me. "Really?" He lets out a little bit of a laugh.

"Bring it."

He swings his fist at me. Thanks to my training ... and glimpsing at what Shilah plans to do through his ability, I manage to block his hits. But his hands are fast, smooth, and each move is calculated.

The loud shouts from the crowd fade out, even though I know everyone is still cheering. I have to block the noise out and concentrate. I don't know how to catch Shilah off guard when I realise I may not have to. All I have to do is distract him enough, while still pushing him backwards. Maybe I can get to the end of the field by taking him with me.

But it only takes a second of lost concentration to do me in. Before I know it, Shilah is on the ground, reaching for one of the guns on the ground, pulling the trigger, and hitting me in the shoulder with a loud and painful pop.

Damn it. "I'm out," I yell, and Shilah runs to the other end of the field with minutes left on the clock. The audience goes crazy, and I find myself pinching one of my ears from the noise.

Chad, after giving Shilah a congratulatory man-hug, walks up to me, lifting my sunglasses off my face and up onto my head.

"I really thought you could've taken him," he says

encouragingly. "Of course, next time I'll know to watch my back, you sneaky bitch," he says, laughing.

I shrug. "What can I say? I learnt everything I know from you. So what does that say about you?"

"Maybe that we're perfect for each other," he says, putting his hand on the side of my cheek and rubbing off some of the paint that sprayed onto my face. He leans down and our lips meet for a brief, sweet kiss.

* * *

We're sitting in the very crowded cafeteria shed, when Cyrus stands on a box at the front, gaining everyone's attention. Everybody's still on a high from the game, talking and laughing about how it all played out.

I get many congratulatory slaps on the back for doing so well and for taking out Chad. He's never been out first and is usually one of the last players in the game, if not the winner. I knew from the beginning it would have been hard to get him out. Anytime he was shot at, he could use his protective ability, so distraction was the only way to defeat him.

It's amazing how a ten-second slip of concentration means the difference between winning and losing. I know it was only a game and it was all done light-heartedly, but if that was a real scenario, distracting someone with my lips isn't going to cut it. The only other person I took out was Drew, and I think that was just from random firing, not actual skill. I'm beginning to understand what Chad meant every single time I managed to defeat him in training. I got lucky.

"Thank you to everyone who came out today," Cyrus yells above the crowd. "It was definitely an interesting match. Here come in these new, fresh trainees, and they manage to take out the two most experienced people in the field first. That certainly won't be overlooked. But I would like to give a special mention to Allira." Suddenly everyone is looking at me, and my cheeks are flushing from embarrassment. "She may not have won, but the fact that she got so close without her ability to use as a weapon ... well, it was an amazing feat. Well done." Everyone claps and cheers in response, and I hang my head, a little embarrassed by the praise. "And a big congratulations to Allira's brother, Shilah, the winner of our match. It seems to me this brother and sister duo could be unstoppable. Maybe we should make sure they're always on separate teams, hey?" Everyone laughs. "So, let's all enjoy our food and then back to the real world of work." He ends his little speech and everyone seems to deflate a notch. Back to work after lunch.

CHAPTER EIGHT

Arriving at my new home I'll be sharing with Ebbodine, I'm surprised it's an underground bunker. There's a small mound in the grass where steps lead down to a giant metal door. It's obvious that at one point a house used to sit on the surrounding land but has since been demolished. What is it with this place and underground? Do they think it's safer to be buried in the dirt?

I suck in a deep breath and tell myself *at least I'm not living with Drew.* Poor Shilah and Dad now have that pleasure— Mum won that argument. They're in an actual house at one of the other properties. To get to their place we have to walk down the hill, past all the farms and the training area, and around the base of one of the mountains. They're tucked away in bushland. If it wasn't for Drew, I think I might be asking to come live with them after seeing what I'm faced with right now.

Opening the door, I find Ebbodine fluttering around in her underwear. I let out a sigh at the realisation I'll be seeing a lot of that from now on. She makes her way over to a small chest of drawers squished in between our two single beds. Mine's more of a foldable cot-type thing. It's kind of dark in here, being underground and windowless, but a light built into the wall above the drawers illuminates the room in a warm tone. Apart from a bathroom door to the left of me, that's all there is. I don't know why Ebb said she had room for me when clearly she doesn't.

"Hey, roomie," Ebb says with a smile.

I dump the bag with my few possessions in the corner of the single room and immediately flop on the foldout cot. "Hey," I reply unenthusiastically.

"Don't get too comfortable, you'll have to vacate soon."

"Vacate?" I ask, wearily. "I was really looking forward to sleeping."

"Don't worry, I'm sure Chad would love to have you over at his place. Hall is coming over."

"Hall? Like, Hall from Eminent Falls, Hall? Really?"

"Yes, really. Why is that so hard to believe?"

"Because you have an entire population of males here and you choose someone you grew up with? Just doesn't seem very Ebbodine-like to me," I say, smiling.

She throws her pillow at me. "Shut up," she says before

getting dressed.

"I don't know why you're bothering putting clothes on, when clearly you will be out of them again soon." I duck out of the way of her shoe that comes flying at my head. "Stop throwing things at me!"

"It's not like that with Hall," she says almost shamefully. "I'm not saying it couldn't be, but he just reminds me of home. Hanging out with him feels as if I'm back there, you know?"

I nod.

"Besides, if either of us is going to get lucky tonight, it will most definitely be you."

I shudder. Not because I think it won't happen, but because I think it will. I sit up on my bed, thinking about the possibility. It doesn't seem like that long ago that I was having this same dilemma but with Drew instead of Chad. How do I know if I'm truly ready? With Drew, it was a reflex to stop it before it went too far. I never felt comfortable enough with him. Maybe deep down I always knew I couldn't trust him. But with Chad it's different. I want to take the next step. I'm fairly certain if Shilah hadn't taken Chad's bedroom a few nights ago, it would've happened already.

"Umm ..." I have no idea what to say. She looks at me with raised eyebrows, awaiting my question. "How did you ... When did ... What ..."

"Spit it out, Allira, Hall will be here soon."

"How did you know you were ready for *that* kind of

relationship?" I ask sheepishly.

"What kind of ... Oh my God. You've never done it, have you?" Her mouth drops open in shock. "I just assumed you and Chad—"

I just shake my head, shyly.

"Not even with Drew?"

"Definitely not with Drew. We almost ... sort of ... no."

"Wow, I was not expecting that," she says, stunned.

I don't know why this is such shocking news to her. She knows all about my lack of experience, and she used to tease me about it constantly. Did she really expect that to change in the seven or so months since she disappeared from Eminent Falls?

"So?" I ask, realising she didn't actually answer my question.

"I don't know what to say," she responds. "It's perfectly okay not to be ready for it. But it's also not that big of a deal. Sex isn't the big, momentous thing that everyone seems to make it out to be. It's a natural, normal, everyday kind of thing."

"Every day?" I exclaim and she laughs.

"Not an *every day* event. Just something that everyone does. It's not a big deal." I nod, a bit confused by her words. "If you think your first time is going to be all romantic and perfect, you're going to be very disappointed," she adds.

I nod again. "I thought you were going to try talking me into it, not out," I say half-jokingly.

"I'm not doing either. Only you can decide if you're ready," she says.

"We haven't been together very long," I say.

"But you've known him a lot longer, haven't you?"

That's true. We've hung out together nearly every day for almost six months. It's not like we just met and started dating. I know him. It's Chad.

"And if he's not okay with wanting to wait, he can answer to my fist."

"I think he will be answering to mine first." I stand up and give her a hug. "I've missed you," I tell her.

"I've missed you too. But I'm not into girls."

"You couldn't just let that one slide, could you?"

* * *

I knock at his door and wait nervously for him to answer. If I chew my nails any more, I may have none left by the time I get inside. His place is another underground bunker, a few hundred metres away from mine. I'm realising now what the "you're welcome" was for yesterday morning when Ebb offered to take me in. After my conversation with Ebb, I can only think about one thing: *that* thing. He answers the door shirtless. *Damn.* I find myself biting my lip so I don't say what I'm thinking. He's not exactly helping to distract me from my thoughts.

"Hey," he says casually, letting me in.

"Hey, I'm kind of homeless," I say, closing the door behind me.

He raises his eyebrows at me. "Homeless?"

"Ebb has company."

He gives a knowing smile and nods. "So, are you wanting a lift to your parents' place?"

"Not so much."

He smiles and closes the distance between us, pulling me close. I wrap my arms around him, and my hands find their way onto his bare shoulders. He brings his forehead down to mine. I suck in a wispy breath before he smiles cheekily and pulls away. I think he knows exactly what he's doing to me and is enjoying it. Grabbing hold of my hand, he leads me to his bed, sitting across it and leaning up against the wall. I sit down next to him.

"I …" he pauses.

"You need to tell me something," I say for him. I don't need to borrow Drew's ability to sense that he's holding something back.

"I figure if we're doing this whole honesty thing, there's something you should know." He hesitates, trying to find the words.

"Okay," I say, but it comes out more of a mumble than a word.

"Paxton knows about you."

"He what?"

"He knows you have a double ability. That's why he worked so hard at getting you out of the Institute, and why he pushed for Shilah to go through the training program quicker than he should have. He knew you weren't going to come here without your brother."

"How does he know? Why hasn't he said anything?"

Chad hangs his head. "I told him," he admits. "While we were still at the Institute."

"Why?" I ask, anger naturally coming through in my tone without consciously putting it there.

"Paxton wasn't convinced you were one of us. You adapted well in the Institute and did what Brookfield asked of you. He wasn't sure you'd want to come with us, or if you were worth the risk. Tate and I agreed that he had to know how important you are."

I breathe in deep. "Why couldn't you just tell him that I was Persephone's daughter?"

"We did. He figured there was a reason why she was with the Resistance and you weren't."

"He's the only one that knows?" I ask, panicked.

"He's the only one I told."

"But he's not the only one who knows," I state, trying to clarify his words.

"I'm starting to suspect Cyrus knows."

"Cyrus?" I exclaim.

"I don't know for sure. It's his other ability. He can tell who's Defective and who isn't and what the nature of their ability is. It's why he asked you if you could borrow abilities when you first met. I thought that by telling him that you can only amplify, he assumed he had it wrong and dismissed his intuition. This is what his ability seems to be—just strong intuition. It's not definite, and he's been wrong in the past. But then today, when he chose you for his team and made that big speech afterwards about you only using your combat skills—I think he's trying to test you. I think he knows."

"Okay," I say, taking in everything. "So what's the worst that could happen if he knew? What's the worst that could happen if the whole council knew?"

Chad thinks for a moment before answering. "They won't let you leave. I know you hate feeling like you're a prisoner, like you don't have any choice. I've heard Cyrus complaining about it before. They don't really let him do much or go anywhere. They don't want him in any kind of danger. He's a council member, but they only want him involved in planning and theoretical things. He's in charge of the training department for recruitment, but he's never been on assignment. I don't even think he has left the compound all that much. Picking us up from the halfway point last night was a rarity. I think that's the farthest he's been in a long time."

"So they'll just keep me here?" I think about it for a moment. "Right now, that doesn't seem like such a bad thing," I say, looking down at our intertwined hands and squeezing tighter.

"Right now, maybe. I just don't want you to feel trapped, making you want to get away."

I sense there is more to the story than he is letting on. "You sound like you know what you're talking about." I fish for an answer.

Chad sighs. "There was a girl."

I nod my head slightly while my stomach ties itself in knots. Do I really want to know what he's about to tell me? It suddenly occurs to me that I don't know anything about Chad's love life before me. He knows my complete history— Drew.

"She didn't like living here," he continues. "She missed her old life and wanted to live a normal life in the city, pretending to be something she's not. She knew I couldn't leave. I had to stay."

"So she left you," I say.

He nods. "I heard rumours that she was arrested a few months later, and at first I thought good. I felt guilty immediately afterwards though. I wanted to know if she was okay."

"You didn't turn yourself over to the Institute just for Tate, did you? You went looking for her. What happened?"

"I found you instead," he says, letting go of my hand and putting his arm around my waist.

"Did you ... love her?" I ask, avoiding eye contact.

"I thought I did. I was a mess after she left. I contemplated leaving when she asked. I contemplated turning my back on my mother and the cause, just so I could be with her."

"I don't know if I want to hear any more," I say quietly.

"But how could I have truly loved her? I found you and completely forgot about her. I fought my feelings for you for so long. I thought that it was impossible to feel things for someone new when I had ruined my life for someone else. It took me a while to realise I needed to follow her, because ... she led me to you."

I feel a blush coming on, and I will myself to stop, but I'm sure I'm failing miserably. "That's why your mother doesn't like me," I state as the realisation comes to me. "She thinks you're going to ruin your life again but with me."

He hesitates but he knows it's the truth. "She doesn't know you yet."

"She doesn't need to know me. To her, I'm just like the last girl. Is that what that very public display was about yesterday in the cafeteria?"

"I needed to show her how serious I am about you. And you're nothing like Jess," he says seriously. "Nothing." He lifts his hand, brushing a strand of hair away from my face and tucking it behind my ear. It's a move I'm becoming all too familiar with. He cradles my head and touches his forehead to mine, our lips so close it's teasingly unbearable not to kiss him.

I breathe him in and hold him close. "So, just how long did you hide your feelings for me?" I ask, smiling.

He pulls away. "Uh …" He stumbles for an answer. "A lot longer than I should have," he says.

Does this mean that this whole time, while I have been annoyed at myself for not telling him how I feel, he has felt the same?

"You know what has just occurred to me?" I ask. He looks at me expectantly. "You really need to learn to communicate better." I smile.

"Me?" he exclaims. "Why didn't you ever say anything? Right up until we kissed two nights ago, I had no idea you were even interested. I thought maybe, possibly, something was between us the night before I left on assignment, but then you found out about the Resistance, and it was as if a wall went up."

It's true. I wanted so badly to kiss him that night before he left, but I kept telling myself it was too complicated. We were being sent to almost opposite ends of the country. I convinced myself that starting something with him that night would've been a mistake, and I realise now that it would've been. I don't know if I would've forgiven him after finding out about the Resistance.

"Sorry. I left my flashing "I heart Chad" sign back at the Institute," I say sarcastically. "How could you not know? I turned the colour of a beetroot every time you touched me. Tate never stopped giving me crap about it. Not to mention, it seemed like you hated me from the beginning. That certainly wasn't making me want to share my feelings."

"I never hated you. Far from it." He grabs my hand and starts drawing circles with his thumb. Looking down at my hands, I fear I may be turning that very shade of beetroot I was telling him about. "That afternoon I first saw you in the foyer of the training office, I knew."

"Knew what?"

"That you were going to be trouble for me," he mumbles. "I thought that by being an asshole, maybe you would stay away. Then it turned out, you were the one that Tate had been helping, and I knew there was no way I could stay away."

I narrow my eyes, trying to work out whether he's full of it or not. "I think you're lying again." He smirks at my accusation. "But the asshole thing worked. *I* hated *you* from the beginning."

"Fair enough. But clearly, you still couldn't resist me."

I laugh before the smile fades from my face just as quickly as it appeared. "Did you ever find her? Was she at the Institute?" I ask hesitantly.

He shakes his head. "Nope. She wasn't. I don't know where she is."

It's clear we've both been burnt before. Did he mean it when he said that Jess ruined his life? Ruin is a strong word. Then again, I do—did—feel the same towards Drew. I run over it in my head—if Drew didn't do what he did, I wouldn't be here. I'm as free as I'll ever be, even more so than before I was arrested.

I remind myself to thank Drew later. As angry as I am at him for the months of torture I endured living in that place, I have to be glad that he did it. I wouldn't have what I do now. I have my mum back, I have my family, and I have Chad.

"What are you thinking about?" Chad asks.

Don't say Drew, don't say Drew. "Drew." *Idiot, idiot, idiot!*

Chad lets go of my hand but I grab it back. He snatches it away, climbs off the bed, and stands up. "It's always going to come back to him, isn't it?"

"Umm, no. If you just let me explain ..." I say, standing up to meet his eyes.

"Explain what? That you're glad he's here? That you're having second thoughts about him, about me?" he yells.

"I'm not glad he's here. I'm in your room, not his. I *was* thinking that you have the right attitude towards your ex, that *maybe* I should try to do the same. If it wasn't for him, I wouldn't have you. You big ... dummy."

Chad loses the serious face and bursts into laughter. "Dummy? Really? You're going to go with dummy?"

"Would you prefer butthead?"

"Get over here, you butthead," he replies, pulling me to him and taking me into his arms. "I'm sorry. That guy just makes me so angry, you know?"

"I know." I nod.

"It hurt when you chose to go back to him over coming here with me."

"But I didn't choose him. I chose Shilah."

"It didn't feel that way. You were so angry at me, I didn't think you'd ever forgive me. I practically pushed you back into his arms."

"Not true. I didn't choose Drew over you. I would *never* choose Drew. And what arms? I never went back to him—not like that."

"I saw the way you two were together. All of those days I watched you out on assignment. Can you imagine how hard it was for me to see that?"

I can only imagine what it would've been like. If I saw a girl with Chad like I was with Drew, I would've been pissed off too. But we were "married," so there were a lot of moments where touching in public was necessary.

"It drove me crazy seeing you with him. It took all the strength I had not to blow my cover, run up to him, and punch him in the face."

Looking in his eyes, I see the depth of his feelings for me. I don't need a supernatural ability to know what I'm seeing is real.

I kiss him, gently at first, but it escalates when I pull him closer, pushing my body up against his. Our mouths come together, fitting perfectly as if they were made for each other. I run my hands down his chest and grab him around his waist. He reaches up, his hands finding their way into my hair. I pull away, summoning all of the courage I have to take the next step. I know this is the moment.

When I look down and undo the top button of his jeans, he lifts my chin gently with his finger. "Are you sure you want to do this?" he asks, just as breathless as I feel, his chest rising and falling in exaggerated movements. "I don't want to rush you into anything."

There's no question about it. "I'm sure."

CHAPTER NINE

I'm awoken by lips touching my shoulder and kisses running up and down my neck. I smile as I roll over onto my back, welcoming Chad's mouth on mine.

"Good morning," he says, climbing over me and out of bed.

"Morning," I say back.

"What have you got planned for today?" He starts getting dressed into his farming clothes: a loose fitting T-shirt and khaki pants.

"I think Cyrus wants us down in the training arena again. Not for another match, but for other things. I don't know what," I reply, sitting up in bed.

Chad nods and walks over, placing his hands on either side of me on the bed. He leans in, kissing me briefly.

He sits down next to me while he puts his shoes and socks on. "Don't show off too much," he says.

"I'll try, but we both know I just exude awesomeness. I can't help it most of the time."

He laughs. "Well, that's true," he says before his face turns serious. "I'm just worried they'll want to send you to recruit others."

"So let me get this straight. I can't tell them I have a double ability because they'll want to keep me here, but I can't show the others up because then they will want to send me away? I'm sensing a bit of a contradiction here," I say with a smile. "You don't want me to go, but you don't want me to have to stay here?"

He laughs. "I guess that is a bit contradictory isn't it. How about this—I want you to stay here but still have the choice to leave this place if you wanted to."

"I guess that's fair. I thought they wouldn't want us recruiting anyway, seeing as we're wanted by the Institute. Wouldn't it be too risky to send us back out there?"

He shakes his head. "They've already asked me to go back to it now that you don't need me as your handler anymore."

"Oh. Can't I just say no, like you did? You did say no, right?" I start to panic at the thought of him going away.

"I said no. But I've been here a lot longer than you. I've paid my dues. I'm in a position to request what I want. For now, I'll be working on the farms, but I know my mum's not happy about that. Something about wasting my ability on a job one of the normals could do. I'm sure she's trying to find me something somewhere else."

"What if you were to change your mind and say yes? Maybe we could go recruit together?" The look Chad gives me tells me there is no way in hell that will happen, although I'm not sure why. "Why do they keep recruiting people anyway? I mean, I know why—to save them from the fate of the Institute—but what's their plan? Do they have a one? Or is 'the Resistance' just a misleading name, designed to create the illusion that they're doing something to fix the world, but in reality, all they're doing is hiding from it? I've been here a few days now, and I don't see an obvious agenda."

Chad purses his lips. "They have a plan. It's just not viable to put into action yet."

"Can you tell me what it is?"

"I'm pretty sure their immediate plan is to build on what we already have. More numbers, more support." He thinks for a moment. "I've also heard rumours about possibly taking Brookfield down and taking over the Institute."

"Just rumours? So what you're actually saying is—you don't really know what the plan is yourself?"

He smiles. "I guess not. Now, get up lazy bum. We've got to get you down to training."

"I think I prefer butthead over lazy bum."

* * *

I decide to go home for a quick shower and a change of clothes before heading to training. When I arrive at my place, I walk in to find Ebb still under the covers. Seeing as she should be on her way to the farms like Chad is right now, I jump on her to wake her up.

"What the hell?" a guy's voice rumbles from underneath me. I let out a scream.

"What's going on out here?" Ebb says as she comes out of the bathroom wearing only a towel. Her face lights up as she sees us and starts laughing. I look down at the body beneath me to see Hall smiling up at me.

"I'm sorry. I'm so sorry," I say to him as I climb off the bed.

"Good to see you again too, Allira." He laughs, sitting up and rubbing his hand over his thick, dark hair. He goes to stand but hesitates. "Uh, Allira?"

"Yeah?"

"Would you mind … umm … turning around?"

"Oh. Right." I turn to face Ebbodine who's still laughing at the whole thing. I feel my cheeks flush. "I didn't think you would remember me?" I say to Hall while completely focussing on the wall in front of me.

"Of course, I remember you," he says unconvincingly. "Okay, you can turn around now." I turn to see him shirtless, but at least he is wearing pants now. "I better get going." He walks over to Ebbodine and kisses her cheek, soft and quick, before grabbing his shirt off the floor and leaving.

Once he's gone, I stand there with my arms folded, waiting for an explanation. Ebbodine ignores me as she saunters over to the chest of drawers that separates our beds and grabs out clothes to change into.

"*Not like that*, hey?" I ask.

"I don't know what you're talking about," she replies smugly.

"Uh-huh. Of course not."

"What happened with Chad last night?"

"I don't know what you're talking about," I mimic her, but I wonder if my face is giving anything away. She studies me, and I tell myself to stay cool, to keep eye contact. She smiles when I find myself glancing away from her analytical stare. "Shouldn't you be on the farms by now?" I try to change the subject.

"I have the added luxury of not having to walk there." Oh, right. "So, was it any good?" she asks, coming to the conclusion that what happened last night did in fact take place.

I shrug. "No big deal. You were right about that." And she was. I woke up this morning feeling absolutely no different than yesterday. I'm the same; he's the same. I don't feel the supposed closeness that I've heard happens after, but I don't feel distanced from him either. I feel nothing. I begin to wonder if that's a bad thing.

"Not what you were expecting?" she asks.

"I guess I didn't really know what to expect." She just nods sympathetically and goes back to getting ready for work. "Okay. I've spilled. Your turn," I say.

"No big deal," she says, but her grin gives away more.

"I'm not going to have to find somewhere else to sleep again tonight, am I?"

She responds with a laugh. *Damn it.*

* * *

I get to the training arena to find I'm the last one to arrive. Licia, Drew, and Shilah turn to look at me as I make my appearance, and I get the sudden cringe-worthy notion they know what happened last night. Ebb could tell, but surely, that's only because we talked about it, right? I tell myself that it's not possible for them to know, reassuring myself to calm down.

"Allira? Come in, Allira. Hello? Anyone home?" I'm brought out of my thoughts by Shilah, trying to get my attention. "The whole council is here," he whispers to me.

"Oh," I mutter, as my eyes size up the group of people huddled near the war games arena.

"Good morning, Allira," Cyrus says to me, walking over to us. He grabs my hand and pulls me into the group. "There's still a few people to meet." I nod and reach out to the first person to my left to shake their hand. Only then do I realise it's Chad's mum and I've already met her.

Smooth as always, Allira, I think as I withdraw my hand.

"Allira," Belle says, nodding.

I nod back and open my mouth to say her name, but then I realise—what do I call her? Mrs. Williams? Belle? Yesterday, Chad introduced her as Belle, but does that mean I have the authority to call her that? Is it disrespectful to call her by her first name? Too much time has passed now to call her anything, so I decide to just say nothing.

Standing next to Belle is a middle-aged man—he'd be at least fifty if his thinning silver hair is any indication. "Hi, Allira. I saw your match yesterday. Very impressive," he says, stretching out his hand to shake mine.

"Thank you," I reply with a smile, taking his hand.

"Allira, this is Connor," Cyrus tells me.

"Nice to meet you," I say politely.

Cyrus moves along the line. The next is a woman, late thirty-ish, with long blonde hair that is curly and untamed. "This is Millie," Cyrus tells me. "Just like Paxton, she's not Defective," he states. I shake her hand too and give her a nod hello. "And this," Cyrus says, moving on to the last person I am yet to meet, "is Marlo." I take her hand, realising I had sort of already met her yesterday. Well, not met her—I saw her with Cyrus. She's Cyrus's other wife. I actually forgot to ask Chad about that last night—the whole two wives thing.

Mum is standing next to Marlo, and as I count down the line, including Mum and Cyrus, there are six council members. I count again, confused.

"I thought there were eight council members?" I ask.

"There are," Mum replies. "There's Paxton, but he won't be back for a while." Oh, of course. Oops. I feel bad that I was able to forget about him—the man who gave me my freedom—so easily. "And Tate ... well ... We haven't really gotten around to replacing him yet."

I actually assumed they had already replaced him. Tate made it perfectly clear three months ago that he wasn't going to come back.

"So what's the plan for us today?" I ask.

"We'll run you through some basic training and see how you go. As the next few days progress, you'll get into more intensive training, and we'll make our assessments next week," Belle replies in a tone that would make you think I asked when the first slaughter would commence. "We will only be observing you today and for your final assessment. Cyrus will be the one working through the training with you."

Cyrus then leads us over to the obstacle course while the rest of the council members remain where they are.

As we start walking, Drew comes up beside me. "Gee, way to

piss off the mother-in-law already." He nudges me and smiles.

"I know, right?" I reply.

"What did you do?" he asks.

"I don't even know." I suspect I didn't do anything and Belle is just using up her leftover resentment towards Chad's last girlfriend, Jess. I don't want to get into that with Drew though. "I think she just has a stick up her ass," I joke. I hear the sound of a throat clearing, and I turn to find that Belle has been following us after all. Drew bursts out laughing, and I hang my head in shame. "Yup. That's about right," I mutter. *Brilliant.*

"Okay. So, how about we get you all running the obstacle course. We'll be observing your fitness and strength," Cyrus tells us as we line up to start. "We'll move onto target practice after lunch to evaluate possible recruiting positions you might be suitable for."

Suddenly I feel as if I never left the Institute.

The obstacle course, while slightly different from the Institute one, is easy to get through the first time round. I take my time, ensuring not to overdo it like Chad instructed. The council stands by, watching us, and it takes all of my concentration to not embarrass myself by falling over or face planting into a pole. Drew and Shilah race ahead of Licia and me, but after a while, even she takes off. I don't think I'll have any worry of being "too good" in front of the council.

"Water. Need water," I pant after running the obstacle course for what feels like the entire morning. I sit on the ground with my head between my knees. A bottle of water appears in front of me and I grab it. Looking up, I see Shilah with a smirk on his face. "Shut up," I tell him, which only makes him laugh.

Licia sits next to me, just as energetic as she was when we started. Shilah and Drew join us. As soon as Shilah sits, a feeling of nerves and desire starts oozing from Licia. I can't help but giggle. Poor girl has a crush. I look to Drew and see he's sensing the same thing.

"So where are you hoping to get placed?" Licia asks quietly. She didn't say it to anyone in particular, but I know who she was directing it at and it wasn't me. But I answer her anyway.

"I'm hoping to work on the farms," I reply.

"The farms?" Drew asks.

"Didn't get enough of that at home, Allira?" Shilah scoffs.

I shrug. "I like it."

"Well, I have a feeling I won't get much say in what I'll do," Drew says. "Clearly, they all think I'm still going to try to escape."

"What about you, Licia?" Shilah asks, and I see her cheeks blush a little. Not enough for a boy to notice—they barely notice anything—but it's there.

"I don't know. I'd love to do what Allira did for me, for others," she replies.

"I was thinking about that, too," Shilah says.

"Really, Shilah?" I ask.

"Why is that so hard to believe?" Shilah snaps at me.

"It's not. I think you'd be really good at it, actually," I say carefully. I want to say I'd miss you and worry about you and would hate that I wouldn't know if you were safe or not, but I know how much Shilah would hate that. "I know they'll be looking for someone to do that. They asked Chad to go back to it, but he said no."

"I think *you* would be great at it, Allira," Drew says. "After all, you did manage to get Licia safe, even though we were watching her like a hawk."

"And I would go into my room every night fretting about being caught, whether or not I was doing the right thing, and if I had the skill to pull it off," I say. "I don't really think I'm cut out for it."

Cyrus approaches us, after having a conversation with the other council members. "Okay, break's over."

* * *

I'm relieved to find my room empty when I arrive home. No Ebb and no Hall. After the day I've had, all I want to do is crawl into bed and go to sleep. My muscles are tight and I'm sore all over. It reminds me of the first few fitness classes at the Institute. I lay down for what feels like less than a minute when there's a knock at my door.

"No one's home," I yell.

"Ha. Ha." Chad's voice booms through the door. Groaning, I get up to let him in. He starts laughing as soon as he sees me, hunched over in pain. "Just like old times, hey?" he says gripping me around the waist and pulling me in for a quick kiss before jumping on my bed.

"Me being sore all over and you laughing at me? Yeah, I'm getting major déjà vu," I say, sitting next to him.

"I missed you at lunch. What did you get up to today?"

"They brought food down to us in the training arena," I reply. "It was non-stop."

"Cyrus will go easy on you the next few days. It's the first and last day that's the worst because you have an audience. So how'd you go?"

"Well, I don't think you need to worry about me showing off. I could barely keep up. Even Licia was fitter than me. I can't believe what three months of no weight training has done to muscle strength."

"You'll get back into the swing of things," he encourages. I hope I do. It didn't take me long to get used to the training at the Institute, but I was also able to borrow Jack's strength ability to help. "So, will you be homeless again tonight?" he asks, wrapping his arm around me and kissing my jawline.

"I don't know. Ebb hasn't been back yet," I reply, reminding myself to breathe properly as Chad's lips move to my neck.

I turn my head to bring my lips to his, wrapping my arms around him as he lays me down.

"Get a room." Ebb's voice interrupts us.

"This *is* my room," I exclaim, sitting up and throwing a pillow at her.

Chad sits up, running his hand over his head and down his neck. "Great timing Ebb, as always."

"How was training, Allira?" Ebb asks me while sticking her tongue out at Chad.

"Eh. It was training. It was pretty entertaining watching the new girl, Licia, fumble for words around Shilah though."

"I can understand that," Ebbodine says. "Your brother got hot."

"Umm, eww."

Ebb shrugs. "Well, it's true."

"What's true?" Hall appears in the doorway.

"That my brother is hot. According to Ebb anyway," I say with a smirk.

"Oh really, Ebb?" Hall laughs.

Ebb mouths "I hate you" to me before turning to Hall to kiss him hello. "He's all right," she says, trying to shrug it off but failing miserably.

"Chad." Hall nods to him. "Glad to see you back."

"Hall," Chad replies with the same head nod. "Come on, Allira, let's get out of their hair." Chad pulls me up off the bed and leads me out the door.

"Have fun," Ebbodine calls out after us in a knowing way.

We walk hand in hand on the way to Chad's, and I feel him staring at me, awaiting an explanation, but I don't give him one.

"So," he says, "you told her what happened?"

"Maybe. Well, technically no. I think that maybe her true ability is having sex-dar. It's like radar that can detect when someone's had sex."

Chad laughs. "I don't care that you told her. Although, I'm pretty sure everyone will know now."

I shrug. "Most of the people at the Institute thought we were already doing it anyway. What does it matter if a few more people think it?"

"True," he says. "I just don't want to be there when your dad finds out." He shudders. "I'm too young to die."

"Meh. I'm sure you can run faster than him. You'll be fine. It's probably lucky you have your ability though." I crack a smile.

We continue to walk, but my muscles are so tense from today's training, I'm starting to ache in places I didn't even know I could ache.

"Are you okay?" he asks.

"Just sore from training."

"Right. Well then," Chad says, picking me up and carrying me in his arms. I laugh at first but can't help wrapping my arms around his neck, snuggling into his shoulder and accepting the gesture. He carries me all the way back to his place.

"So what's the deal with the council?" I ask after reaching his room and he sets me down on his bed.

"What about them?"

"What can they do? What's with Cyrus and his two wives, one of whom is also on the council? How long have they been with the Resistance? Why haven't they replaced Tate yet? What's with the old dude? Why is Millie with us if she's not Defective? And Paxton for that matter? Is that enough questions to start with?"

"Oh," he replies sitting next to me. "Well, to begin with, Cyrus actually has three wives."

"Three? Do they know about each other? Is polygamy common here? What the hell kind of place is this?"

"He's the only one. I think it's the whole double ability, plus council member thing, that draws them to him. They know about each other, but they don't seem to care. It's not as if they all live together. The three of them are on separate properties. I think they feel it's an honour to be with someone so strong and powerful."

I screw up my face. "Really? Because whenever I see him, I can't help but laugh. His wardrobe is atrocious."

"I'm pretty sure his wives are more interested in what's under his clothes," Chad jokes, and I screw up my face again.

"I don't see it. I just don't know how they can be okay with sharing their husband."

Chad shrugs. "Well, they're not really married. Everyone here technically doesn't exist, so legally, they aren't married. They just call each other husband and wife. I wouldn't choose that kind of life either, but I don't see anything wrong with it if they all agree to it. They knew what they were getting themselves into."

"Well, at least I won't have to worry about having to share you," I say playfully, brushing my lips against his. He lets out a groan as I pull away. "So, next person. What's the deal with the old guy?"

"Connor? He's a first generation. When it became public that Defectives existed, Connor's parents kept him hidden instead of coming forward. They had a feeling it wasn't going to end well. He was one of the first people to come here. He's getting slower now that he's aging but could still outrun anyone here."

"So his ability is that he's fast?"

Chad nods. "Pretty much."

"And Millie?"

"Her husband was Defective."

"Was?" I ask.

Chad just nods again and says, "Yes. Was."

I lay down on my side, feeling heavy from the day. I have more questions, but I can't seem to keep my eyelids open right now. Chad lies down behind me and wraps his arm over me. A moan escapes me.

"Are you really that sore?" he asks.

I can't see his face but I know he is smiling, mocking me. "Mmm" is all I can answer.

"Okay, roll over," Chad commands.

"Roll over?"

"Yes," he says, pushing me onto my stomach. He starts massaging my aching muscles. It feels amazing as his hands start kneading my back and shoulders.

"Why didn't I get this kind of treatment when I was sore after training at the Institute?"

"Because I couldn't do this at the Institute," he whispers, leaning down and kissing my neck.

I moan again, only not from pain this time. "I'm sure you could've tried."

He lets out a laugh, but I barely hear it. My eyes are closed, and I know I'm about to fall asleep.

CHAPTER TEN

Four days of training, four nights of sleeping at Chad's to escape Ebbodine's sexcapades, and ninety-six hours of concentrating on hiding my double ability. I've had to focus on being good enough to get placement on the farm, all the while making sure I wasn't so good that they would want to send me on assignment. It all comes down to this.

The four of us newbies are sitting in the front row of the town hall. Cyrus, Marlo, Millie, Belle, and Connor sit at a long table in front of us, each with their own expression of seriousness on their faces. Mum was called away to help one of the recruiters yesterday. She should've been back by now, but she must've been held up. Paxton hasn't made it for the meeting either, but there are enough of them here for a majority vote, Chad said.

Chad and Dad are waiting outside. This is a closed session,

and even though the council knows that everyone will find out as soon as we leave here, they won't allow anyone else in to see the decision being made.

"Let's get started, shall we?" Cyrus's voice echoes through the hall. "Licia. You're up first." I squeeze her hand in support. Nervousness surrounds her. She stands and walks to the podium, which is centred between the rows of chairs. "We asked you a few days ago what your preferences were, and we've taken that into consideration. Are you still wishing to become a recruiter?" Cyrus asks.

"Yes," she replies, a bit unsteady.

"We've all agreed to let you continue with training towards that goal," Cyrus says with a smile. "It may be a while before you get out there, but after your match and observing your training over the last few days, we think you'll fit in well. Congratulations."

She comes back and sits down with a giant grin on her face.

Marlo stands. "Shilah. Your turn," she says. Shilah is more confident than Licia in his composure as he takes to the podium. "You too have the desire to become a recruiter, with the second preference of being trained as a handyman?"

That's news to me, but it makes sense. Shilah was always helping Dad fix things around the house. He never was big on the farming side of things; that was all me.

"That's correct," Shilah replies politely.

"To be honest, this decision was split. We see a lot of potential in you. You would be great at recruiting, but you would also be great as a jack-of-all-trades, too. We do have concerns about you going out into the field when we know the Institute would be looking for you." I see Shilah's face fall from happy to disappointed. "Having said that, we are willing to put you through training for both and make a future decision when we can further develop your skills. If you can build on your ability, there should be no reason why you couldn't go into the field. Does that sound okay with you?"

The smile is back on Shilah's face as he thanks them for their consideration.

Millie is next to stand up. "Drew," she says and nods towards him. He gets up and stands at the podium. "You informed us that you have no preference and will be happy with whatever we think is best. Is that correct? Have you thought of anything since then, that you might want to do?"

"Whatever you think is best," Drew replies. I think he knows there's no way in hell they're going to let him recruit. I don't know why he hasn't chosen something else as a preference though.

"We have voted, and all agree that a young, strong man like you would best suit us working in the farms, harvesting."

Drew nods and comes back to sit.

The butterflies in my stomach suddenly appear when I realise it's my turn. They kick up a notch when Belle is the one to stand up to deliver my verdict. "Allira," she says. I take to the podium, sweat dripping off my brow. "Are you able to tell us why you did not preference work as a recruiter? With your proven experience in this field, I would've thought you would jump at the chance to do it again."

My mouth drops open in shock. Why am I the one to get an inquisition? Drew has a lot more experience than I do, and he didn't get questioned. "I honestly don't think I have the nerve for that kind of work," I try to explain. "It's true that I have training and experience, and I do like the idea of helping people, but … I just don't think I can give one hundred percent when a big part of me would always be worried about being caught by the Institute." I take a deep breath before getting out this next part. "I don't want to go back there." I hang my head, avoiding eye contact with the panel.

When I look back up, I see the panel of council members discussing between themselves, quiet enough that we can't hear.

"We're going to have to vote again," Belle says. "I still vote to make you a recruiter," she says. Of course, she does. If I were to do that, I wouldn't be here with her son. My face turns angry, but I try to conceal it. "We could use your skills, and with added training, I'm sure we could get your nerves under control."

Cyrus stands up. "However, knowing your feelings about being in the field, I'm putting forward that you assist me with training. With your amplification ability, we think you would be really beneficial in helping us reach the trainees' full potential. Plus I've been thinking about getting someone trained up to take over if I'm ever needed elsewhere—to spend more time at home perhaps."

"Which home?" Marlo—his wife—jokes, making the panel laugh.

I can't believe everyone is okay with his … situation. And to actually make jokes about it? I just can't wrap my head around it. I tell myself to stop being so judgemental. It has nothing to do with me.

"Does that sound like something you'd be interested in?" Cyrus asks me, ignoring his second wife.

I think about it for a moment. Why are they offering me this? Is it so Cyrus can keep a closer eye on me? Prove to them that I'm just like him? Why haven't they offered Chad or Drew this position? Again, they are much more qualified for the job.

"This is an honour of an offer, Allira," Belle interrupts my train of thought. "Either you want us to vote on this or we'll assign you to be a recruiter."

I breathe in deep. "I would love to help with training," I say with the most forced smile I've ever had to fake. The council talk amongst themselves again, and it feels like forever until I get my answer.

"Welcome to the training team," Cyrus says with a smile.

* * *

Sitting at the dining table of my parents' house, I'm silent as Mum, Dad, Shilah, and Drew talk about our placements. I try to change the subject numerous times, but it keeps making its way back into the conversation. Mum made it back from assignment this afternoon, so she said she wanted to have a celebratory dinner with us. I'm just waiting for Chad to come pick me up to take me back to our place … his place. *His* place. I have to keep reminding myself of that fact so I don't casually let it slip that I'm not exactly living where Mum and Dad think I am.

"So you're not happy with your placement?" Dad asks me.

"It's not that. I realise I'm really lucky to be given such a great position," I say hesitantly.

"But?" Mum asks.

"I guess I'm wondering why they have offered it to me, when Chad—or even Drew—is more qualified for it."

Drew lifts his head from his food. "There's no way they'd offer me that kind of position. They don't even trust me to live on my own." He looks over at Mum. "Sorry. No offence. I don't mean to talk about you like you're not here."

"That's okay. You're actually pretty correct on that one. We want to trust you, but … well …"

"No need to explain," Drew says. "It's okay."

Mum smiles at him. I want to tell her to be wary of Drew's charm. He's sucking her in, I can tell.

"But back to you, Allira," Mum says. I take a deep breath in and try not to sigh when I breathe back out. "Why do you feel like you don't deserve it? As Cyrus said, you'll be helping him out. You won't be in charge or anything."

"I know. I just …" I can't tell them my real concern which is that I think Cyrus suspects I have a double ability, and the more I'm around him, the more chances he will have of proving it. Maybe I should just tell everyone and get it out of the way. If the worst they can do is keep me here, I'm okay with that. I don't want to leave anyway. At least if I'm forced to stay here, I won't ever be assigned as a recruiter.

"You deserve it, hon," Dad says. "Watching you during the games, seeing what you have achieved since ..." He gives Drew a deathly stare. "You've grown into someone I am proud of. You're strong and selfless, but you're too modest for your own good. You *deserve* this."

I don't respond to that, continuing to shovel food in my mouth as an excuse to stop talking about this. I'd really like to talk about something else right now.

"So how is living with Ebbodine going?" Shilah asks, a wry smile on his face.

I take it back. Let's go back to the placement conversation. I'm fairly sure Shilah knows I haven't been spending my nights with Ebbodine.

"It's fine." I shrug. I decide to get him back for asking that though. "She thinks you've gotten hot, Shilah. But I told her you were taken."

Shilah practically chokes on his food, which makes me smile. Mum and Dad look at Shilah, awaiting a response.

"Nah. I'm not taken," he says, giving me a glare that could break glass. "But she's not really my type anyway."

"Easy isn't your type?" Drew jokes.

I reach over the table and slap him over the head. I can't help but notice Dad out of the corner of my eye trying to suppress a smile. "Not nice," I say. Granted I've said similar, if not worse, but it has always been in her presence and as playful banter. It's one thing to say it to someone's face, but saying it behind their back is not only mean, it no longer classifies as a joke.

"Sorry," Drew says unconvincingly.

We continue to eat, now in silence, with the occasional small chatter thrown in here and there. I think it's impossible for Mum to sit and not talk for longer than five minutes. She does a lot of *"Oh, wasn't the weather wonderful today?"* and *"Even though it's winter and hardly any crops are growing, isn't this food wonderful?"* Lots of random weather-related things.

"I might head to bed early," Shilah says. "Had a big day of nerves and all that."

He starts making his way to his room, and I have a feeling I may have stepped over the line by announcing to everyone that he's taken. He still hasn't opened up to me about the mystery relationship he had back at the Institute. Whenever I've asked him about it over the last few days, we've been interrupted or he's wormed his way out of talking about it.

I think I need to go apologise. It's obviously a sore subject, yet I brought it up anyway.

"Excuse me," I say to the others at the table, following Shilah into his bedroom. When I get to his room and open his door, I find him climbing out of his window. I clear my throat and smile.

"Oh. Hey," he says, quickly climbing back in.

"Going somewhere?"

"No?" he replies.

"Was that a statement or a question?"

Shilah sighs. "Okay, I was going out."

"Out where?"

"Apparently, there's a hangout up the mountain, for those in recruitment."

"Oh. Okay," I reply with a shrug. "Can I talk to you for a minute, before you go?"

"You're not going to stop me from going? Are you going to tell on me?"

I shake my head. "I don't care what you do in your spare time," I say in a tone indicating that if he doesn't say anything about my extracurricular activities, I won't say anything about his. "But if Mum and Dad catch you, I can't help you."

"You could probably come if you want? Technically, you're in recruitment too," he says. "I'm sure Chad could come as well. He used to be one of us."

"One of *us*, hey?" I smile. "I'm happy to see you excited about something."

"You're not excited?"

I shrug. "I'm definitely happier here, but I don't know. It still doesn't feel like *home*. I'm beginning to think I'll never have that feeling again. Or if I've ever had that feeling to begin with."

"It's only been a week. I'm sure it will grow on you," he says, putting his arm around me.

"I wanted to make sure you were okay. I didn't mean to blurt out that you were taken ... okay, maybe I did. But I didn't mean to upset you." He doesn't respond, but he does remove his arm from around my shoulders. "How are you going with all of it? The whole being separated thing? I was only separated from Chad for a week and I hated it. We weren't even together at that point either. I can't imagine how hard it's been for you." I'm fishing for information again, and I think he knows it, but he answers me anyway, finally.

"I don't know. I guess I'm just upset I didn't realise the last time would be the *last* time, you know? I had no idea about any of this until I was on my way to my assignment. That's when I first saw what was going to happen and I realised I didn't get a proper goodbye. I thought I would be back."

"If you ever want to talk about it, I'm here. I know that sounds cliché and overbearingly sisterly of me, but I want us to be able to talk to each other about anything."

Shilah scoffs. "Right," he says sarcastically.

"What?"

"It's a two-way street, Allira. Tell me, where have you *really* been staying? Why are you not over the moon about getting the highest and most sought after job they could possibly offer you? Why do you cringe every time Cyrus says your name? Why does Belle hate you? Shall I go on? You expect me to spill everything to you, but you haven't once confided in me since we got here. No, actually, since we were living at the Institute."

I breathe in deep. *I want to answer your questions. Every single one of them. But I can't.* "I—"

"Don't. You don't have to. I'm just saying, I know I can confide in you. Just like you know you can confide in me. But both of us choose not to because, why?"

I shake my head. "I don't know. I want to. I really do ..."

"But?"

I don't answer him. The truth is, I don't know why I haven't told him my secret. At the Institute, I was too worried he would tell—it took a long while, almost two months of being there, for him to realise how evil the place was. I guess I just don't have that trust in him that I once had, and that makes me feel horrible on the inside. I have absolutely no reason not to trust Shilah. In fact, out of everyone, he should be the person I can trust the most. Everyone else has lied to me; he's the only one who hasn't.

"Good talk," he says sarcastically before climbing out the window again.

* * *

"I'm contemplating telling them," I say as Chad and I get into the car to drive back. He arrived to pick me up right after Shilah went out.

"Telling who what?" he asks.

"Everyone. About me. Shilah knows something's going on. It's only a matter of time before everyone finds out. Why not just tell them and get it over with?"

Chad looks at the steering wheel in front of him. "I don't think it's a good idea." He puts the keys in the ignition, and we pull away.

"I can't keep lying to Shilah. I don't want to, and I think Mum should know. I—"

"Can you at least wait until Paxton comes back? See what he thinks? It's pretty obvious he doesn't want the rest of the council to know or he would've told them already."

"We don't even know when that will be. Aunt Kenna said it could be weeks or even months before they can risk coming back."

"Just think about it? Please?"

"Okay," I say. He reaches for my hand, bringing it to his lips without taking his eyes off the road. I can't help but smile. "So, want to go to a party tonight?"

"A party?" he asks.

"A gathering … I don't exactly know what that means. Shilah is going. Apparently it's on the hill somewhere? For the recruiters? He was very vague about it—said you would know about it, seeing as you used to be one of them."

"I guess we can go if you want, but it's usually just a hangout for hook-ups." He raises his eyebrows at me. "We can just go home for that." He smiles and I smile back but not before rolling my eyes. "Okay, fine, we'll stop by before things get messy." He does a U-turn and heads back the way we came.

"Messy?"

"Yeah. They usually sneak alcohol up there."

"Where do they even get that? I can't get coffee, but they have access to alcohol? That's pretty screwed up."

Chad laughs. "There's always a way. Whenever we do a trading run for things we need but can't grow or make ourselves, they usually bring some sort of alcohol back with them. But they all mainly drink wine from our vineyard."

"There's a vineyard too?"

"Sort of. It's a pretty poor one, but it's also a necessity to keep most people sane around here." He laughs as if he is joking, but I'm wondering if there is some truth to it.

"We don't have to go if you don't want to," I say.

"We'll go. It'll be good for you to meet your students." He smirks.

"Students." I shudder. "That just feels weird. And I still don't know how they're going to learn from me. Most of them are probably more experienced than I am."

"You have to stop that."

"Stop what?"

"Thinking you're not good enough."

"It's not that. I know I can do it. I just think they have ulterior motives for giving it to me."

"Cyrus?"

"Yeah, Cyrus. I know he's Mr. Popularity and everyone loves him, everyone is his brother, and blah, blah, blah. I just can't shake the feeling that he's up to something. I keep telling myself it's the double ability thing, that he suspects. But then I think about his wives, his kids, and wonder …" I stop my train of thought. I shouldn't be expressing my paranoia.

"Wonder what?"

"I don't know." I shake my head. "Maybe my brain is just creating drama. I don't think I truly believe this is real. That I'm finally here and that I'm free. It's too good to be true. I'm just looking for faults so I know it's real … Does that make sense?"

"It does. But we're not perfect here. We're far from it. We keep recruiting yet we're running out of room to put people. There's enough food for now, but we'll need to start new crops if we keep gaining numbers, that could take years. The council don't seem to have any future plans of getting us back into the real world; none that they've spoken to us about anyway. There's plenty to worry about other than Cyrus preferring the company of three different women."

"Oh, well, great. Thanks for adding that to my thoughts."

Chad laughs. "You're welcome. We're here."

We get out of the car and make our way down a pathway that has clearly been made from feet constantly walking back and forth over a long period of time. The smell of smoking wood and the sound of insects envelop me, reminding me how far out in the woods we really are. We come to a clearing on the edge of the mountain and make our way through the gathering of people. Chad leads me to the rough-hewn bench seats made out of rock that surround a campfire. We're high enough on the mountain to see the lights of the city, hours away. It's hard to believe that everything is going on as normal down there. As if we never existed. I can almost hear the bustling sound of the city—the cars, the people. I know it's only my imagination, but it seems so real.

There are fifteen or so others here, and I spot Shilah standing with three others. Shilah sees me and raises his cup, an offering. "Drink?" Just as he does this, two cups are placed in front of us. Cyrus stands above me, a smile on his lips.

"Glad you two could make it," he says. I don't really want to drink, but maybe if I do, I won't find every word out of Cyrus's mouth creepy and sleazy. Grabbing the cup, I drink half of it in one gulp. "Impressive," Cyrus says.

Looks like I'm going to need a lot more if I have to spend the rest of the night near Cyrus. I down the rest of my drink in the hopes it fades him out.

"Thirsty?" Chad asks.

"I guess I was, yeah," I reply with a smile, grabbing Chad's drink and drinking that too.

Cyrus sits next to me, no, practically *on* me. I take the opportunity to inch closer to Chad and put my hand on his leg.

Chad wraps his arm around me, and I feel bulletproof … well, Cyrus-proof. Although, technically, I would be bulletproof sitting here with Chad—if I were to borrow his ability anyway. Hmm, is his ability bulletproof? I don't think I've ever asked to what extent he's protected. Is his force field made of Kevlar? I laugh at my funny thoughts.

If I'm beginning to ramble in my head, I'd hate to see what is about to come out of my mouth. Maybe the drinks are working … and maybe it wasn't the best idea that I drank them.

"I might go say hi to Shilah," I say as politely as possible before getting up and walking over to him. When I get over there, three fresh faces of boys I haven't met stare me down.

"So this is the new boss lady?" one of them asks.

"Boss lady?" I ask, confused.

"Your Cyrus's right-hand man now, right?" another asks, with a tone of annoyance.

"Uh … I guess … sort of?"

"This is my sister, Allira," Shilah adds. The three of them just continue to stare.

"No, no, don't use my real name. I'm liking this 'Boss Lady' title," I joke, hoping to break the tension lingering in the group. "I may get everyone to start calling me that." The three boys smile, their stances relaxing a little.

"Well, as long as you're as cool as Cyrus, we'll get along," the third one states. "I'm Hayden, by the way, and this is Loccie and Arlo."

I shake each of their hands. "So Cyrus is a pretty good trainer? Good to work for?" I ask.

"Well, he pretty much lets us do whatever we want," Arlo says, gesturing to our surroundings. I don't know if that really answers my question, but I won't push my limits with the guys who are obviously asking the same question I am—why did Cyrus choose *me* over everyone else?

I feel a presence appear beside me. Turning around, I find Licia inching her way closer and closer to the group.

"Licia," I say. "This is Arlo, Loccie, and Hayden ... did I get that right?" I ask. Hayden nods. "This is Licia." I pull her into our circle as she shyly says hi to each of the boys.

"Another newbie," Loccie says.

"And a girl this time," Arlo says. You can see his excitement as he widens his eyes, staring at Licia's ... assets.

I suddenly feel overprotective towards Licia. The looks on the boys' faces lets me know that they haven't been introduced to many new girls, and I can see them staring her down as if she was a piece of meat.

"My eyes are up here," she sasses Arlo, while pointing to her face.

Maybe I don't have to worry about her after all.

Hayden shakes his head at the other two who are practically drooling over Licia. "Ignore them, Licia," he says. "Want a drink?" Ah. It's pretty clear who the smooth one of those three is. Licia nods and walks with Hayden to go get a drink. Arms wrap around me from behind and lips find my shoulder.

"Ready to get out of here?" Chad asks.

"Sure." I didn't exactly get to meet a lot of people, but if I'm met with the same kind of reaction that the three boys gave me, I don't want to spend my night trying to prove myself. I'm sure there will be plenty of time for that at training.

I lean in to Shilah before leaving. "Can you just keep an eye on Licia for me? Make sure she doesn't drink too much or make a mistake?" I say, nodding my head towards the boys. He agrees but he doesn't look too impressed with my request. "Nice to meet you," I say to the boys as Chad grabs my hand and drags me away.

"Is there a reason why you wanted to leave so early?" I ask as we get into car and he starts driving us home.

Chad shrugs. "Just did."

I can't tell what his tone means. "You're not telling me something," I say.

"Not telling you what?"

I think for a moment. "I don't know what it is, but I know it has something to do with recruiting." He doesn't respond. "Why did you choose to not go back?"

He sighs and shifts in his seat. "I wanted to stay here, with you."

Lie. "As romantic as that is, I'm calling bullshit."

He scoffs. "Really? And why is that?" His tone reaches a whole new level of annoyed.

"You didn't know where I was going to be placed. As everyone has already pointed out—especially in my placement meeting—I would've been suited to recruiting, meaning I probably would've been placed in recruiting with you. You chose to leave recruiting." *I don't think I have said the word recruiting more in one sentence before,* I think before shaking off my thoughts and telling myself to listen to Chad's answer.

"I just felt like I was done. I did it for close to eighteen months. I was done. Does it really matter why I don't want to be part of that world anymore?"

"I guess not. I just wanted to know why. You don't even want to hang around the others who you used to work with. You—"

"I only ever worked with Tate. I only ever saw those guys during training, which I didn't even have much of. Mine and Tate's abilities complemented each other so well, we didn't need it ... *thought* we didn't need it."

It's perfectly clear why he wants nothing to do with recruiting. I've just been too wrapped up in myself to see it. "It's not your fault," I say. Chad doesn't respond. "Chad, it's *not* your fault. None of it. It's not your fault he was arrested, and it's not your fault you couldn't get him out. He chose to stay there."

"Just stop," he asks quietly. Something about his tone makes me stop talking. I want to get through to him, but I know it's not going to happen, and I'm not going to waste my breath.

We arrive back home after a long silence in the car. We park the car in its designated bay in between two others and put the keys in a box that sits on the fence line. Cars are a shared commodity here and are only to be used when needed. Having Mum and Dad living on the other side of the compound, we're entitled to use them for social purposes, so long as they aren't being used for work means. There's usually always at least one car available, but if we all started using them just because we can't be bothered to walk somewhere, there would never be any available. That's what Mum told me anyway when I asked why everyone walks everywhere.

"I might go back to my place," I say. I don't really want to, but there's tension between us that I haven't felt since before we got together. He isn't being completely open with me, and making him talk will be next to impossible.

Before I can start walking off, he is at my side, pulling me into him. "Stay with me, please?" he asks, his tone boyish and vulnerable. "I'm sorry. It's hard for me to talk about him. You understand that, don't you?"

"I do. It's hard for me as well. I just wish I could make you feel better."

He smiles. "I can think of one way."

My lips curl upwards in an involuntary action as he leans down, touching his lips against mine and holding me close.

"Okay. I'll stay."

He kisses the end of my nose and leads me inside, straight to bed.

CHAPTER ELEVEN

"Everyone, this is Allira," Cyrus says, addressing the group of trainees and recruiters in front of us. It's a warm spring morning. The dew has already dried, and everyone sits on the ground just outside the obstacle course in the training area. Everyone except for me. I tried to sneak in and sit down with the rest of them, hiding between Shilah and Licia, but Cyrus pulled me up front to stand in front of everyone. "She'll be helping me keep you lot in check," he jokes. "Allira, would you like to say something about yourself?"

I shake my head. "Nah, I'm all good, thanks."

"Aww, she's shy," Cyrus says condescendingly. "Don't worry, we'll get that out of you." Everyone laughs. I can feel my face redden—I just want this to be over with. "Okay, let's get to it. I figure we haven't been paying much attention to our ability training. Not as much as we should. So I think we'll be focussing on that today. Everyone pair off and let's go."

"What would you like me to do?" I ask Cyrus.

"You can just stand there and look pretty," he replies. I try to hide my automatic reflex to cringe, but I don't think it works. "Or you could use your ability to help others realise their potential. With an ability like yours, it's bound to help them realise the extent of their capabilities."

The group spreads out as each pair starts practicing their abilities. Some are putting on protective vests they picked up from a crate at Cyrus's feet, and some are putting on protective sunglasses like the ones we used for the games. It's only then do I realise that we must have some pretty strong abilities here.

The first person I recognise is Hayden from last night. I would prefer to help Licia or Shilah, but I can't see them in the group anywhere. The sheer number of people here surprises me. There were only about fifteen at the gathering last night, and I thought that must have been the majority of us. There's at least double that here now. Some are older, mid-to-late twenties, but most are younger. Some even look as young as fourteen or fifteen. It seems the Resistance has taken a page out of the Institute's book on training.

"Hey, boss lady," Hayden says with a smile, and I can't help but return it.

"You're already my favourite, Hayden. No need to suck up."

"Allira, this is my younger brother, Brayden."

I give him a look. *Really? Hayden and Brayden?*

"And yes, our names rhyme, you don't need to say it."

I shake Brayden's hand and go to say hello, but when we touch, a sharp pain runs up my arm as if a zap of electricity is running through it. "Ah, f—ar out," I say, trying to cover what I was actually about to blurt out.

"Sorry," Brayden says quickly, pulling his hand away. "I didn't mean to."

Hayden leans in to me. "He hasn't quite got the hang of things yet."

"That's okay," I say. "It probably doesn't help that I amplify abilities."

"That's what you can do?" Brayden asks. "That's so awesome. Can we try again?"

"Uh, maybe later." My arm's still tense and sore from his last jolt of power. "What about you, Hayden? Show us what you've got."

Hayden runs his hand over his white-blond hair. "All right." He reaches out his hand for me. I hesitate for a second. *What is he going to do to me?* I give him my hand reluctantly. *'Tell me I'm awesome,'* I hear telepathically.

"You're awesome," I say, the words flying out of my mouth before I can stop them. "What was that? Are you a Telepath like Tate?"

"Not quite," he says. "I can control what people say."

"That's really impressive."

"It's okay, I guess. It would be better if I could force more than a sentence out of someone."

"I can work with you on that."

"Really?" he asks, surprised.

"That's what I'm here for."

Hayden smiles at me, and for the first time since being handed this job, I'm excited to help.

* * *

"So how many recruiters are actually out in the field at the moment?" I ask Hayden as we break for lunch.

Hayden sighs. "Six."

"Only six? Only three teams? But there's so many at training. Why are there only six people out there?" I ask.

"Cyrus says none of us are ready, we don't have abilities that complement each other enough to be sent out there by ourselves. He wants abilities like mine matched with ones like Brayden's. A passive ability with an active."

I nod. That's the same sort of combination the Institute would go with as well. It makes sense: one to investigate and find

Defectives, and one to approach and proposition while being protected. It's why Tate and Chad worked so well together. Although, now that I think about it, Drew and I both had passive abilities, and that didn't stop the Institute from pairing us off. I'm beginning to think they really did partner us together to punish us like Drew first suspected. They knew our history; maybe they did it to emphasise the amount of control they had over us, maybe they did it for pure entertainment—who knows.

"Well, if you can get control over your ability, I'm sure you'll be out there before you know it," I say encouragingly, trying to put the Institute out of my mind. But now that I have said this, I begin to wonder just how Hayden's ability would help in the recruitment process.

"We'll see," he replies unenthusiastically.

"You don't think so?" Maybe he knows he won't be all that helpful out there, too.

"I … never mind. I'm sure you're right," he says walking off and catching up to the others who are heading towards the cafeteria shed. It's as if he thinks he'll never be put in the field.

I follow the others up the hill to go to lunch, only to see Chad coming the opposite way. He nods to some of the trainees on the way down, grabbing my hand as he reaches me and leads me back towards the training area.

"Lunch?" he asks, holding up a bag of food.

"Is there a reason why we can't have lunch with everyone else?" I ask, following him over to the obstacle course.

He throws the bag of food up onto a ledge and starts climbing up the ropes course onto the little square platform where the horizontal rope section begins. He sits down and pats the spot next to him. "Maybe I wanted you all to myself. So, how's your first day going?"

"Really good actually," I reply, climbing up after him. "That Hayden kid is pretty good."

Chad smirks. "That 'kid' is seventeen. Only a few months younger than you."

"Oh," I reply. He seemed younger to me for some reason. Maybe I just feel old. I'm sure I've aged years over the last six months. "How did you do it?"

"What do you mean?"

"How did you become a teacher when your students were your age? Wasn't it weird?" I know it's weird for me to think that at some point Chad may have taught one of my classes back home and I just don't remember it.

"It was even harder when it was my old school and my 'students' were friends. But I guess I just … I don't know. I just did it."

"Thanks for clearing that up."

"You don't really need to look at them as if they're your students. Look at them as people you can help. It might be easier if you treat them as an equal, rather than trying to get them to look up to you. They have Cyrus for that."

"The impression I get is Cyrus loves the admiration he gets from them. He seems to feed off it."

"That's probably true."

"I also get the impression that Cyrus has no intention of sending any of these trainees into the field," I say hesitantly.

Chad raises his eyebrows. "Really? What makes you say that?"

"Do you know how many people are in the field right now?" I ask.

"There's usually about eight teams, sixteen people at one time."

"There's six."

"Six isn't that bad."

"No. Not six teams. Six people, total. There are only three teams out there. Hayden could be ready for it. We made so much progress this morning, and it was only a couple of hours' work. But when I told him that he'll be out there in no time, he got doubtful about the whole thing. Said Cyrus doesn't believe any of them are good enough yet, but what would he know? He hasn't been out there, he has no idea."

"He's probably right though. They probably aren't ready. They're not going to send anyone out there until they are absolutely prepared for it. It's not like the Institute where they don't care what happens to their agents once they're out there. It's safety first here."

"I guess that's a good thing."

"It's a really good thing."

"I don't know. I just … No matter how much I try, I just feel like something else is going on here." Maybe deep down, I want something to be wrong here. Isn't that what most screwed up people do? When something good happens in their life, they sabotage it any way they can because they don't know how to be happy? "Maybe I'd feel less self-conscious if everyone knew about me," I say, trying to cover other reasons for my insecurities.

Chad rolls his eyes. "Not this again."

"I know, I know. Wait until Paxton is back. Fine."

We're silent after that. I pick at my food and look out across the Fields. I look anywhere but at Chad. I can see some of the crop fields beyond the training arena. It's eerily deserted while the workers are at lunch. Half-full bins of ripe food sit intermittently around the crops. Rakes, shovels, and other tools lie anywhere but on their racks.

I start wondering what this place would look like to an outsider. What would someone see if they came stumbling upon us? I know the chances of that happening are small—miniscule in fact—but I am fascinated by the possibility anyway. They would discover a community of people, completely self-sufficient and separate from the rest of the country. We live by the rules of the council, our very own government, and we train our fittest and fastest to become the strongest people they can be. Something snaps in my brain as this thought comes to mind. *I know what Cyrus is doing.*

"Are any of Cyrus's kids in recruitment?" I ask casually.

"He has two in recruiting. Twins actually. Wife number one's kids. Ada and Alec."

"What are their abilities?"

"To be honest, I don't see how their abilities will help in recruiting. I think Cyrus persuaded the council to send them here so his kids didn't have to work too hard. I remember everyone being disappointed when the twins finally realised what they could do. There were rumours that they could possibly be the strongest out of everyone. Double ability parent, having twins? Everyone had high hopes for them. Unfortunately, having a double ability doesn't necessarily mean your kids will inherit that kind of power. One of them controls the air around them—they can create wind tunnels, tornados—that kind of thing. The other is a fire-starter."

I think for a moment. "So together, they would be pretty good at containing and controlling a fire," I suggest. Chad raises his eyebrows at me. "Fire needs oxygen to grow, right? Twin A starts a fire, Twin B feeds it the oxygen it needs to take over a whole area … for instance."

"I guess, but I don't see what that has to do with recruiting?"

"Neither do I," I mutter.

"What?"

"Never mind. I'm just rambling. So how many kids does Cyrus have?"

A voice comes from behind us, startling me. "A lot." I turn to see Cyrus. He has returned from lunch already. Did he even leave? "Why do you want to know?" he asks, a little snarky.

I shrug. "I was just curious. I saw you with your little ones last week, and Chad just told me about the twins." I hope I'm pulling this nonchalant attitude off, because on the inside, I'm trying not to fall apart with nerves.

Cyrus climbs up and takes the spot on the other side of me. Again, sitting far too closely and completely ignoring personal space boundaries. Seriously, don't they teach this kind of stuff to you when you're a child? *"Do not invade another person's personal space. It's rude."*

"Well, there is Ada and Alec, the twins. They're fourteen and the eldest. Then there's Benji, who's twelve, Bianca's ten, Bronte, nine. Brent's seven, and Bailey and Char are four—"

"Oh, more twins?" I ask.

Chad shakes his head as Cyrus answers. "Uh. No. Sort of had some overlaps that year."

"Oh." I cringe.

"Then there is Catharine who is almost three and Camryn, the baby, who's almost one. And, I think that's all of them," Cyrus says with a smile. *Ten.* Ten children. *Ten.* I think I'm in shock. *Ten?*

"Well, you don't look old enough to have ten children," I say. It's really the only thing that came into my head that seemed polite enough to say.

"Thanks, beautiful," he responds. *Don't cringe again, don't cringe.* "Sorry, Chad. I may just have to steal your woman away."

I freeze at his words, glancing sideways at Chad to see how I should react to that. He doesn't seem fazed by it. Was it a joke?

"What I mean is: we have to get back to work. Lunch is over," Cyrus says.

"Oh," I say, letting go of the breath I was holding in.

Chad kisses the side of my head before climbing back down the course and walking off.

"Help me set up for the next challenge?" Cyrus asks when Chad disappears over the hill.

"Sure. What is it?"

"I want to set targets up around the place so those with the really active abilities have some target practice."

"You know, I was working with Hayden this morning. He's doing really well. And with my amplifying his ability, I think he's improving."

"Really?" Cyrus asks excitedly. "And just how much were you amplifying his ability by?"

"How much? I don't know. It's not a measurable thing."

"Of course, it is. Everything can be measured. Have you not been shown how to use different strengths of amplification?"

"No. I just ... amplify."

"Just like that, huh?" He leads me over to the war games arena. "You have to think of your ability as a muscle. The more you use it, the stronger it becomes. So if you think about it, there are many different strengths and fitness levels your ability could have. Come, I'll show you. I wouldn't want you practicing with someone with an active ability like Brayden and accidently electrocute someone. You need to be able to control your ability."

"Okay." I guess I never thought of it like that before.

Cyrus takes my hand. "Okay, I'm going to lift one of these cement barricades with my telekinesis, you try to amplify it until it's only a few feet off of the ground. Don't make it go any higher."

I breathe in and concentrate on getting the barricade to float a little off the ground. It gets to that point quickly but keeps going. "How do I pull it back?" I ask.

"Don't concentrate so hard. Look at me, not at the barricade." I turn to look at Cyrus, and the cement falls to the ground with a thud; I swear I feel the ground shudder.

"It seems to be all in or nothing," I say.

"All right. Maybe we'll start from the other end. This time, go as hard as you can, and then we'll try to pull it back."

I nod. "Okay." I concentrate again, and the barricade flies high into the air.

"As hard as you can, Allira."

"I am," I say. The barricade is really high, and I get the sudden fear that if I lose my concentration, this will turn into a real safety hazard.

"Now try to pull it back," Cyrus says.

I'm concentrating so hard, I don't even notice when Cyrus lets go of my hand. By the time I do realise, it's too late. The giant slab of cement falls to the ground in a swift, quick descent but not before it remained hovering in the air for longer than it should have. It crumbles as it hits the ground, cracking in numerous places with debris shooting out. I look at Cyrus, my eyes so wide they feel like they're going to pop out of my head.

He gives me a stern look. "You have some explaining to do. Do you want to tell me exactly how you were using telekinesis?"

"I wasn't," I lie.

"Your amplification ability allows you to amplify only when touching someone, correct?"

"Maybe it's getting stronger? Perhaps that's even part of my amplification ability?"

"Cut the crap," Cyrus says with an uncharacteristic scowl on his face. "I know you have a double ability. I've known since the first time I met you. What I didn't know is if you knew. I really hoped you were just naïve and innocent and had no idea about it, but the look on your face right now tells me that you've known about it for a long time."

What do I do? Do I continue to deny it anyway? Or do I just give in? I've wanted to tell them ever since I got here. It's been Chad who has been preventing it from getting out. I could continue to deny it, knowing full well that Cyrus will never believe it, or I can admit it and that way it came out through no fault of my own. Cyrus worked it out; he confronted me. Chad won't be able to dispute that.

"How did you know?" I ask him, my chest already feeling

lighter from the weight of my secret holding me down.

"It's my second ability. I don't know how you thought you could keep it from me," he says in a much calmer tone than he'd been using. "You should've been honest with the council."

"Two council members know. Well, three, including you now." I hang my head.

"Two? Your mother and who?" he demands.

"Mum doesn't know."

His eyebrows fly up in surprise before furrowing in thought. "It has to be Paxton and Tate then," he concludes. We both stare at each other, unsure of what to say next. "Why did you feel the need to hide it from us?"

"I don't know. Tate told me from the beginning to keep it to myself. He said it wouldn't work out too well for me if people found out, especially people at the Institute."

"We're not them," Cyrus says.

"I know that."

"But?" he asks.

"But what?"

"You still haven't answered me. We need to be able to trust everyone here, and right now, I can't think of one reason why we should trust you. Let's look at the facts: you and your family—with the exception of your mother—refused to join the Resistance, landing yourselves at the Institute. You trained with them, became an agent, again refused to join the Resistance when the opportunity presented itself. You said you would join us after we got your brother out; we do that for you, but somehow, your Institute boyfriend tags along as well. When you finally get here, you're skilful, you're smart, and yet you request to be placed working in the Fields in a menial position that is clearly beneath you. And the biggest issue of all, your inability to put any trust in us."

"I don't know what to say to that," I answer. "Except that, I didn't know about the Resistance until I was already an agent for the Institute. Hell, I didn't even know I was Defective until I was arrested."

Cyrus sighs. "I don't know what to do with you."

"Do with me?" I retort, narrowing my eyes.

"I need to take this to the council—"

"No. Don't, please don't," I plead. "I should be the one to tell the others."

"I agree, but you haven't yet. Why should I believe that you will?"

"I will. I promise."

Cyrus thinks for a moment. "I'll give you a few days but no longer. If you don't tell them, I will. You need to start being honest about who you are. There's nothing wrong with having two abilities. If anything, it makes you more important and more valuable to us. For lack of a better word, it's what makes you *special* to us. To me. We're the same, you and I."

"I don't think I'm any more important than anyone else here, and I don't want to be. We're all playing a vital part in our fight against the Institute."

"Do you really think the Institute is our only obstacle? Our only enemy?"

We're interrupted by the recruiting trainees appearing over the hill, making their way back for the afternoon classes. I wipe the tears from my face that I've only just realised were there. Cyrus doesn't say anything else as we start setting up for the afternoon.

Focussing is next to impossible as I watch and help those with active abilities shoot at targets. I'm easily distracted and have to tell myself to concentrate harder. I catch glimpses of Cyrus staring at me, his expression unreadable. Sometimes he looks quizzical, other times just flat, no expression at all. If there was ever a time I wished Drew was near, now was it. You would think that after months of sensing emotions, I would have some natural instincts about the meaning of facial expressions. Apparently, I'm a slow learner.

Before I know it, I find myself sitting alone, back up on the platform of the obstacle course. Everyone has gone home for the evening, even Cyrus. He didn't say a word to me all afternoon. I should start heading home, but facing Ebbodine right now—and most likely Hall as well—doesn't seem all that appealing. I'm not really looking forward to telling Chad about my day either. The sun has just touched the horizon. It'll be dark soon, and yet I can't make myself get up.

I see someone coming down from the hill. At first, I think it's Chad, and he has worked out where I am. But it's not. The person walking towards me doesn't walk as confidently or as tall as Chad. Once upon a time, he did, but not here. I don't say anything as Drew walks past me, and I let out a sigh of relief as he keeps going. I guess he must not have seen me.

"You sure you want to be alone right now?" he asks, his voice echoing through the silence as if we were standing on the hilltop. I flinch from the fright—I thought he kept on walking. He starts climbing the rope ladder to get to me.

"Are you freaking kidding me?" I say, pushing him, almost causing him to lose his balance. "Don't you know it's insanely rude to scare the crap out of me?"

He just laughs. "I'll try to mind my manners next time." He gets onto the platform and sits down next to me. "Want to talk about it?"

"With you?" I don't mean for it to come out as harsh as it does.

Drew shrugs. "You don't have to, but you can, if you want."

"What are you even doing here? Walking through here, I mean."

"It's how I get home from the Fields."

"You don't get a lift with Dad?" I ask.

"I wouldn't even if he offered," he replies.

"Things still aren't going well between you guys?"

"It's all right. Shilah isn't so bad now, and your mum is really nice, but I guess that's because she wasn't there for the whole … thing."

"I think Dad will forgive you. Eventually. Even I'm coming around," I say, nudging him with my elbow. "And I think if Shilah and I can forgive you, surely he will be able to. I was actually thinking the other night that I owed you a thank you."

Drew pulls his head back in shock, a look of complete mock horror across his face. "A thank you? Really? Then by all means, please, go ahead," he says, smiling.

"In a roundabout way, I have you to thank for all of this," I say, gesturing to the view before us. "If you didn't do what you did, I wouldn't be here." Drew smiles and puts his arm around my shoulders. It's the first time I haven't pulled away from him since we were together, or pretending to be married, but it also doesn't feel like anything other than a friendly embrace. "Then again," I add, "if I'd worked out that I was Defective on my own, maybe Dad would've gotten in contact with Mum sooner, and we could've come here first and skipped the whole torture thing they're so fond of at the Institute."

Drew pulls his arm away. "I hated that they were doing that to you," he says quietly. "I couldn't be there, for any of it. I couldn't watch that. They ordered me to, but I just … couldn't."

"Well, it wasn't much fun for me either," I reply, my tone surprisingly soft.

Drew changes the subject. "So you've successfully distracted me with this conversation for a few minutes, but how about you tell me why you're sitting up here, alone, in the dark."

"Just stuff," I answer.

"Stuff can be a bitch," he replies.

I hesitate, debating internally whether to tell Drew about what's going on. I know I shouldn't; that was the deal we made at breakfast last week. Don't tell Drew any important information. However, Drew is an outsider, and as such, he might have a different perspective than someone who's been here for years, like Chad.

"What do you think of the council?" I ask. "Honestly."

He shrugs. "To be honest, I haven't paid a whole lot of attention."

"You're lying."

"I am? How do you know?"

"You think living with you for the past three months hasn't given me any insight into how you work? I watched you investigate Licia every day. You're lying, I can see it in your face."

"I don't think they're much better than Brookfield," he says.

Borrowing his ability, I know he's telling me how he really feels. And the scary part is, I think I agree with him.

"Granted, they aren't as harsh or as strict as Brookfield, but what kind of life do we have? We work seven days a week just trying to feed ourselves. I don't know what it's like down here in training, but on the farms, it's literally hard labour for eight, nine, ten hours a day. We eat, sleep, farm. Eat, sleep, farm. Don't get me wrong, I do like it here and I'm technically free, but I guess I didn't realise that freedom would come at such a cost," he says.

"A cost?"

"I just wonder how everyone out here hasn't died of boredom," he says.

"Says the ex-agent who's used to action and drama on a daily basis. I think you'll find anything boring after doing that." I certainly haven't been bored, but I also have a boyfriend, a best friend, and my family. Drew has no one. "The games were fun," I say, trying to find something to fill him with some kind of hope for making things better for him.

"Yeah, the one time we've had the chance to play."

I don't respond to that. All this time I was thinking Drew must be so happy and so grateful to be here, I didn't stop to actually think of what it must be like for him. But I do know what it's like for him—I went through it at the Institute. He's right, we aren't much better than them.

"So, are you ready to go home yet? I'm starting to freeze over," he says. The icy chill of night time in early spring has hit, and he isn't wearing a jacket.

"Sure. How about you walk me to your house? I need to tell my mum something."

CHAPTER TWELVE

Drew and I walk in to find Mum, Dad, and Shilah eating at the dining table.

"Lia? What are you doing here?" Mum asks, surprised. She then looks to Drew before I have a chance to answer. "Sorry. We had to start without you, it was getting cold."

"No problems, Seph. I ran into Allira on my way home. Got held up a bit." Dad shoots us a stare. If I didn't know Dad any better, say if he was a stranger and I saw him in a dark alley in the city and he gave me this look, I would assume I wasn't going to make it out of that alley alive. "Talking," Drew clarifies. "We got held up talking." Dad doesn't say anything and goes back to eating.

"Join us," Mum says. I pull up the chair next to Mum as Drew sits at the head of the table, opposite Dad. Shilah seems oblivious to anything around him and keeps shovelling food in his mouth as if he's worried he won't get enough now he's sharing with me as well as Drew. "How was your first day working with Cyrus?" Mum asks.

"Uh … fine." Geez, if I go at this rate, I'm never going to tell her about me. "Could have gone better." I tell the nerves that have started to build in my stomach to calm down. Like Cyrus said, this will make me more valuable to them. They're not going to be angry, right? For me lying to them? A high-pitched singsong tone starts ringing in my ears. *"Hypocrite. H-Y-P-O-CRITE."* Ugh.

"Did I miss you falling on your face or something?" Shilah asks. "I thought it was a pretty good day."

"Something like that," I reply, while shoving a forkful of charred roo meat and salad into my mouth.

"So you're not going to elaborate?" Dad asks me.

I just shake my head and eat. I don't have the words. Blurting out I have a double ability seems extreme. Easing them into it by announcing I have something to tell you seems unnatural.

"Mum?" I ask, putting my fork down.

"Uh-oh. That sounds like a pretty serious *Mum* tone," she replies, smiling. If only she realised what she was saying was the truth and not so much a joke.

"What's the plan? The big plan. The whole point to the Resistance?"

"Whoa," she says, putting down her cutlery. "This did just get serious. Why do you want to know?"

"Just something I noticed today in training. It started to make me think."

"What did you notice?" Dad interjects into the conversation.

"I just got the feeling we aren't really training for recruitment purposes only."

Mum goes stiff. "What makes you say that?" she asks.

"Just a few of the things Cyrus said. Plus the fact his eldest two kids are being trained when their abilities would be absolutely no benefit in recruiting people. Actually, there's a few like them. Also the fact that there used to be eight teams of two out there at any given point, now there's only three."

Mum puts her hand up to stop me. "We've had a run of misfortunes lately with recruiting. Our best team, Tate and Chad, obviously can't recruit anymore. We had a few people pull out after what happened to Tate. I think they finally realised they aren't invincible. We don't have many out there at the moment because the majority—as you would've seen in training—are young. Too young for such a big responsibility."

"And Cyrus's kids?" Drew asks, suddenly interested.

Shilah is sitting across from me, taking it all in. He's also giving me a stare similar to Dad's earlier. I can almost hear him thinking "Why can't you just leave well enough alone?"

"I'd like to say they deserve to be there," Mum says. "We do always need people who can defend themselves. But I'm going to be completely honest here and say Cyrus wanted them there. And usually what Cyrus wants, Cyrus gets."

"Because of his double ability?"

She looks at me, contemplating how to answer that. Instead of answering, she starts picking up the plates and tidying the dining table. I'm pretty sure that means "yes."

"I'm just curious, because there's something you all don't know."

I remind myself to breathe; I didn't even realise I had stopped. I'm about to tell everyone, when I hear footsteps behind me. I didn't hear the front door open though.

"Allira." Chad's voice startles me. "I've been looking for you. When you didn't come home. I ... Ebbodine got worried."

"But not worried enough to come herself?" Shilah asks. "Wouldn't it have been much faster for her to come and check?"

I shoot Shilah a "shut up" look.

"I had to come here first," I say to Chad. "I had an interesting afternoon. I was just about to fill my parents in. On *everything.*"

"Can I talk to you for a minute? Outside?" he asks.

I sigh as I get up from the table and follow him out the front door, closing it behind me. "Want to fill me in on what happened today?" he asks.

"Not really."

"Why's that?"

"Because I'm scared you'll try to talk me out of it."

"Why are you going to tell them? I thought we—"

"Not *we*. You. *You* decided we shouldn't tell them. But you were right. About Cyrus. He knows. He tricked me into borrowing his ability, confronted me, and told me I had a few days to tell the rest of the council before he did."

Chad runs his hands through his hair and down his neck. He must be really nervous. He goes to say something but stops himself. He opens his mouth again to say something, but nothing comes out.

"What?" I ask.

"I don't know. I don't know what to say. I guess I wasn't expecting you to expose yourself so easily."

"Did you really just say that to me? *Really?*"

"Well, I don't know what else to say," he says, clearly pissed off. "The only reason you haven't told them yet is because of me, because I asked you not to. Maybe you were hoping to slip up. Maybe you weren't using your usual amount of caution."

"And you think Cyrus would be the first one I would choose to show my abilities to?"

He pauses, thinking. "I guess not. I just … I'm sorry. I guess we'll just have to see what happens now. It's done. There's not much else we can do but admit it."

"We?"

"You think there won't be consequences for me knowing and not telling them? Not telling my mother?"

"Is *that* what you're worried about? Getting into trouble with your *mother?*"

Chad sighs. "Of course not. I mean, that won't be fun, but I'm more worried about you."

"What about me? Why? Please explain it to me."

"I don't know what they're going to do with you, and that scares me, okay." He takes a breath before slowly speaking his next words. "I have a bad feeling about this. I don't want to lose you." He pulls me in close.

"I thought you said the most they'll do is just keep me here, like they do with Cyrus."

"That's just a theory. What if, for instance, they *are* planning a takeover of the Institute? With your borrowing capability, they'll use that to their advantage. They'll spare everyone else by putting you in the line of fire. You have the potential to use numerous abilities at once."

"Well, both of my abilities could come in handy that way."

"And here you are almost volunteering for such a position!"

"It's a hypothetical situation."

Chad runs his hand over his head again. "Let's just do this," he says, exasperated. He begins to walk inside, but I grab his hand and pull him back.

"Tell me we're okay," I plead.

He shakes off my hand. "We're okay," he says, walking into the house.

Yeah, really sounds like it.

Walking back inside, we find everyone staring at us as we appear through the entryway.

"Everything all right out there?" Drew asks, knowing full well it's not. The amount of frustration coming from both Chad and me could fill the entire house.

"Perfect," Chad answers, putting his arm around me. I roll my eyes at the obvious manoeuvre. "We have an announcement."

"If this is about you two living together, we already know," Mum says.

"What?" I respond, my cheeks embarrassingly flushing, giving away my guilt.

"Please. We knew the minute Ebb asked to be your roommate in a single bunker," Mum says.

"Well, no. It's not that. Although, that's actually true too," I say. Chad turns his head to smile at me. I don't think he was expecting me to ever tell my parents where I've actually been sleeping.

"Then what's the big announcement?" Dad asks.

I feel as though my dinner is about to come back up.

Mum's face turns to brief elation. "Oh, are you getting married?" she asks excitedly.

"What? No! Really no. Really, really, really, no." I can't seem to find other words right now.

"Oh. That's probably for the best anyway," Mum says, slight

disappointment in her voice.

"Just tell us already," Shilah says.

I look to Chad, and he gives a small nod.

"Okay," I say. "So, I told everyone I found out I was Defective because of the incident with my guard. That's actually not entirely accurate—I knew before then. A few days before, actually. I … I was in my cell the first night after being arrested and I heard a voice. Tate's voice. Only it wasn't his voice, it was his thoughts. So at first we thought I was telepathic, right? That would make sense. Only, when I was being interrogated, I couldn't do it. I couldn't hear anyone's thoughts. Tate and I just figured it was too stressful or something—I couldn't focus on it properly. Then we discovered I could amplify other abilities around me through touch. But it wasn't all I could do. Am I making any sense at all?" I don't even know what just came out of my mouth.

"You're saying you're telepathic *and* you can amplify?" Drew asks.

"A double ability?" Mum asks, her eyebrows rise in surprise.

"No. Yes. No to being a Telepath, yes to having a double ability." Silence fills the room. "I can borrow other's abilities if I'm close to them … and amplify through touching."

All I can hear is crickets. The four of them are looking at me as if I'm some kind of freak.

"Why didn't you tell us sooner?" Mum asks. I can tell she's trying to stay calm, be diplomatic. She's holding back anger, hurt, and worry. I wish Drew wasn't here so I didn't have to feel it, too.

I look at Chad. "That's my fault," he admits. "We knew it would've been dangerous for her to reveal herself while at the Institute, and so Tate and I advised her not to say anything. When we came here, we didn't really know what to do. Paxton knows and he didn't tell the council, so we figured it would be best to keep it a secret."

"But Cyrus found out," I say. "He told me I need to tell the council or he will."

"Well," Mum says, "The rest of the council will want to know. It probably would've been a good idea to have filled us in on that particular piece of information when you first got here."

"Allira was just following my advice," Chad says. "We were going to talk to Paxton about it when he came back, but he hasn't been here."

"Okay. We can probably work that angle with the others." Mum thinks for a moment. "I think it should work out okay."

"Angle?" I ask.

"The council won't like being betrayed like this," Mum says.

Dad, Drew, and Shilah are completely silent, sitting there with nothing but shock across their faces.

"Betrayed? That's a bit extreme, don't you think?" I ask.

"Being lied to about the nature of your ability? Sorry, abilities—plural. That's a big issue. The way they'll see it is, if you have hidden this, what else are you hiding? Could you still be an ally to the Institute? And the fact that it's something as big and important as a double ability … I don't know how they're going to take it. I'll talk to Cyrus tomorrow. Maybe this doesn't need to get out."

I should've just announced it the minute I arrived.

Drew excuses himself from the table and goes to his room, slamming the door behind him. Shilah sits at the table, his eyes focussed on me.

"So that's the thing?" he asks. "The thing you've been hiding from me?"

I nod. "That's the thing."

He gets up from the table, walks over, and hugs me. "I wish you felt like you could have told me," he says.

I don't reply. I don't know how. I wish I had told him.

"I don't really see what the big deal is. That Cyrus bloke has a double ability, and he does fine," Dad says.

"Thanks, Dad. I think." The way he said it almost sounded like he thinks I'm more broken than I already was.

"I'll talk to Cyrus tomorrow," Mum repeats herself, a lot calmer this time. "If I get to him soon enough, I could maybe erase that he found out in the first place. Hmm … but if he has already told one of his wives, they would know I tampered with his memory." Mum looks up at us as she mutters her words to herself. "You two go get some rest. I'm sure we can work something out with him."

* * *

After driving home in silence, going to sleep next to each other but not facing one another, I wake up alone. It's pretty clear that not all is as "perfect" as Chad described to Drew last night.

There's a knock at the door. The clock on the bedside table tells me it's really early. I get up to answer it and find Mum standing there looking tired … no, she looks wrecked. She actually appears older somehow.

"Cyrus has called a council meeting," she mumbles. Her words shoot through me like a cold shiver.

"Already?"

"I've come to collect you to take you down there."

"But he said we had a few days? You were going to talk to him? You were going to sort it." I know I shouldn't be blaming Mum for this, but it's just all coming out.

Mum takes me in her arms. "We'll work it out," she says, trying to shush my fears away.

The short walk to the town hall feels longer than it did yesterday. I concentrate on putting one foot in front of the other in fear my legs will just give out on me. I have that feeling in the pit of my stomach where I don't know if I'm hungry or just nervous. I should've grabbed something to eat.

We enter the hall, finding it completely empty except for the six council members lined up behind their table at the front of the room plus Mum and I. Even Paxton has come back for this. *I am so screwed.*

Mum leads me to the podium where I stood to get my work assignment and joins the rest of the panel. Belle stands up. I tell my leg to stop shaking; it doesn't listen. I focus on setting my jaw. I will not let them see me upset.

"Good morning, Allira," Belle says with her usual icy tone. "I assume you know why we've asked you to come here today?" I glare in Cyrus's direction. "I take that as a yes. So cutting to the chase, I will hand it over to Cyrus," she says before sitting back down.

I look over at Paxton; his eyes are sympathetic and tired. He doesn't hold my gaze for long before he looks away, avoiding eye contact.

"I know I told you I would give you some time, Allira. I'm sorry I had to call this meeting, but after thinking it over, I decided it needed to be done," Cyrus says without bothering to stand up. I concentrate on trying not to get upset. "I have filled the other council members in on what I found out yesterday, and we have a few questions for you, if you don't mind."

"Okay," I manage to get out, wondering what they'd do if I said no.

"Why were we not informed of your double ability?" Belle asks formally.

"I was advised by Tate that I should never tell anyone the true extent of my abilities," I state. I'm not lying.

"While you were at the Institute?" Belle asks, more of a statement than a question.

"That's correct. I trusted him, I took his advice." Trusting Tate has to equal trusting the council, right? He's one of them.

"You didn't think we should've been told?" Marlo asks.

"I did. I was going to. I—"

"I'm afraid she was given some poor advice," Mum interrupts. "By her boyfriend, Chad." Now it's Mum's turn to get the icy stare from Belle.

"Well, no matter how it happened, the fact of the matter is, you hid this from us, and now the question of trust has arisen," Cyrus says. "But the thing is, someone like you is so important to our cause. You could be vital to our success here."

"Success?" I ask.

"Of our future plans," Cyrus says. Out of the corner of my eye, I see Paxton roll his.

"Which are?" I ask.

"Well, our immediate plan is to build in numbers. *Strong* numbers," Cyrus responds.

"And that makes me important how?" I ask, confused.

"Well, to produce the best possible offspring, the best should procreate with the best. Don't you agree?" Cyrus asks.

I furrow my brow. "Are you saying what I think you're saying?" Surely, they aren't expecting me to—

"A courtship, with Cyrus," Marlo, Cyrus's second wife, says.

Paxton finally talks for the first time. "Are you friggin' kidding me? Really? I mean, are we activists or a matchmaking service?"

I somehow manage to stay upright, though my jaw is practically on the floor.

"You would do this, to your own son?" Mum asks Belle.

"He'd be better off this way," Belle snaps back.

For a moment, I think I see Mum about to rise to her feet, as if she's preparing to attack Belle. I almost want to shout, "Do it, Mum. Slap the bitch!" but I don't, and she doesn't move.

I shake my head. "You can't force me to procreate. It's like you're looking at me like a prized dog to breed."

Millie, the non-Defective one, responds. "There are other ways to go about that these days. We're not forcing you to *be* with Cyrus—"

"Just have his eleventh, twelfth, thirteenth child?" I yell in between trying not to dry retch. "He's already got ten children, are any of them any stronger than anyone else here?"

"I'm just saying there are medical ways around it, if you weren't interested in a courtship."

"Interested in a relationship with a man who has three wives already? Gee, where do I sign up." I can't hold back the angry sarcasm any longer. "Are we really having this conversation? Is this actually happening, or should I start pinching myself and try to wake from this screwed-up nightmare?"

"Watch your tone, young lady," Connor says. "I can tell you now that I don't agree with this plan either. This is not what we're about, but we're still your leaders, you will contain yourself and your manners."

"Fuck manners!" I yell.

"I agree," Paxton says. "This isn't what we're about. We can't continue to grow in numbers without building more accommodations, planting more crops. It's not viable. Not to mention we'd be forcing an eighteen-year-old girl into becoming a mother. A mother responsible for another human being. And for what? In the hopes of producing another double ability? We're not about gaining power, we're not the Institute. We shouldn't be about who's the most powerful. All we should want is to be treated fairly."

Paxton talks as if he's one of us, but he isn't. It makes me wonder why he's here again. Who does he know that's Defective, who is he doing this for?

"You're not even Defective, Paxton," Belle retorts.

"We need all the strength we can get. We need to be able to defend ourselves if they come," Cyrus says.

"We need to put my plan of action in place," Paxton says. "I keep bringing it up—we need to take over the Institute. We'll have all the numbers we need, plus government funding, plus a chance to change the laws. I don't see how building in numbers here will help any. It will also take years. Are you really willing to keep living like this for generations to come?"

"It already has worked for generations," Belle replies.

I take a deep breath as I blurt out my crazy theory about Cyrus. "Cyrus is building an army." I feel all seven pairs of eyes on at me at once. *Here goes.* "He has people training whose abilities are not suited to recruiting. He keeps having babies with different women, trying to produce another double ability—which I'm assuming hasn't happened, considering you want me to be the next in line to try. It's clear to me that he's power greedy. He lets the trainees drink, party, play games, all so they form some sort of bond with him. And when it comes time to choosing a side, who do you think they will pick? I have no doubt that he's trying to take over the Resistance. Why else would he need an army?"

"Are you done?" Cyrus asks.

I can see that I've surprised some of the panel but not everyone. Belle and Cyrus's wife don't look at all surprised. In fact, they look rather bemused.

"Well, that was a delightful tale of fiction," Belle says. "But we do have a vote to make."

"A vote?" I ask with raised eyebrows.

"Yes. Spouting crap about an impending internal war is not going to get you out of this," Belle replies. "The bottom line is that you lied to us. You hid how powerful you are, making us question your dedication and commitment to the cause. You will need to earn our trust again. You'll need to make sacrifices, as we all have."

"You can't make me have a child I don't want."

"I vote yes," Belle says, ignoring me.

"We're not voting on this," Mum yells. "This is not going to happen. I won't allow it."

"I'll take that as a no then, Seph?" Belle says, ignoring Mum's actual words.

"I vote no too," Paxton adds.

"Yes," Cyrus says.

I don't know if that was purposefully sleazy or not, but it certainly came out that way. I'm lucky I didn't eat breakfast because I'm sure it would've come back up.

"Yes," Marlo follows. Really? His own wife wants me to procreate with her husband? That is all kinds of messed up. Then again, she does share him with two other women, what's one more? I shake my head. I keep telling myself this isn't actually happening.

"No," Connor says, and I let out a sigh of relief.

All eyes are on Millie. "I think we need to try it. If not for ability reasons, then for science. Maybe a baby with two double ability parents will give us more insight into how Defective people are genetically made up." I think I'm about to collapse. "I'm not saying it has to be right away or it has to be done the old-fashioned way. There are ways around it to make everyone happy."

"I'm not bringing a child into this world with someone I despise," I say through gritted teeth.

"Whoa. Hey now," Cyrus says. "No need to get nasty."

"I beg to differ," Paxton says. "I think she has every right to get nasty. This isn't right. And you know that if Tate was here, he would be voting no. I say this is a tied vote."

"Well, Tate isn't here, is he?" Belle bites at Paxton. "And who do we have to thank for that?" She glares at me.

"I had nothing to do with Tate staying where he is. *Nothing.*"

"Well, that doesn't matter anyway. He's not here, so his vote doesn't count," Belle says. "You will obey our ruling. Unless you want to join Tate back at the Institute? I'm sure they'd love to get their hands on a double ability again. I do believe it's been a while."

Did my boyfriend's mother just threaten to have me killed?

CHAPTER THIRTEEN

I find myself outside the town hall. I don't remember leaving, but I'm here, sitting on the ground using the wall for support. Groups of people walk by me on their way to the cafeteria for breakfast. My name is being casually called every now and then, and people wave as they go by me. Am I waving back? I don't know. I mean to, but I don't think my body is capable of performing such a simple task right now.

Did I say yes to their insane plan? I can't remember. Not that I had much of a choice.

"Allira," Paxton says, suddenly standing at my side. "Come on, let's go."

"I am not going back in there," I state with more confidence than I was expecting.

"You don't have to," Mum's voice comes from behind me.

"Go with Paxton. He'll take you back to his place." She turns to Paxton. "I'll get the others, and we'll meet you there. I'm not going to let them go through with this," she says quickly before she's gone. Just like that, swift and silent.

"The others?" I ask.

"I'll explain when we get there," he says. "Come on, Allira. Let's go." He gently grabs my arm, lifting me off the ground, and moves me towards his car. I didn't realise I wasn't moving. Before I know it, we're speeding off down the street.

"So did that really just happen?" I ask after a while, after I've had a chance to reach some sort of calm and focus my thoughts.

"Yeah. That happened," Paxton says flatly. "But I think you're right. I've suspected for some time now that Cyrus has been working towards his own agenda."

"And you haven't done anything about it?"

"I haven't been able to. With Tate gone, I only have your mother on the council who seems to listen me. The others all follow Cyrus. I'm actually shocked that Connor went up against Cyrus in this vote. That's not like him."

"I thought the idea of a council was so there was no clear leader. No personal agendas."

"Yes, but when one person on that council seems to be more powerful and superior than the rest, some are bound to believe whatever he says. I always get the 'you're not even Defective' line whenever I disagree with him."

"What are we going to do?" I ask.

"I'll explain everything when the others arrive. Things have gone bad at the Institute since you all left. I need everyone involved to come up with a plan."

"A plan?"

"Let's just go inside and wait for the others," he says parking the car. I hadn't even realised we'd arrived.

Paxton's house is surrounded by trees, sitting under a blanket of forest. It's well hidden on the side of the mountain. The design is identical to the house we stayed in the first night. Same weatherboard double-storey house, just in a different location.

"This is your place?" I ask.

"Yeah. We're halfway back up the mountain that leads to the city. It makes sense to be closest to the way back. It cuts off about twenty minutes of travel time to the Institute. So I can get there in relatively good time if I have to."

"Do you usually spend much time here?"

"No, not a lot. If I'm not at the Institute, I'm generally at my apartment in the city."

I nod my head. Aunt Kenna has an apartment, too. I guess they need to have a place of residence on file, working for the Institute.

"Would you like a cup of tea while we wait?" he asks.

"I guess so." Watching him in the kitchen, moving about as if he's somewhere new, it's obvious he doesn't quite know where everything is. "You really don't spend much time here, do you?" I ask, walking over to the cabinet where the mugs are kept in the Welcoming House. I assume the kitchen is laid out the same, like the rest of the place.

"It's probably why I don't have much influence here, I guess."

"Why *are* you here?" The words come out before I have a chance to really think through what I just asked. "Don't take me the wrong way—you're an asset here. What you've done to bring me and my family back together is amazing. I'll be forever grateful, but ... why? You're not even ..." I stop myself when I realise I'm about to say the same thing he has been told by the council every time he doesn't agree with them.

"I have a daughter," he says but doesn't elaborate.

"Have a daughter. Present tense?" I don't know if I should pry, or even if I want to, but words keep falling out of my mouth. "Is she with her mother?"

Paxton scoffs. "Her mum didn't want anything to do with Nuka once she found out she was Defective."

"Nuka?" I exclaim. "That little girl in the Institute is your daughter?"

I think back to when I met Nuka. The Institute had just discovered my ability but wanted me to prove it. Out walked this adorable, curly-haired girl around five years old with the ability to heat things. Through my amplification ability, we ended up blowing up a car battery. She beamed with happiness, and I'd always wondered who would leave their child in such a horrible place. Now I know.

"I didn't want to send her there," Paxton remarks quickly, as if he could read my mind. "I went to work one day, came home, and *she* had dropped Nuka off at the Institute. Just like that. She knew I was against it, so she did it when I couldn't be there. Nuka was only twelve months old. I was so mad. No, mad doesn't even begin to describe how I was feeling. I left my wife that day." Paxton pauses before letting out a sigh. "I tried to convince myself that she did it because she was young. She was only twenty when she had Nuka; I was twenty-two. I don't think she was ready to be a parent. I guess, in a way, neither of us were. But I never once considered giving Nuka up, turning her in. Young or not, I just don't understand why she did it."

"That's when you started working for the Institute?" I ask awkwardly. I don't know how to handle other people's emotional baggage. I have a hard time just trying to handle my own.

"I kept applying for jobs with them through all the right channels until one day, about a year later, I finally got a call saying they had a spot available. They didn't know she was my daughter at the time. And then after seeing what they do there, I found the Resistance. Through your aunt, actually." He stops and shakes his head. "It's not right—what goes on. I want Nuka out of there but they know now. Brookfield found out about her a few years back. He knows she's my daughter. Which is why something needs to be done, and soon."

"Done about what? Does he know about you, about us out here?"

"No. At least, I don't think he does. Not yet. He knows that there's some sort of rebellion happening. Protests throughout the city, agents disappearing. He's on the lookout for moles within the Institute. We need to make our move, and we need to make it soon."

"That's why you need us to make a plan?" I ask. He nods in return. "But what can we do?"

"I'll wait for the others to get here. I don't want to repeat myself, and there's something you all need to know."

Paxton hands me the cup of tea he promised, and I sip it slowly, trying to get my hands to stop trembling as they bring the cup to my mouth. Somehow, I think my day has only just begun to suck.

I'm shocked to see Chad, Shilah, and Drew walking in, tailed by Mum and Dad. When Mum and Paxton said the others, I assumed they meant people, Resistance people, not *my* people. *Whoa, did I just call Drew one of "my" people?* Chad avoids eye contact with me as they pile into the kitchen with Paxton and me. I really hope the fate of the Resistance rebellion isn't in our hands alone.

"I don't exactly know where to start," Paxton says. "Come. Let's all go sit down." We make our way into the living room, which has a fireplace, just like the Welcoming House. This house is carpeted, while the Welcoming House had floorboards.

These aren't important things to notice. Focus on what Paxton is saying. I want to tell my inner voice to shut up but it has a point.

Paxton sits in a single seated armchair, and my parents take the double. I go sit on the floor next to the fireplace, even though it's not lit. Shilah sits next to me, Drew next to him, and Chad takes the second single armchair. Time seems to be going ridiculously slow. The simple movement from the kitchen to living room is excruciatingly long. I'm on the verge of screaming "Let's just do this before I give birth to the baby they're forcing me to have." That's probably not the best way to start this conversation.

"I guess we should start with what's happened this morning," Mum says. "Chad, I don't know if you've had a chance to talk to your mum this morning or not, but ..." she doesn't know where to start. I'm sure as hell not going to tell my boyfriend that I've been ordered to have another man's baby. I shake my head. I can't believe I just thought that sentence.

Chad shakes his head. "I haven't seen her."

Paxton speaks up. "The rest of the council aren't happy with Allira. They've given her an ultimatum."

The room is silent. Mum, Paxton, and I don't want to say the actual words.

"Just say it already," Shilah exclaims.

"Basically," I begin to explain, "they've ordered me to procreate"—I shudder—"with Cyrus as some kind of messed-up science experiment. They want to try to create another double ability. It's what Cyrus has been doing with his other wives."

No one reacts.

Seriously? This is not worthy of swearing, jumping up and down, and screaming obscenities? It's just me who wants to do that?

"Are you serious?" Drew asks, finally. "You're not just being dramatic?" *Since when did I get the reputation of being a drama queen?*

"It's true," Paxton says.

"That's messed up. Capital M, messed up," Shilah says.

"I think that's an understatement," Dad adds.

"You said it was an ultimatum?" Chad asks, "What's the other choice?"

"Being sent back to the Institute," I say. I'm about to tell him just whose idea that was before I stop myself. Putting Chad in the middle of his mother and me is a not good idea right now. Partly because I think it's unfair, and partly because I'm worried I'll lose if it came down to him making a choice.

"About that," Paxton says before anyone has the chance to react. "There's something else you should all know."

I suck in a breath and it catches in my throat. I don't think I can handle any more today.

"Things at the Institute have hit a whole new level of intense. Chad disappearing was one thing, but since the three of you disappeared on the same night, things have gotten worse. A lot worse. Everyone with access to the outside world is being scrutinised. I wasn't sure I was going to make it back for the meeting this morning. Not that my vote seemed to make a difference anyway."

"You all voted on that?" Drew asks. "On whom Allira gets to

have a family with?" The disgust in his voice is unmistakable.

"What were the numbers?" Chad asks. "How many for and how many against?" His leg starts bouncing nervously.

Mum, Paxton, and I exchange looks. "Four to three," I say, refusing to elaborate.

"You know what I'm asking, Allira," Chad says. I hang my head, refusing to tell him what he wants to know. He stands up, making his way towards the door, when Paxton speaks.

"I can't locate Tate," he says, his voice full of desperation.

Chad stops dead in his tracks. "Brookfield killed him?" he asks, his voice cracking.

"I don't know for sure. All I've been told is he's not in his cell. The rumours are that he has been executed, but I can't confirm it. With all the finger pointing and paranoia about a mole, I haven't been able to look into it further. Not without exposing myself and the Resistance."

It's one of those big news moments, the kind of news that washes over you at first. You nod as if you accept it, but deep down, you know it hasn't sunk in. My initial reaction is to say "okay," but that doesn't make sense. What kind of reaction is that? Tate is the one person who always understood me, the one who got me through the worst time in my life, and the one I always thought I'd see again someday. And now he's dead.

No, *possibly* dead.

What if he's not dead? Until we know for sure, I don't know how I'm meant to feel. I just feel numb. My hands start to shake, and I don't know if the temperature in here has suddenly dropped a few degrees or if I'm in shock. I'd guess it's the latter.

"Brookfield could be trying to flush us out," Chad says, walking back to his chair and sitting.

"That's a very good possibility," Paxton replies. "He could also be testing us, the ones on the outside. If you suddenly go back now, it *proves* there's a mole."

"Or he could've killed Tate to punish you all for leaving," Drew states. We all turn and glare at him. "I'm not saying that's definitely what happened. I know you want to hope for the best, but the truth is, Brookfield is a spiteful man. If he thought you were never going back, he ..." Drew pauses. "He doesn't like losing."

I look at Chad, tears filling my eyes. He knows it too—Drew's right. I don't see why Brookfield would keep Tate alive. He wants to punish us, get revenge for crossing him. Not only is Tate gone, but it's our fault.

I hear blubbering, sobbing cries and take a deep breath to quieten myself, but then I realise the sound isn't coming from me. I look up at Chad, but it's not coming from him either. It's coming from Shilah. It's evident by the way he has broken down that he visited Tate a lot more than he let on.

"He's the one, isn't he? He's the one you've been seeing?" I ask. After seeing the state Shilah's in, the answer is pretty clear. He doesn't respond; he just puts his head in his hands, guttural sobs emanating from his chest. "Why didn't you tell me?" I wrap my arm around him, trying to comfort him, but I don't know if it will help.

Shilah wipes the tears from his face. "I'm fine," he blubbers. "I'm fine." The second time he said it was an improvement, but it's obvious he is not fine. "I didn't tell you because he's your best friend."

"Exactly, he's my best friend. I would've been nothing but happy for you both. But I didn't even realise you were—"

"Could we maybe talk about this later?" he asks, starting to break down again.

I rub his back awkwardly. "Of course." I look at Mum and Dad, but they both seem equally as shocked and clueless as I am.

"What are we going to do?" Shilah whispers.

I don't know if it was rhetorical or not. "We have to go back," I say and feel a shift in everyone as they look up and stare at me. "If there is any chance—even the slightest—that Tate is alive and being used as bait to lure us back? We have to take it."

"And if he's already dead?" Drew asks. "Chances are we'll join him."

We could be walking to our death. It's stupid of us to go back, right? Tate wouldn't do it. He wouldn't want us to do it. Then why is everything inside of me screaming to go back?

"You know that if we go back and Tate is alive, he'll kill us himself, right?" Chad says with a pained smile. One that says "should I be joking at a time like this?"

"Brookfield won't let us be agents anymore," Drew says. "We'd be given crappy guard jobs or janitors or something …

that's if he doesn't throw us in The Crypt forever."

"There might be a way to solve everything. We could save Tate, take over the Institute, and save Allira from becoming the fourth wife of an egotistical narcissist," Paxton says.

"How do you propose we do that?" Mum asks.

A gleeful smile starts on Paxton's face. "If we can take over the Institute, we'll have the power to prove that Defective people are still *people*. We could free everyone and stop the propaganda of the dangerous and unpredictable Defectives."

"Do you really think that taking Brookfield out of the equation will fix that? What about the laws that state we belong there?" Drew asks.

"Well, there's clearly ways around those laws, or Brookfield wouldn't have a full team of Defective agents, would he? Taking Brookfield out is a necessary step towards where we have to go," Paxton replies. "And if nothing else, it will stop the poor treatment of everyone there. We may not be able to accomplish freedom and equality in measurable time, but we can take steps towards getting there."

* * *

After the last few hours of trying to sort out some sort of plan, we seem to be going in circles. Part of me is about to give in and let Cyrus do whatever he wants with me ... okay, no, I'm definitely not at that point yet, but I am considering the artificial way of becoming a mother—what Millie was suggesting.

"Maybe I should just do it," I say in exasperation. "I could be a mother." I don't know if I'm trying to convince everyone else or myself. If I comply, we can keep on living here. Like Belle said, everyone here has made some sort of sacrifice. This could be mine. I've never rejected the idea of kids; I've just never really given it any thought—any proper thought.

Chad stands up, frustrated, muttering something about going to yell at his mother before walking out, still avoiding eye contact with me. I don't think he's looked at me all day. Maybe this is his way of saying I told you so. He knew nothing good would come of telling everyone about my double ability.

"I think we need to take a break," Paxton suggests.

"We'll go get some food and bring it back here. It's probably best if no one knows what we're doing," Mum says. I look at the clock and realise that we've lost track of time, it's almost two pm. No wonder everyone is getting frustrated, we're all hungry.

After Mum and Dad leave to get food, I slip onto the veranda where Shilah is leaning against the balcony, looking into the surrounding forest. He excused himself from the group about half an hour ago.

"Hey," I say, trying to sound sympathetic.

"Hey." His response is flat, distant.

"What do you think we should do?" I ask, hesitantly.

"I don't know," he replies, shaking his head. "I really don't know. Everything in me wants to run back to him, make sure he's safe. Everything except common sense, that is. I've tried to get a vision of what would happen if we were to go back, but I get nothing. I keep telling myself I'd be foolish to go back. We'd never see the light of day again. We'd probably end up dead, too."

"Too," I say quietly. "You think he's dead, don't you?"

He hangs his head. "I don't want to, but yeah, deep down, I think I do." A tear falls on his cheek.

I wipe it away with my thumb before taking him in my arms.

"But I have to know for sure. What if he's alive and we don't do anything? If Brookfield is using him as bait, he won't wait forever before he does kill him. Once he realises we aren't coming back, Tate will be killed. We have to do something."

I give a half-smile. Not because of his words—they are scaring the hell out of me—but because of the look in his eye when he mentioned Tate's name.

"You two … you're pretty serious then?" I ask.

"I've never felt this way about anyone."

"I didn't realise you were—"

"Into guys?" he interrupts. I nod. "To be honest, neither did I. Before we were sent to the Institute, I couldn't allow myself to feel anything for anyone, so I never gave it much thought."

"You must have sort of known, right—on some level?"

"I guess." He shrugs. "You'd think I would've had a crush on someone at some point, but I can't recall anyone in particular, male or female."

"He's a bit old for you," I say with a smile. Tate is twenty-four, and Shilah just turned seventeen a few months ago.

"I told him you'd say that." He laughs. "But he said you once told him that age shouldn't be a factor when it came to loving someone."

I swallow, hard. "You ... love him?" I have never used the L word. I thought a long time ago that I may have loved Drew, but that was when I was wrapped up in first love, having a boyfriend, and his ability to always make me smile. Finding out he was an agent sent to arrest me ruined me for Chad. I'm not saying I don't love Chad, maybe I do ... I don't know. I feel more connected to him than I ever did with Drew, but saying the words? Out loud? I don't know if I could do it.

He nods. "I do. I love Tate." Shilah clearly doesn't have my problem.

"Then I guess it doesn't matter, does it?" I say, my half-smile appearing again.

"I should have told you sooner," he admits.

"I should have told you about me sooner." We look out at the surrounding bushland, at its peacefulness, with clean slates. No more hiding; no more lying. I reach over and put my hand over his.

225

"We have to get him out of there, Allira. We just … have to," he says, beginning to tear up again.

I nod. "I know. Let's go back inside and sort out this plan."

"So we're going back?" he asks.

"Yes. We're going to take over the Institute and save Tate."

CHAPTER FOURTEEN

"So you're just going to go back?" Chad yells at me in front of everyone. He returned not long after Mum and Dad came back with some food.

"What other choice do we have? You want me to stay here and have a baby with another man? You're *okay* with that?"

"That's better than sending you to your execution."

"You're Tate's cousin. How do you not even care that our actions—or lack thereof—could get him killed?"

His expression turns cold. "He's probably already dead," he says without emotion. "He's not in his cell. Where would they have moved him? He's gone." His face is blank.

I don't know how he can just switch off like that.

"I know where he could be," Drew says. We all stare at him. "There's another level to The Crypt. I've only been down there once. No one is housed down there usually. It's reserved for …" he hesitates.

"Double abilities," Paxton finishes for him.

"I thought you believed double abilities were a myth?" Shilah asks Drew.

"Well, no one was ever housed down there, so I assumed they were. Obviously," he says, looking pointedly at me, "that's not the case."

"We could have this same conversation for hours. Bottom line is we're not going to know Tate's status until Shilah and Allira go back," Paxton says.

"And me," Drew says. "I'm going back."

"Of course, you are," Chad directs at Drew. "I'm not going back," he says, pacing around the room. "I've already risked my life and spent months imprisoned for him, and he chose to stay anyway. I don't see how things will be different now."

My shoulders slump forwards in disappointment. I can't believe the words he is saying—not when it comes to Tate.

"Allira, can I talk to you outside?" he pleads.

"I think our time will be best spent in here, trying to sort out the finer points of the plan," I say. I don't want to face whatever he wants to say to me right now. I don't want him to try to talk me out of this.

Chad storms out.

"He'll come around," Paxton says, breaking the obvious awkward silence that's always there when two people have a public argument.

I shake my head. "Maybe. But let's not worry about him right now. I want to make sure this plan will work."

"I've asked the council many times to put this to a public vote but they refuse. We need numbers. We need a list of people who we think can help us—both at the Institute and here. And we'll need to do it behind the council's back," Paxton says.

"I can give you some names of the people at the Institute," Drew says.

I exchange a look with Paxton, mentally asking, *Are we really going to trust Drew on this?* Not that he can hear me.

"Are you sure they'll want to help us?" I ask Drew.

"Well, they all pretty much think I'm the worst person in the world—apart from Brookfield, of course—so yeah, pretty sure they'll be happy to help. Just don't tell them I'm involved."

"And who do we have here that can help?" I ask, looking to Mum. She's the only one who's been here long enough to know.

"There's a few people I have in mind. Allira and Shilah, you should scope out the recruiters—especially the younger ones. I haven't had a chance to get to know them all that well."

"Do we really want to send the young ones into the Institute?" I ask.

"We may have to for the numbers," Mum says reluctantly.

"Well, I know of a few already that could help. Licia, Hayden, maybe a few others. It will just be a matter of getting them to agree."

"Okay, so let's make a plan," Paxton says with a hint of hope in his eyes.

* * *

"Okay, so can we go through this one more time?" My question is met with groans from nearly everyone.

After a full day of brainstorming, planning, and arguing, we're just about ready to put our plan into motion.

Paxton throws his head back on the headrest of the couch. He keeps his eyes trained on the roof as he talks—going over the plan for the millionth time this afternoon. "You recruit from within, behind the rest of the council's backs. Assemble a team of forty—or as close to forty as you can manage. While you do that, I'll be recruiting at the Institute. You, Drew, and Shilah return to Brookfield claiming to feel remorseful for abandoning your posts and that you want to come back. You will convince him that living on the outside was too tough, you didn't realise how good you had it, how well he treated you. Then when we can organise it, the Resistance will infiltrate the Institute. We let them in, they'll be armed, and we'll take Brookfield down."

"And if you're all caught?" Dad is sitting in the corner of the living room, where he's been practically sulking all afternoon.

Dad seems to be on Chad's side on this. He's been throwing his objections at us all day.

"We'll most likely be killed," Paxton says quietly.

"They'll be okay," Mum says, putting her hand on Dad's shoulder.

"How do you know, Seph?" Dad puts his head in his hands. "I haven't worked as hard as I have at keeping them safe, only to send them to the one place that will hurt them."

Dad starts sobbing, successfully breaking my heart.

"We'll be fine, Dad. This will work. We'll make it work," I try to reassure him.

"I think we should leave it there for now," Mum says.

I lie down on the floor and stretch out, completely mentally exhausted from the day.

"You can stay here tonight if you want," Paxton suggests. "I've got a spare room that's already made up."

"Sounds good," I say.

Mum and Dad offer up the couch at their place, but at least here I'll get an actual bed. Mum, Dad, Shilah, and Drew leave as I sprawl out in front of the fireplace. We lit it when the sun started to go down to provide warmth throughout the house.

"Chad *will* come around," Paxton says, sitting next to me in front of the fire and handing me another cup of tea. I think it's about my fifth cup for the day. It's nowhere close to being as good as coffee, but it'll do. "He's just worried about losing you. I can't say I wouldn't act the same if I was him."

"I know. I just thought he would want to do whatever he could to try and save Tate."

Paxton sighs as if he's deliberating about what to say. "He's probably weighed up the risks and has worked out that risking your life for Tate's isn't worth it. He could end up losing both of you. We don't even know if Tate is able to be saved; we don't even know if he's alive. It's true what Chad said—Tate chose to stay where he is. He knew Brookfield may find out about him, and he knew that he could be executed for it. They both grew up in this world. They've been taught to weigh up the options and choose accordingly. The basic rule of life out here is to survive. It's all they know. It's all they do."

"You think I shouldn't go back?"

"I'm not saying that. The more of us that can go back, the better this plan will work. I admire you for wanting to go back, but I can also see where Chad is coming from. Can I ask you something though?"

"At this point, I don't think any questions are off the table." There have been some pretty personal questions tonight.

"If it wasn't for Cyrus, would you be risking your life to do this? I only ask because if that's why you're doing it, you may want to re-evaluate your decision. There are ways around the baby issue—it would be easy for your aunt to claim that you're infertile. I just want to make sure you're doing it for

Tate and the Resistance and not purely for yourself, because I can tell you now that when you end up back in The Crypt, you may start to wonder why you didn't just have the baby."

I take a sip of tea, concentrating on Paxton's words. "I believe in what we're doing. I was talking to Drew the other night about our freedom. As he put it, he does nothing but eat, sleep, and work. What kind of life is that? I want to be able to do what I want, when I want. I want the freedom to walk down the street and not be seen as a threat or feel everyone staring at me for being different. I think you're right. We need a starting point, and the Institute is the perfect place to get started."

"But is anyone ever truly free? Let's just say everyone is released from the Institute. Then what? People still need to work to support their families, there are still social obligations to abide by, laws to follow. You know what it was like for your dad to raise you and Shilah—working seven days a week on a farm; before that, he was a janitor six nights a week. I'm sure there were a lot of times where he felt that all he was doing was eating, sleeping, and working. I work five days at the Institute, more if I have to, just to ensure Nuka's safety. True freedom is a bit of a unicorn, isn't it?"

"A unicorn?"

"You know, majestic horse-like animal with a horn. Farts rainbows and all that."

I can't help laughing. "I know what a unicorn is. I just don't understand what you mean."

"You want the freedom to make your own choices, but sometimes your choices—even when you are completely free—are between two evils. Again, I'm not saying you should stay here. I'm just giving you other options if you wanted to take it. Walking to your possible death or becoming a mother … from the outside, it seems like a pretty easy decision. You could choose to have this baby and have nothing to do with it afterwards. It was easy for Nuka's mother to do that to her."

I give him a sour look. "I don't think I could ever do that to my child, even if its conception was less than ideal or unpleasant. It would still be a part of who I am. You've seen how protective I can be over Shilah, and he's just my brother."

Paxton smiles. For a moment, I begin to think he was testing me to see what my response to him would be.

"And it's not just that. If I were to have Cyrus's baby, I'd be connected to him for the rest of my life." I shake my head. "I can't do it."

"It would be interesting, though," he says.

"What would?" I ask, one eyebrow raised.

"To see if you produced another double ability."

I give a nervous laugh. "You're not going to make me stay now and find out, are you?"

He smiles back. "No. I'm not *that* curious."

"Is that how Cyrus chose his other wives? By their ability?"

"I'm not actually sure. He was on wife number three by the time I got here. I get the feeling that she—just like you—felt pressured into doing it. The first two seem to be more in love with him than Nina does."

"And she's the one with the cloaking ability, right?"

"Yeah. The one who has Char, Catharine, and Camryn."

"We could use her. Do you think she would help us?"

"I don't know. She'd have to leave the three girls here, and that would be asking a lot of her. I could get your mum to ask though. That way, if she reacts inappropriately, your mum can erase the fact the conversation ever happened in the first place. We have to be careful with who we approach for this mission. A wrong choice could have us all punished by the rest of the council for what we're doing. The last thing we need is the Defective population to split and start warring against each other."

We sit in silence, watching the flames of the fire flicker and work their way around the burning wood in the middle of the fireplace.

"So you and Drew are getting pretty close again? Do you really think we can trust him?" Paxton asks, changing the subject.

"First of all, no, Drew and I are not getting close again. I think I'm just finally accepting that he did what he thought needed to be done. I may be able to forgive him for lying to me, arresting me, and doing nothing as they tried torturing information out of me, but I can't look at him as anything more than a friend. Even the word friend is stretching it a bit. As for trusting him? Jury's still out. He hasn't given us reason to *not* trust him, but he hasn't exactly given us reason to start trusting him either."

"Fair enough. I think we should still be wary of him." He looks at his watch before leaning forwards and rubbing his hand over his head. "It's getting late. I might go to bed."

"I think I'll stay up for a bit. Goodnight."

Paxton gets up and starts to walk out. "Night. See you in the morning."

"Oh, Paxton?" He turns around to face me. "In case I forget, thank you. Not just for letting me stay here, but for … well … everything." He smiles and waves me off, as if there's no need for my words, and goes to bed.

* * *

Paxton drives me to another early morning council meeting that he scheduled yesterday after our planning.

"Nervous?" he asks.

"Wouldn't you be?"

He laughs. "Fair enough." He looks over at me and then back at the road. "You know, I was thinking last night that it might be an easier getaway for you if you leave from my place. I'm going back to the Institute today, so you and Chad can have the place to yourself if you want. It beats that bunker you're living in now."

"You're giving us your house?"

"Well, it's not really giving it if it's not even mine to begin with, is it? It technically belongs to the Resistance."

"I was so wrong about you," I say, smiling.

"Wrong?"

"When I first met you, my first impression was that you were just another Brookfield—working for the Institute to make your way through the ranks and into the political world. I didn't think you cared about us at all."

He gives me a wry smile. "Then I guess I'm good at what I do. I have to be like that when I'm there. And I guess you're half right. I am working my way through the ranks so I can have a political advantage, but it's not the only reason I'm there. We're going to do it, you know. You, me, the others. We're going to change the world."

I can't help but admire the certainty to his optimism.

When we walk into the meeting, everyone is already in their places. Paxton makes his way to the panel, and I step up to the podium. There are no pleasantries or greetings today.

"I'll do it," I say confidently. Five surprised faces stare back at me, and two pretend shocked faces join them. We'll need some time to put the plan we came up with yesterday into motion, and to recruit some possible helpers to come with us, so until then, I have to play nice. "I'll do this baby thing." It's hard not to gag on the words. "However, I do request that this is taken purely as a science experiment. I'm not interested in a courtship. I'm not interested in becoming Cyrus's fourth wife. I would like to do this without even being in the same room as him." I force myself to look at Cyrus as I say this. I hope to see evidence of his ego taking a hit, but he doesn't look surprised.

"That's understandable," Millie says.

"We'll get started on it this month," Belle states. "Where are you in your cycle?"

"Excuse me?" I exclaim. I said the same thing when Paxton asked this while making this crazy plan. He needed to know how long we had before I had to be out of here, before they could try for this baby. "I think I'll leave timing up to the doctor. I can discuss such matters with her."

"Just give us a timeframe for when this could take place, Allira." Belle sighs.

"About two weeks," I reply, rolling my eyes. I'm totally lying though. The perfect time to do this would be now, but there is no way I'm going to admit that. They would drag my aunt here this afternoon to get this started.

"Well, that certainly explains the current surliness," Cyrus jokes. It takes a confident man to make such a comment when the women in the room outnumber him five to one. The two other men on the panel know better than to laugh at that.

"Okay. Well, until then, you're still assigned to recruitment," Belle says. "Your abilities are still an asset to us, so punishing you for keeping them hidden will only punish *us*."

"To be fair, I only hid one from you," I mutter under my

breath. Paxton stifles a laugh, and I realise I wasn't as quiet as I thought.

"This also goes without saying," Belle continues, "but you'll no longer be permitted to share a residence with Chad."

My mouth falls open.

"We can't risk an accidental pregnancy," she clarifies.

"You can't—"

"That's not an issue," Paxton cuts me off. "I've already offered Allira a room at my place." He glares at me, his icy stare telling me to let this go.

"Thank you for showing leniency," I say, turning and walking out before Belle has a chance to say anything else.

The warm air hits me as I walk outside in the morning light. The street is as it usually is—busy with people going about their daily business. Some are heading to work and some to breakfast. None of them is aware that their whole world is about to be turned upside down.

I make my way down to the training arena. That nervous feeling in the pit of my stomach churns harder the closer I get, and I know it's because of what I'm going to have to do. It's so familiar because I had it for three months working as an agent for the Institute, all the while relaying information to the Resistance.

I'm greeted by stares, a lot of them. I'm guessing the news of my double ability has gotten out. Hayden comes running up to me, along with the other kid from the other night, Arlo.

"Is it true?" Arlo asks.

"Do you really have a double ability like Cyrus?" Hayden asks.

"News travels fast around here then," I say, trying to pass it off as though it's no big deal. "So what do you think? Am I a total freak now?"

"What?" Hayden asks. "Hell no—you're a badass."

"Just like Cyrus," Arlo adds.

That is what I'm afraid of.

I need to gauge just which of these trainees will come with us and who are loyal to Cyrus. I look around at everyone, and I get a sudden pinch of guilt rush through me. I don't know how the military does it—how they choose who to march into the line of fire. Who decides which ones get to live and which ones most likely get sent to their deaths?

CHAPTER FIFTEEN

Chad comes to find me after training ends. It's been a long and exhausting day, and I don't really have the energy to deal with him right now. We approach each other, both of us just as cautious as the other. We look into each other's eyes, waiting for the other to speak. I'm about to concede defeat and break the silence when he beats me to it.

"So I hear you have a new residence," he says, emotionless.

"Uh, yeah. Who—"

"Paxton came to see me. Are you ready to go? I've organised a car."

"I just have to get stuff from the bunker first—clothes and things."

"Okay." He holds out his hand, and I take it in mine. The

gesture, so normal and reflexive, feels so foreign and forced in this moment.

We walk back to our bunker in complete silence, politely smiling and nodding to others as they walk by.

"I shouldn't be long," I say as we arrive to the claustrophobia-inducing room. I think I've only put up with it for as long as I have because there hasn't been anywhere else to go—and wanting to be with Chad, of course. "Were you going to get some stuff too? Come with me to Paxton's? I know we're not supposed to sleep in the same place anymore, but I couldn't care less what they think. They can't stop us from being together."

"I'm not … I can't …" he struggles to find the words. "I'm going to stay here," he chokes out.

I sigh. "Can we not be *that* couple?"

"What couple?" he snaps.

"The couple who fall apart because of a little fight. Can't we just ignore the metaphorical elephant in the room and be happy for what we have?"

"What *do* we have? You're leaving me."

"Paxton gave his place to both of us," I reply before realising he is not talking about tonight. I'm leaving him to go back to the Institute, and I don't know when or if I'll ever return.

"You know that's not what I mean. I figure why put off the inevitable? I may as well just stay here."

I shake my head in shock when I realise what he's saying. "So you are willing to end this now, instead of spending what time we do have left together?"

"I think it will be easier this way," he says quietly.

"Easier? How will it be easier? Because you'll be able to move on quicker if you're still angry at me for doing this?"

He winces but doesn't reply. He really *does* think it will be easier that way.

"It doesn't matter how you're feeling right now. If you do this, if you end us, I ..." I don't know how to finish that sentence. I don't know what will happen. I'd like to say he'd regret it, but maybe he won't. "If our plan works, it won't even have to be goodbye. It's a good plan. Have you even spoken to Paxton about it?" I ask, clinging to any last grasp of hope.

"Anything that puts you in the line of danger is not worth it," he says.

"I don't know why you're being like this. You know what I had doubts about when we first got together? That I wouldn't be enough for you."

His eyebrows go up at this, as if it surprises him.

"Ever since I met you, you've been all about this cause. Everything you've done, everything you've worked towards, has been for the Resistance. I was worried that if it came down to it, you would pick the Resistance over me. Now you have a chance to really do something, and you won't."

"Maybe I don't think this is what's best for the group as a whole. Maybe I found something I want more than equal rights. I want a life—any life—with you." He pulls me in close, wrapping his arms around my waist. Tears start falling on my cheeks as I realise this could be the last time I feel his touch, his skin against mine, his warm breath on my cheek. He leans down, touching his lips to mine. "Stay with me?" he asks, breaking our lips away for just a moment.

I don't know if he means just tonight or indefinitely, but I seize the moment to cherish what time we do have left, even if it's only a few hours. Tomorrow I will carry on with our plan, and he will go back to being angry at me for leaving him. But right now, he's mine and I'm his.

I force myself to go slow, to memorise every contour of his body, his lips, his hands, and the way he holds me close. I take my time, knowing that once it's over, I have to walk out that door.

* * *

I feel horrible sneaking out in the middle of the night, grabbing my things and the car keys, and just leaving while Chad sleeps, but I'm beginning to think he's right. It really is easier this way.

But as soon as I start to drive, I realise what truly just happened. I finally know what it's like to be connected to someone so deeply. To feel the kind of closeness that's too hard to articulate. I've heard others try to describe it, but it just doesn't compare.

I tell myself I should go back, but I don't end up building enough nerve to make the U-turn. After arriving at Paxton's house—well, I guess it's *my* house now—I light the fireplace. There's no point in trying to get to sleep right now.

The sound of footsteps and voices startle me, and I turn to see Paxton, Drew, and Licia coming out of the kitchen. I quickly wipe the tears from my eyes. "What are you guys doing here? Paxton, I thought you were going back today?"

"I was meant to, but Drew …" He pauses. "Is everything okay?" He cocks his head to the side, examining my face, which I'm guessing is blotchy and red from crying.

"Oh, I'm fine. Just tired I guess."

"Where's Chad?" Paxton asks, and I burst into tears again at his name. Ugh, I really need someone to slap me out of this. "Oh, I'm so sorry, Allira. I really thought he would come around."

I guess it's obvious Chad and I broke up. "I don't really want to talk about it. Can we change the subject, please?"

Drew sniggers. "How about this for a subject change: want to infiltrate the Institute tonight?" The hint of excitement in his voice suggests he isn't joking.

"Are you serious? I thought we weren't going to leave for a few more days?"

"The plan we worked out has some merit," Drew says. "But for it to work, we need a few things to go our way, and chances are they won't. I don't really see Brookfield buying that we escaped to be on our own and have since decided that it's too hard and we want to come back. He's not going to just welcome us back in, especially not as agents. I thought of an alternative but didn't want to mention it in front of everyone until I asked her if she'd be okay with it."

"Who?" I ask.

"If we were to return from assignment with our target"—Drew gestures to Licia—"it will be much more believable."

I look to Licia. "You're okay with that?"

She nods. "I want to help. You helped me when my only future was being arrested. You gave me another chance at life. I want to do that for every Defective person out there."

"Are you sure you want to do this? You'll be giving up your freedom," I say.

"And working towards the freedom of others. Besides, it's not like I'll really be giving anything up. Not the way we've planned it, anyway."

I smile. I'm impressed, proud of her even. I think about the logistics. "But we were going to recruit from here and inside the Institute. How will we do that if we go tonight?"

"Your mum will put the plan to everyone tomorrow, publicly—after everything is already in motion. I know there will be a lot of people who want to help, we just need to give them a little push. This is a way of recruiting people without going behind the back of the council," Paxton says.

"How do we explain the absence of our tracking bracelets? It made sense in the original plan that we got rid of them so we could escape," I ask.

"Ah," Paxton says, standing up and walking to his bedroom. He returns with a square metal box. He opens it to reveal four tracking bracelets inside.

"What are they doing here? How have they not come to find us?" I ask, worried.

Paxton takes one out and points to where the clasp is covered with some kind of thick metal. "They can't find you if there's no signal. They use old satellite technology to track you. With very few satellites left—and even less that our country has access to—it's fairly easy to hide from them. They don't tell you about that though. If agents knew how easy it was to get away, I'm sure more would attempt it. I went back to your place the night you first arrived, disabled the tracking mechanism and cleaned up the house. That broken chair, the tracking bracelets, I took care of it all."

"I knew you were thorough, but damn, that's borderline obsessive," I say. Paxton smiles as if he took that as a compliment, even though I didn't really mean it as one. "Okay, so we go back with Licia, and then what? How do we get everyone who's willing to help us from here to there?" I ask.

"That's the brilliant part." Drew smiles. "We get the Institute to bring them in themselves."

"We're going to turn them all in?" I ask. "What about those who aren't willing to help? They'll take all of them. We won't be giving them a choice. That's not what I want."

"Anyone unwilling to help will go underground in the desert.

We'll give the Institute the coordinates to the Fields. They'll do a small radius search in the area, but they will realise there isn't anything close. Everything a small group requires to live is in that vicinity. They won't go searching any further."

"But how long can they live in the desert? There are no crops out there, and we'll be giving up the location of their only food source."

"They'll have enough to get them by for a few weeks, even a few months. I'm sure this will all be over by then, and if not, there are other places they can get food from. They can hunt roos—there are plenty out that way. The woods provide enough greens, and we'll be sure to give them the chickens from the Fields. All precautionary, of course. Because, Allira, we are going to succeed," Paxton says.

Drew clears his throat. I've let my guard down since not spending much time with him lately, and I realise he can sense my distrust in him and this alternate plan of his. "It's understandable that you feel that way. I'd like to say that it doesn't bother me, but you know it does. Let me prove to you that I'm not the same guy I was six months ago."

I want to believe him, but can someone really change in only six months? Can someone really change at all? Deep down, aren't we the same person we've always been? Someone may be able to change their attitude or their actions, but on some level, aren't we who we are, who we'll always be?

"Sometimes you just meet someone, and they make you want to be a better person," he continues.

I awkwardly glance away and look at Licia who's staring at Drew as if he just said the most romantic thing ever. I roll my eyes. She looks at me, and I swear it's like she's asking me, *"Why aren't you two together, again?"*

I know what Drew means though. For me, the guy who makes me want to be a better person is Chad. And here I am, taking that step to being a better person and breaking his heart in the process. I take in a deep breath. "So when do we leave?"

"We're ready when you are."

He could have just as easily punched me in the stomach; it would've had the same effect.

I nod. "I'll just gather my stuff."

When I walk to the bedroom, I realise I have to leave everything behind. I left my job as an agent with nothing, so I need to go back with nothing.

* * *

"What's it like there?" Licia asks from the backseat of the car as Paxton drives along the sloped winding road on the other side of the mountain.

I'm feeling lightheaded and weird. It's an odd sensation, but I assume it's from the curves in the road, even though I didn't get carsick on our trip to the Resistance. Maybe it's because we're in Paxton's hatchback and not the monstrous four-wheel drive this time. I try to shrug it off and focus on Licia's question. I turn and look at Drew who's in the back with her, and we exchange looks, deliberating on what to tell her—the truth? Or a lie to ease her mind?

"If you cooperate, it can be quite pleasant," Drew says.

"And if I don't?" she asks.

"You don't want to know," I respond. "Unless you enjoy pain and lots of it."

"Oh," Licia replies.

I begin to wonder what the others at the Resistance will think of us. All three of us have only been there a couple of weeks and we are about to betray their whole lifestyle, the whole system.

"What are you smiling at?" Paxton asks.

"The council's reaction to me leaving," I reply. "I wish I could be there to see it."

"I guess this will really stuff up their 'super baby' plans." He laughs.

"Super baby?" Licia asks.

"So you didn't fill her in on that part?"

He shakes his head.

"It's a long story," I reply to Licia.

As we get closer to our drop-off point, my right leg jumps like a jackhammer against the car floor. Paxton grabs my leg hard, holding it down.

"Stop," he says. "Please stop."

"Sorry. I'm just nervous. I can't believe I'm going back. Voluntarily, I might add."

"I know," he says, gently squeezing my leg before putting his hand back on the steering wheel.

We drive through the outer rural suburbs. The first signs of civilisation appear in the form of run-down farmhouses, abandoned storefronts, and neglected streets.

Paxton pulls over to the side of the road, just off the shoulder. He kills the engine and turns to look at me. Drew and Licia open their doors and get out. I tell myself to move, but my body doesn't cooperate.

"You can do this," Paxton reassures me. I nod as a tear rolls down my cheek. I don't know why I'm crying though. I will myself to stop but fail. I look at Paxton and see the concern in his eyes.

"I'll be fine once I'm out there." I smile. "I faked my way through three months of being an agent, right?"

He reaches over and wipes my tear away with his thumb. "You'll be great," he says. He reaches behind his seat, pulling out the box that contains the tracking bracelets. He pulls two of them out and hands them to me. "Take the metal off at sunrise. It won't take long for them to come." I pocket the trackers and open the car door. "I'll see you in a few hours," Paxton says with a smile.

I nod and force myself out of the car. Drew, Licia, and I start walking as Paxton speeds off in the direction of the Institute.

We walk a few kilometres in complete darkness before anyone says anything.

"So how far do we have to walk?" Licia asks.

"The farther we get, the better. We need to be as far away from the compound as possible."

"What's the time?" she asks.

"The car clock said 3:04 a.m. when we got out," I say.

"So we have about two and a half to three hours until sunrise," Drew says. "Maybe we should pick up the pace." He sounds way too excited and way too optimistic for three o'clock in the morning.

"We should have slept before we left," I complain.

"Come on, the run will do you good," he replies. Even though it's pitch-black out here, I can feel his smile mocking me.

"It's as if I'm back already," I say, starting a light jog. It feels exactly how it was a few weeks ago: Drew and I going for a run before our daily tasks as Institute agents, watching Licia and every move she made. In this moment, it's hard to believe we even left at all. It gives me hope that Brookfield and the others at the Institute might feel the same. I start to falter after a while when I can no longer contain the thoughts running through my head, slowing down, trying to catch my breath.

"You okay?" Drew asks.

"I've just been thinking," I say. "How do you know Brookfield won't just kill everyone instead of arresting them?" Fear shoots through me at a level I didn't even know existed.

"We'll make sure he won't," Drew replies, as if that's meant to make me feel better.

"How?"

"A proud man like Brookfield won't let this arrest go down like some sort of genocide. Imagine the political advantage he will gain from an arrest this big."

"He will want to be seen as a hero, not a dictator," Licia adds.

They're right. It's too big of an opportunity for Brookfield to turn down.

I nod to Drew. "Ready to jog again?"

* * *

"So are we ready to do this?" I ask as I notice the sky begin to turn a shade lighter. "I doubt they have someone watching us right now, just waiting for our trackers to start flashing, or beeping, or whatever they do. It might be a while before they notice, right?"

"I guess here is as good as any," Drew says. "We can keep walking until they come, just to keep getting that little bit further away from the compound."

"I don't understand why Paxton couldn't have just dropped us off closer," Licia complains.

"Because this way, they can blame our location and the faulty trackers for our disappearance," I explain, reaching into my pocket and pulling out the two bracelets. Drew takes the thinner, more feminine one and removes the metal. The clasp falls open, and he wraps the bracelet around my wrist, fastening it to my skin. I do the same to him with his.

"Ready?" he asks.

"As ready as I'll ever be," I say.

"Sorry about this, Licia," Drew says, taking zip ties out of his pockets and tying her hands behind her back. "We need to make it look real." She nods in reply. "One last thing," Drew says, digging into his pocket again and pulling out six pills. "As soon as we see them, we need to take these." He hands me two and goes to hand two to Licia before realising he had just cuffed her. "I'll give you yours when the time comes."

"What do they do?" I ask.

"One of them is pure caffeine, the other is a drug they used to prescribe to hyperactive kids to calm them down. Apparently it works in reverse if you don't have a hyperactive disorder," he says. "They'll make you unreadable to a lie detector. They'll no doubt question us for a few hours, so we need to take them as late as possible."

"Lie detector? Why was I never given a test when I was arrested months ago?" I ask. It would have saved a lot of trauma.

"You did," Drew says. "Zac is the lie detector. He can analyse your respiration, pulse, and blood pressure just by looking at you. Any slight variance in your stats indicates you're lying. That's why you confused us so much. We were so sure you were Defective, we didn't understand how you couldn't have known. You were covering for your brother at the time, so I assume that's why your stats showed you were lying. It's not an exact science, but he's pretty accurate. Hence the pills."

"So if our stats are erratic—"

"He won't be able to get a definitive read on us," Drew interrupts me.

"Where did you get these?" I ask, referring to the pills. I'm beginning to wonder just how much Drew has left out in this plan of his.

"From that poor excuse of a clinic the Resistance has. Ebb thought they would come in handy when I told her about the plan."

"So Ebb knows about the plan, too?"

"Yeah. She left to alert your mum of the new plan so Paxton and I could continue to iron out the smaller details."

This information doesn't sit well with me. I thought they had already told Mum and Shilah before I agreed to this. If this plan fails, we are putting everyone at risk.

We continue to walk, sudden silence filling the air. The sun starts rising behind us, and light starts hitting the dry desolate land ahead of us. We pop the pills when we see the two four-wheel drives speeding towards us.

CHAPTER SIXTEEN

We stand with Licia in the middle of us, Drew and me on either side of her holding on to the spot just above her elbows.

"Here we go," Licia says, smiling.

"Yes, but for this to be believable, you may want to stop grinning like you just won the lottery," I say. "We're supposed to be being mean to you after all."

She nods and tries to look serious, but a strong case of nervous giggles begins to come out of her.

Drew shrugs. "Maybe we can just tell them she's insane." He tries to hold back a smile, but he too can't help it.

Both four-wheel drives are getting closer with every breath, and Licia still doesn't have herself under control. I kick her hard behind the knee making her stance falter, throwing her off guard.

"Ah, shit," she mutters. "Well, that worked. She regains her footing, the laughter gone from her voice.

"Sorry. Had to," I say.

The monstrous cars come to a screeching halt about thirty metres shy of us. Four agents file out and aim guns at us. *Yeah, great plan.*

"Finally! Where the hell have you guys been?" Drew yells, taking a few cautious steps towards them.

"Don't move," one of them—who I can see now is Lynch—yells. "Put your hands up and get on your knees."

"Is this really necessary?" Drew asks, abiding to her demands. He looks over to me, encouraging me to do the same.

"You, in the middle, get your hands up," Lynch demands.

"Uh. I can't," Licia says, turning slowly to show them she's cuffed.

"Get down on the ground," Lynch yells back.

They approach us in a swift manner, the front two making sure they focus their weapons on us and the other two flanking them on either side. As Lynch approaches, she lowers her gun.

"What the hell, Jacobs?" she asks Drew. "Where have you been?"

"Where have *we* been?" Drew exclaims. "We've been doing our job. What have you guys been doing?"

"We've been looking for you," she replies angrily.

"We've been waiting to be picked up. We've had our target in custody for days now without a way of getting back. We thought if we just stayed in the one spot you'd track us."

Lynch looks confused. "But your trackers have been inactive for weeks now," she says.

"What?" Drew exclaims again. It's scary how well he lies. Even I believe him right now. "How could that even happen?"

"We don't know. We thought you worked out a way to do a runner," she says.

A throat clears behind Lynch. It belongs to Costello, the driver of the van on the day of Licia's unsuccessful arrest. "We better save the questions for Zac," he says to Lynch.

"You're right." Lynch nods. "Okay, get up you two," she says to Drew and me. "You two go with Costello and Bek. Eugene and I can take the target."

"No, I need to go with her," I say. I need to stay close to Licia.

"We're not going to give her to you and have you take credit for her arrest," Drew remarks hastily.

"Look, I was woken up in the middle of the night to come get you two. Just cooperate okay?" Lynch says and rolls her eyes. "You'll get your recognition. Relax, we'll be right behind you."

Drew and I reluctantly climb into the back of one of the cars while Licia is assisted into the other.

"Welcome back," Bek says.

"Funny. We didn't even realise we had left," I say.

"So where did you find her?" she asks.

"I think we should wait until we get back to the Institute before giving any answers," Drew says. "No doubt there will be an investigation. I can't believe our trackers weren't working. We're lucky she didn't kill us. You never would've found us. I thought these were for our protection?" he says, gesturing to his wrist. I try to suppress a smile. He's laying the act on pretty thick.

The closer we get to the Institute, the more I start to freak out. I start running over details in my head of what we have to do once we're inside. If I feel prepared, I won't freak out as much. That's the theory anyway. I should be worried about finding Tate, but right now, he's a few priorities down the list. My first priority is convincing them we've been working this whole time.

When we eventually arrive at the Institute, my stomach is in knots and the nerves have taken over. My heart is pounding through my chest, but I'm not sure if it's from the nerves or the pills Drew gave me. The place itself looks the same. Tall mid-rise building, and no windows apart from the atrium at the front of the building and the first few levels where Brookfield's and the administration offices are. It all screams evil. I'm on edge and just the sound of Drew opening the car door makes me jump. I tell myself to calm down, or I will never pass this questioning.

I hope that Licia doesn't have to endure what I did when I was first arrested. Just thinking about it is making me flashback. I can almost feel the swell of my cheek, the ache of my muscles, and the ringing in my ears. *Please, Licia, just cooperate with them.*

We're greeted at the car by guards. Lynch lied, they aren't right behind us. I don't know if that car has already arrived or if they're still on their way in. We're escorted to agent headquarters, taken to the locker rooms, and are told to get dressed into our old uniforms. This is probably a good thing— we still have our four-stripe ranking on our clothes, which means they believe us so far, at least.

When we come back out, we're escorted over the walkway to the main building and to where the interrogation rooms are. My jaw tightens. I don't want to be back here.

Drew and I are led into a small room. A light flicks on and I can see through a window into the next room. Licia sits at a table, hands still bound behind her back. Six months ago, I was on that side of the two-way mirror. Drew and I are left alone in the little viewing booth. Carefully sneaking over to the door behind us that leads to the hallway, I open it a crack and double-check there's definitely no one out there.

"What do you think they'll do to her?" I ask as I make my way back over to Drew.

"Do you really need to ask that question?" he responds, not making eye contact.

"What do you think they'll do to us?"

Drew sighs. "Right now, I'm not sure."

"Do you want to tell them together or separate? About … you

know where."

The door swings open, interrupting us. My interrogator—the one who was there for all of my torturing—struts in. His monobrow is still as impressive as the last time we came face to face.

"Agent Jacobs." Monobrow nods. "Miss Daniels. Oh … I guess it's *Agent* Daniels now, right?"

"You remember Zac, Allira?" Drew asks.

"Yeah, I do," I reply through gritted teeth.

"Well, I'll get started then, shall I?" Zac says, entering the interrogation room. "Hello, Miss Henry," he starts as the door clicks closed behind him, leaving us to observe through the two-way mirror. He puts a file down in front of him, sits down, and leans back in his chair confidently.

"My name is Licia," she says casually. If she's scared at all, I can't tell. She's hiding it well.

"All right. So, Licia, are you aware of why you have been arrested?"

"Yeah, it probably has something to do with the fact I'm Defective." *Good girl.*

"If you knew you were Defective, why didn't you turn yourself in? Why send our agents on a wild goose chase?" he asks.

"I wanted to be free," she says, and I feel myself wince.

"So you think it's okay for you to be free but not other

Defective people?"

"I think they should be free too," she replies. I face palm.

"Maybe we should've spent more time on prepping her answers," I mutter to Drew.

He smiles. "She's doing fine. She has to show a little reluctance, or it won't be believable."

The door behind Drew and me clicks open, and Lynch steps through the threshold. "How's she going?" she asks. "Did I miss much?"

"Nothing important," Drew says. "I don't think she'll be any trouble for us. She's already admitted she's Defective. If only all interrogations were this easy," he says, sweeping his hand in my direction.

"To be fair, I seriously had no idea I was Defective," I argue.

"Yeah, that's what they all say," Lynch says. "Only in your case, it did seem to be true."

We all watch Zac continue his interrogation. "Okay, so can you tell me where you have been for the last two weeks?"

Licia looks into the mirror, as if she knows we are behind it.

"I ... Well, my parents, they heard of this place out west. Not like here out west, more north and more west than here. It was beyond the radiation perimeter. We were looking for it."

"That's probably why your trackers lost their signal," Lynch tells us. "Basically nothing works if you're that far inland." *Yeah, that's why.*

"What place?" Zac asks Licia.

"A refuge." *Here we go.*

Zac shakes his head as if he thinks Licia is crazy. "Where are your parents now?" he asks.

"They left me a few days ago. They said they could no longer live on the run and that I was on my own. They said they wouldn't turn me in but encouraged me to do so."

"And why didn't you?" Zac asks.

"I still had hope of finding them," she says.

"Finding who?" he asks.

"The refuge, the people who live out there," Licia says.

"I can assure you, no one lives out there," Zac says. Licia doesn't respond. "Are you able to tell me about the nature of your defect?" he asks, taking a different angle.

"I thought your agents would've told you?" she responds.

"They did, but we want to hear it from you."

"I can project," she says simply.

Zac just stares at her for a moment. By the looks of things, he doesn't really know where to go from here. "Just sit tight, I'll be right back," he says, getting up from his chair. He walks into the room and looks at Drew and then me. "She's lying through her teeth," he says accusingly.

"About what?" I ask cautiously.

"I don't know yet. Her stats are all over the place." The pills Drew gave us are working. "She seems pretty adamant that there's something out there though—people. Did you two ever see anything that would indicate that?" he asks. This is it. It's time to come clean.

"About that …" Drew stammers, his voice unusually shaky. "Uh, yeah … we're going to need a meeting with Brookfield."

* * *

We're escorted by guards who come to collect us from the interrogation rooms, Zac trailing us. As we near Brookfield's office, I start trembling. I look at Drew, and for once, I'm actually happy he's with me. I reach out my hand for his, taking it and intertwining his fingers with mine. Drew tenses with surprise but then relaxes into it. I just really need to not feel alone right now. I need a symbol of solidarity.

We're escorted into Brookfield's office. We stand at the doorway, waiting for Brookfield to notice us. He's behind his desk with his head in some paperwork. He looks up but remains seated, not bothering to come and greet us.

"Allira," he says, looking at me before glancing at Drew. "Andrew. We're so glad to have you back."

I look at Drew with a raised eyebrow. *Andrew?* He shakes his head and mouths "Just Drew." He lifts his chin in the direction of Brookfield. "Dickhead." I try to contain my giggle. He gives me a half-smile before looking down at our hands. His brow furrows and he lets go of my hand and enters farther into the office. I follow him in, confused by the look he just gave me.

"So," Brookfield says as we take our seats in front of his desk. Zac walks over and stands next to a still seated Brookfield, his arms folded in a defensive stance. "Are you ready to fill us in on what *really* happened out there?"

I don't even know where we should start. I can still feel the presence of the two guards behind us. Brookfield sits forwards, leaning his elbows on his desk, waiting for us to begin.

I look over at Drew. "Well," I say, turning back to Brookfield. "A lot happened out there." I'm trying to be elusive, and Brookfield knows it.

"This group of people. Who are they?" Brookfield asks.

"We don't know," I answer.

"She knows about them," Drew says. "Her mother is one of them."

Asshole, bastard, Goddamn sonofabitch. What is he doing? Before I have a chance to say anything, I feel the guards take a step closer. I pick my jaw up off the floor, take a deep breath, and prepare myself for what's going to happen now. They won't believe me if I dispute Drew. It would be his word against mine, and he has a lot more influence here than I do.

"My mother is one of them," I admit.

"And her Dad, and her brother," Drew adds.

If looks could kill, he would be dead right now. I sigh through gritted teeth and feel my leg start to bounce uncontrollably. What is he doing? I should've known better than to trust him. He's throwing me under the bus. Well, to be literal, he may as well be throwing me into my old cell downstairs and throwing away the key. Brookfield is looking at me. I need to say something.

"It's true," I say quietly.

"Why did you come back?" Brookfield asks me.

Drew is the one to answer. "It's like some weird commune out there. Sharing everything, even women," he says, gesturing in my direction.

"Apparently, I caught the eye of one of the men there," I say. Is this where Drew is wanting me to take this?

"Ah. So everything isn't so rosy on the outside then?" Brookfield says. He has a small smile upon his lips, but it fades quickly. "How many?" he asks.

"How many?" I repeat his question.

"How many people are out there?"

We don't know how to answer this question because we don't know how many have agreed to fight with us. I try to count how many people I know would help but lose track easily with Brookfield staring at me, his eyes almost trying to pierce my skin.

"I don't know for sure," I stall.

"I think I met about thirty to forty," Drew says. "I can't give a definitive number. There may have been more that I didn't meet."

Brookfield's eyes light up. "Thirty to forty people? All Defective?"

"A few of them aren't. My dad for instance," I say.

Brookfield looks at Zac with raised eyebrows.

"Are you feeling okay, Agent Jacobs?" Zac asks.

"Actually, I'm pretty exhausted. We've been walking for days, trying to get back here. I haven't had much sleep," he replies. The pills must still be working.

Zac looks back at Brookfield and shakes his head, as though he can't get a definitive read on Drew.

"So what are you proposing we do about this, Agent Jacobs?" Brookfield asks.

"Mass arrest," Drew says confidently.

Brookfield scoffs, "And walk my people into an ambush? Not going to happen."

"From what I can tell, they aren't well armed out there. All they want is to live on the outside, but deep down, they know they could be brought in any minute. They're prepared for that to happen. I think they know it's inevitable. And now that the three of us have escaped them, they'll know you're coming."

Brookfield rubs his hand over his head in thought. The manoeuvre reminds me of Chad, and it makes my heart sting a little.

"Exactly, they'll know we're coming," Brookfield says. "They'll have time to prepare an attack."

"Not if we move on this as soon as possible. We only left last night, and no one knows we're missing. They shouldn't know until later today. They may have time to assemble in their safe house, but they won't have time to formulate a plan. But we need to move on this, now," Drew says.

Brookfield takes a moment to think it over. I'm really hoping they don't pull Drew up on his lies. A minute ago, he said we've been walking for days, now he's admitting to only leaving last night. Maybe it's my training kicking in, or maybe it's just that I know he's lying. Either way, Brookfield and Zac don't seem to notice, and I let out a silent sigh of relief.

"Imagine the publicity you'll get on this," Drew entices him. It's all the words he needs.

"We'll need everyone on this," Brookfield says. "Including you two. And to make sure this isn't a trap, you two will lead the arrest. Be the first in line."

"Me?" I ask. I haven't even had a single arrest under my belt, let alone a mass one—apart from Licia's, which was faked.

"I don't think bringing her is such a good idea," Drew says. "She's too close to the targets. Some of them are her family."

"She defied them by coming here, didn't she?" Brookfield

asks.

"Because she wanted to get away from unwanted advances from old guys. Like thirty-year-old guys." Brookfield almost flinches. If thirty is old, then Brookfield is ancient. "She didn't come because she missed this place—no one would do that," Drew says, and I try not to laugh at Brookfield's insulted face.

"She still goes. She's obviously here for a reason, and I know if she wants to keep her family safe, she'll want to bring them in herself," Brookfield says.

"Trust me, you don't want to send her," Drew says.

"Why not?" Brookfield asks.

I want to say 'Yeah Drew, why not?' but I have a feeling I'm about to find out and I'm not going to like it. I have a feeling the small amount of trust I've put back into Drew is about to be crushed.

"She has a double ability," Drew states loudly and confidently.

Of all the things I was expecting, *that* was not on the list. How could he do this to me? *Again?* How could I have trusted him? *Again?*

The two guards—who have been remarkably quiet in their corners—step even closer to me now, so close I can feel their presence just inches away from me.

"You're a dead man. If I don't get the chance to do it myself, you know one of them will. You know which one, too," I say, referring to Chad.

"A double ability?" Brookfield asks excitedly. "Are you sure?" he asks Drew but doesn't take his eyes off me.

"I'm sure. It's the reason she was so desired by everyone at that weird commune thing, whatever it was. I doubt anyone would like her for her personality."

Ouch. I'm livid. I'm outraged. I'm trying ever so hard not to throw myself at him, attack him from every angle. The real Drew is back. He hasn't changed—he never will. Why would he do this to me? What's the point? I close my eyes as tears fill them, but just as I'm about to break down, something inside of me builds up. I don't know if it's courage or just plain anger, but it propels me into Drew. Tackling him out of his chair, I pin him to the ground. I punch his face as hard as I can, and I get in a few good hits too, before the stunned guards finally come to Drew's aid. They pull me off Drew and pin me on my stomach on the floor next to him, my face in the carpet and my hands restrained behind my back.

Drew leans in and whispers something barely audible. I can't be sure, but I swear he says, "I've got this."

"You know where to take her," Brookfield orders the guards. They pull me off the floor, my hands now bound by cuffs behind my back.

They escort me out of the room, back to the elevator, and down to the old hallways I used to walk every day. They're taking me back to The Crypt.

My feet stumble and flounder as a dreaded understanding of defeat courses through me. Drew screwed me and my family over once again, and we were all fools for trusting him.

We walk down the stairs to reach The Crypt floor, and I'm expecting to be taken to a cell. My old cell is on the left, but by the look of it, it's occupied by someone else now. They lead me to the very last cell and open the door. Where I'm expecting to see a bed, a toilet, anything that should be in a jail cell, I see nothing. There's nothing but a cold cement floor in front of me.

They push me into the room but file in behind me. My initial reaction is to tense for a beating. But instead of an assault, we walk to the opposite end of the cell where the guard on my right punches a code into a keypad on the wall. I try to see what numbers he pushes, but he blocks my view by turning his back to me. The entire wall, which I now realise is actually a door, slides completely to the left, revealing yet another set of stairs leading down.

One guard walks ahead of me, and the other puts his hand on my shoulder, pushing me down the stairs. I take them slowly and cautiously.

We reach the bottom and turn right into another cellblock. Only six cells are in this room, three on each side, cramped together with only a narrow walkway between them. Ahead of us, across from the entry, is a set of double doors. I can see through the two windows on the doors to what looks to be an operating theatre—like what hospitals have.

I've been so busy wondering why Drew exposed me that I didn't even remember what I'd been told about what they do with double ability Defectives here. Until now. The guards escort me to a cell on the right and un-cuff me as they lead me in. They walk away as I sigh and throw myself onto the cot along the right-hand wall of the cell. The dank air, the cold concrete walls, and the very real feeling of confinement only makes me realise I truly am back.

"Yeah. You are," an angry voice startles me. "And I want to know why."

"Tate?" I jump up and run to the door of my cell, not that I have to run far—are the cells even smaller down here than in The Crypt?

There he sits, in the cell opposite me, right at the door. He's alive. I slide down and join him on the floor, both elation and worry crossing my face, if that's even possible. I can see only anger on his. He looks thin, too thin. He has bags under his eyes that I can see from here and old bruises that haven't quite healed.

"Thanks for that. You know you don't look too crash hot yourself. What the hell are you doing back here? And more importantly, why are you down here, with me?" he asks.

"We thought you were dead," I exclaim. "And by the look of it, a few more days and you would be."

"Please don't tell me you came back for me?"

"You were part of the reason. Actually, a big part of my decision," I admit. "I'm so happy you're alive. You have no idea what I've been thinking, what Shilah's been thinking."

Tate's head snaps up at me. "Shilah?" He starts to shift his position, as if he's suddenly uncomfortable.

"He's really worried about you, and I'm sure if he knew I was here right now, he'd want me to tell you that he loves you."

"He told you about us?" he asks quietly, and I nod. "And he didn't come back with you?"

"He was going to, but it ended up just being Drew and me … for now."

"Drew? Please don't tell me that you're back together with him, just because … is Chad dead?"

I shake my head. "He's alive and well. I told Paxton to tell you, but I guess with everything going on, he didn't get the chance."

"I didn't think he was dead. I hoped he wasn't. But when I didn't get word that you had gotten away, I couldn't be sure. It didn't stop me from blaming myself for it," he admits.

"Chad's definitely alive," I reassure him. I neglect to tell him that things between us are weird, that he ended things with me because I agreed to come back here. I sigh. *I guess you heard all of that though, didn't you? I'm going to have to work on blocking you out again.*

"Well, at least I don't have to kick his ass too then. He did the right thing in not coming back. But he ended things? Meaning there was something to end between you two?"

"I think there are bigger issues to deal with right now than me and Chad," I say.

"I've missed you so much," he suddenly says.

"I've missed you too. So much."

"Well, I didn't think it would end like this," Tate says.

"Like what?"

"You and me in the chamber of death," he says with a sigh of defeat.

"It's not the end." *If everything goes according to Drew's plan, you'll be out of here by tomorrow* I tell him telepathically—a little worried someone might overhear otherwise.

After a bit of silence, Tate furrows his brows as he looks at me. "Drew's plan?" he whispers.

Well, it was Paxton's actually. Drew just made it better. At least, I think that's what he's done. I'm not so sure now. Until I saw you, I was convinced he'd screwed me over again, but now I realise he did it so I could find you. That's what I'm hoping he's done, anyway.

"So he ended up being a good guy after all?" Tate asks.

"I really hope so," I say. *Otherwise, I've just given everyone in the Resistance a death sentence.*

"So, can you tell me something?" Tate asks.

"Always," I reply.

"Why can't you hear my thoughts? I've been thinking some very inappropriate things that you would've normally called me on."

I give him a smile. "Because … I'm not really here."

CHAPTER SEVENTEEN

When I come to, I wake in my bed in Paxton's house. Just the mere admission of being in a projected state seemed to have triggered bringing me back. I'm disoriented for a moment until I look and find Licia next to me, our hands still touching. She's still out of it. I find Ebbodine sitting at the end of the bed, smiling at me.

"Hey, you're back," she whispers.

"Water," I say. My throat is dry and my body is tired. It actually feels like I walked that far, that I have been awake this whole time, even though technically, I haven't.

Ebb runs to the kitchen to get me a glass of water, and I turn and look at Licia passed out next to me. I wonder where she is right now. What are they doing to her other self, back at the Institute? According to the bedside clock, it's a little after eleven a.m. which means she's been out for almost twelve hours. That's the longest she's ever gone. If I were to let go of her hand right now, it would bring her back immediately. We told her to come back as soon as she had the chance, so I guess there's nothing to do but sit and wait for her to come back. What if she was still being interrogated and I brought her back? I hope she comes back soon, because I really have to pee.

Ebb comes back with the water and I'm torn. My bladder is full but my mouth is dry. I take a small sip, hoping to quench my thirst without affecting my bathroom situation. I sit up and cross my legs—but keep a hold of Licia's hand.

"So what are you doing here anyway?" I whisper to Ebb, like maybe my voice will startle Licia, even though I know it won't.

"Moral support. It's all happening, isn't it?"

"And you're here to help?" I ask, a little surprised.

"Anything to get me back home," she admits, a hint of sadness in her eyes.

Licia takes in a deep breath, gasping as she wakes. She sits up, looking around disoriented.

"Whoa, are you okay?" Ebb asks, rushing to Licia's side.

"Yeah, I'm fine," Licia chokes out. "It's a bit of a jolt sometimes when you've been out for so long. I'll be fine in a minute."

"Oh, good," I say, getting up and rushing to the bathroom.

When I return, Licia looks calmer and is back to breathing normally. "So, how did you leave things? Was it a clean getaway?" I ask her.

"Yeah, I think so. They had me in that interrogation room for ages, but I was finally sent to one of the dorm rooms, given a uniform, and was told to rest. I went to the bathroom and came back here."

"Okay, that's good. It gives us a few more hours. Hopefully they'll be so wrapped up in arresting everyone here, they won't check on you for a while," I say.

"What happened to you?" Licia asks.

"Drew outed me for having a double ability. At first I thought he was double-crossing us, but then I realised he was giving me the chance to find Tate. I may have reacted a little irrationally. I kind of attacked him," I say with a small smile. Ebb and Licia look at me a little shocked but also smiling. "It was as if I totally forgot if I ran into trouble I could just come back here—to my real self. I think I was overwhelmed by everything and I wasn't thinking clearly."

"Did you?"

"Did I what?"

"Find Tate?" Licia asks.

I nod with a smile. "He's okay. For now."

"So what's the next step?" Ebb asks.

"I need to let the others know to get ready. They're going to be coming for them, and soon. Have you heard from any of them this morning?" I ask Ebb.

"No, I haven't. I didn't want to leave your side in case something happened."

I brace myself for this next part. Mum would've filled them in on the situation this morning. Everyone will know that Drew and I returned to the Institute, that we've put into motion what Paxton set out to do. A lot of people here will think we've betrayed them, and I guess in a way, we have.

"So are we going?" Licia asks.

"Ebb and I are. You've already helped us in more ways than I ever could have expected." I walk over to her and place my hands on her shoulders. "You did so well. Thank you," I say, hugging her.

"I can still do more though. I want to help," Licia says.

"There's not much else you can do. Unless ... Well, I'm guessing you can't project back to the Institute, can you? It doesn't work that way, right?"

Licia shakes her head. "It doesn't work like that. When you project, you always project from where your host body is—like we did last night. I'm not like Ebb, I can't teleport."

"We'd be able to take her though," Ebb says to me.

"We can?" I ask.

"Yeah. I worked out one day I can take living things with me. I teleported and noticed I had a lady beetle on me that came along for the ride. Hall let me try it on him once."

"Whoa, he's brave," I say.

"Well, I figured that if I can take inanimate objects with me, surely I could take living things also."

"But what if it didn't work? You could've killed him."

"But it did work," Ebb argues.

"Like that makes my point invalid," I argue back. "Then why can't we just teleport everyone into the Institute?"

Ebb shakes her head. "I've teleported with Hall before, but that's all. Even taking one person puts a bigger strain on me. I wouldn't risk trying to take two people."

"But we could go one by one? It would take some time but—"

Ebb sighs. "It takes a lot out of you—teleporting all the time. You'll see what I mean."

"So are you sending me back to the Institute or what?" Licia interrupts. "What did you want me to do there?"

"It would just be buying us time. Because you were with Drew and me last night, we can't send you back in with the rest of the group. I'm sure Lynch and the others who came to pick us up will be part of the arrest crew, and we can't risk them spotting you and realising something's not right. If you decide to go back to the dorm, at least you won't be discovered missing. But you don't have to do that. We can take you to the safe house out west if you want." Licia looks unsure, as if she doesn't know what she wants to do. "Want to come with us to get the others prepared and make a decision then?" I ask. Licia nods.

Ebb walks over to us and grabs Licia's hand. She looks at me with a wicked grin. "Are you ready for this?" she asks wryly. I'm suddenly nervous about borrowing Ebb's ability. What's going to happen to me?

"How does this teleporting thing work?" I ask.

"Just think about where it is you want to go. Sometimes it's easier to focus if you close your eyes and picture where it is you need to be. We'll be right behind you," Ebb replies. I take a deep breath, close my eyes, and think of the town hall shed—where the arrest is set to take place.

When I open my eyes, I'm nowhere near the town hall entrance. I can see it from here, but I'm up the road quite a bit. A rush of nausea runs through me, and I begin to stumble. How does Ebb get around like this? I feel woozy and carsick. Ebb and Licia come out onto the road from inside and laugh.

With a blink of an eye, Ebb's right beside me. "Not bad for your first try," she remarks. She puts her arm around me as I hunch over, feeling as if I'm going to vomit. "It gets easier," she says, rubbing my back. "Are you ready to come inside yet?"

"I think so," I say, still trying to catch my breath and trying not to dry retch.

I stand upright and immediately lose the contents of my stomach. Fortunately, it's only water since I haven't eaten since last night.

"Oh. I probably should have told you to eat. Even I get woozy teleporting on an empty stomach."

"Thanks for the tip," I say, dry retching again, kneeling on the ground. "How come she didn't react like this?" I cough out, pointing at Licia who is approaching us.

"I don't know," Ebb says holding my hair back from my face in case I vomit again. "Maybe she's used to weird sensations, being able to project and all. It's probably a similar experience."

"Projecting didn't make me feel anything like this," I reply, still unable to stand.

Warm, strong arms wrap around me, bringing me to my feet and then lifting me into the air. I look up, in hopes to find Chad, only to be a little disappointed when I see Shilah. I'm grateful for the help, but I guess I was just hoping I'd find Chad here and that he'd changed his mind about doing this with us.

"What happened to you?" Shilah asks, carrying me over to a bench seat just outside the cafeteria shed.

"I popped her teleporting cherry," Ebbodine boasts.

Shilah laughs. He sets me down on the bench, and I turn and lie down, one arm coming up to my head to try to stop the dizziness.

"Come on, Licia, we'll go get her some food," Ebb says, disappearing with Licia into the cafeteria.

"Are you going to be okay?" Shilah asks.

"He's alive. Tate's alive," I say, ignoring Shilah's question. I'm sure I'll be fine in a minute.

"He is? You saw him?" he asks shakily.

"We kind of became cell neighbours again. But, Shilah," I say, gathering the strength to sit up and look him in the eye, "we need this plan to work, or he's not going to make it."

"Allira, we need this plan to work, or *no one* is going to make it," he replies, taking a seat next to me.

"Have you seen it? What's going to happen?" I ask.

He shakes his head. "I've tried. I haven't seen anything since I found out about Tate. I don't know why. I can't get any vision, none at all—not what's going to happen in five minutes, or even in thirty seconds."

I reach out and quickly slap him across the face. I laugh when he doesn't attempt to move. "You really have lost it, haven't you?" He usually would have dodged such a simple attack. Shilah grimaces at me. "Sorry. What if we try together?"

"Are you sure you should try to do anything? You're not going to throw up again are you?"

"That's a very good possibility, but let's try anyway. I can just barf all over you if need be." I'm joking, but part of me wonders if I might actually do it. I touch his hand trying to amplify his ability and also focus on borrowing it to see if I can get something, anything, but I too get nothing. "What is going on?" I ask.

"I have no idea. This kind of thing used to happen to me all the time before I learnt how to control my ability, but it hasn't happened since before I was arrested," Shilah says.

I realise Shilah uses the same life timeline I do. Everyone

tends to have one big event in their life that they measure time and events against. It used to be divided by Mum's disappearance, but now our lives are split into before our arrest and after.

"Maybe we're trying to force it too much?" I suggest. "I know that when I first discovered I could borrow abilities, I'd find myself just doing it without even focussing on it. Maybe we're both too stressed about today and it's clouding our abilities."

"Maybe even the universe or fate—whatever it is that gave us our abilities—doesn't know how today will play out. Maybe we both die and we have no future. Maybe that's why we can't see anything."

Shilah's words scare me more than they should. "Well, unless we're going to die in less than thirty seconds, we should at least be able to see that far, right? But we can't, so your theory is invalid," I argue, reassuring myself in the process. Still, Shilah and I sit and count to thirty just to be sure. We both look around for another ten seconds until finally he nods, accepting my response. "We can try again later. Where's everyone else?" I ask.

"Inside. We got a lot accomplished this morning actually. We harvested extra crops for the safe house, got them all prepared. They should have plenty of stored food to last them until this whole thing blows over," Shilah says. He must see the question in my eyes because I don't need to ask him. "Chad went to the safe house. I thought, out of everyone, he'd be first in line to fight with us."

"Yeah, me too. He says he's staying out of it for 'us,' but that doesn't make sense to me. He says he's not okay with any plan that puts me in harm's way, but I think that's crap. If he was to join us, I'd have access to his ability, making it a lot safer for me."

"Do you think his mother has anything to do with his decision?"

"The last time he carried out a crazy plan that landed him in the Institute, he was chasing a girl and Tate. That plan didn't exactly work out the way it was meant to—he came back with neither. I don't think his mum would forgive him if he made the same mistake twice. I don't know if he would forgive himself."

"Well, we just better make sure we're successful so you can come back to him," Shilah says.

"Yeah … I'm pretty sure we broke up last night."

"What?" Shilah exclaims.

"He asked me to stay, and I left in the middle of the night to go to the Institute without even saying goodbye. I'm pretty sure he won't forgive that one."

"I'm sure he'll come around, once this is all done."

"That's what Paxton said too. I'm just not so sure."

Ebb returns, Licia in tow, and puts a plate of food in front of my face. "Eat," she says. I take the fork to my mouth, but the food is cold. "Oh yeah. Sorry about it being cold. I'm guessing it's leftovers from this morning."

"Ah. Probably from last night actually," Shilah says. "We

informed everyone first thing this morning. No one has eaten; we've all gone into emergency mode."

I spit the food back out and place the plate on the seat next to me. "Let's go inside," I say.

"Are you sure you're okay?" Licia asks.

"Yeah, I feel all right now. Just needed to sit for a bit, I think." I'm starving, but there are more important things to tend to before my stomach, and I'm clearly not hungry enough to eat leftovers that have been sitting out for eighteen hours.

We walk to the town hall, and as I enter, my face drops in disbelief and disappointment.

"Where is everyone?" Licia asks.

"This is it," Shilah replies.

"Shit," I let out in frustration, just loud enough for everyone to hear. I haven't counted, but there's about half the amount of people in here that we were expecting. Half as many as Drew told the Institute there would be.

"What is it?" Mum asks, walking over to us.

"There's not enough. Drew told them there are at least thirty to forty of us." I finally focus and count. There's only twenty-two. "I guess we had higher hopes that more people would want to help."

"Well, I can't say I blame them," Mum says. I look at her confused. "You blindsided them, Lia. You forced them to make a choice instead of taking this to them first like we originally planned."

"But Paxton was getting nowhere with the council. They never would've allowed us to put this plan to vote. You know that," I say. "We had to do it. For Tate."

"Why is Tate's life more important than any number of ours?" Mum asks.

"It's not just that, though. We have a chance to save others. Isn't that what this whole cause is about? Or at least, meant to be about?"

"They're all scared," Mum emphasises.

I look at the people around us. A few faces I recognise—Hall, Hayden, some others from recruiting, and some who I don't recognise at all. "What are we going to do?" I ask. "We don't have enough. They'll know there are others hiding. They'll go searching." I start to panic.

"You're going to have to convince them," Mum says.

"Me?" I exclaim.

"Well, Drew and Paxton aren't here to explain themselves. You're the only one." I'm suddenly wishing I had actually gone to the Institute last night as opposed to projecting there. "Ebbodine," Mum turns to Ebb who has been standing here along with Shilah and Licia just listening to Mum and me argue. "Lia needs to go to the safe house. Can you take her? We don't know how much time we have left before they come for us, and we need to get more bodies in here before they do."

Ebb looks at me as if she doesn't want to be the one to take me to my execution. It feels like that's what Mum's asking her to do. I wasn't even this nervous last night when I was actually walking to my possible execution. Although, I guess that doesn't count because it wasn't really me.

Ebb grabs my hand, and we teleport to just inside the entry of the safe house. I arrive in the same spot as Ebb this time, but I think it's because she still has a hold of me. She drags me down the underground hallway past all the apartments to the open courtyard at the end. I don't even have time to pay attention to the nausea from teleporting this time, but I do notice it's still there. Not as bad as earlier though.

In front of us, huddled inside the safe room courtyard, is everyone who decided to stay. Nearly the whole Resistance is in there, and I have to face them. I tell myself to be a big girl—it's true what Mum said. Drew and I did blindside them, just as he did to me once we got to the Institute. But just like his actions, I'm doing this for everyone. And I have every intention of telling them that … I just don't know where or how to start.

"I don't think I'm able to face all of them in there," I say, pulling back from Ebb.

She turns and looks at me. "I know," she says sympathetically. "But you have to."

I throw my head back, look at the roof, and fight off the tears that are threatening to start flowing. *You can do this. Stop being such a chicken shit. This is your fault—you need to deal with it.*

"You'll be fine," Ebb reassures me.

I take a deep breath and enter the common room. No matter how many times you walk into a room and have every pair of eyes turn on you, you never get used to it.

"Well, look who it is," Cyrus announces. "The girl who screwed us all."

I ignore him and give Ebb a look, one that says "I told you so."

I scan the room, looking at the numerous faces staring at us. My eyes find Chad. He's standing in the back corner of the room next to his mother, avoiding eye contact with me. He looks pained, and I know that's my fault. I search for words.

"It's obvious you're all angry with me," I say stepping forwards. I may be addressing this speech to everyone, but really my words are only for Chad. I don't care what everyone else thinks of me. "It's understandable you feel that way. I just need you all to know why I've done this. I don't expect any of you to forgive me or change your mind about helping us, but I need to explain."

"So you can make yourself feel better for ruining everyone else's lives?" Belle steps forwards, moving in front of Chad in a protective stance.

"They say blood is thicker than water," I say. I can tell I'm about to start rambling, but I try to reel my thoughts in. I'm not exactly ignoring what Belle just said; I'm just hoping to find a better reason as to why I'm explaining myself. I don't want her to be right, but I don't know if there is another reason. "And yet, all of you have formed bonds with each other, stronger bonds than most normal families have. You are all family here, even though there are hardly any blood ties between you. I know deep down that you all want to do what's best for your family, just like me.

"Six months ago, my entire life was about protecting my brother, Shilah. We grew up not knowing our mother, we were raised by a man who worked his hands to the bone to provide for us, so he wasn't around as much as other dads. Shilah and I only had each other, so I would have done anything for him.

"While I was imprisoned by the Institute, I met someone who I consider to be just as important to me as my brother; someone who isn't tied to me by DNA. When I first met him, I was recovering from an aggressive arrest, interrogation, and beating. Our connection was instant, but I get the feeling he's like that with everyone he meets. I've never met someone so thoughtful, so insightful, so selfless and kind. He taught me that being Defective doesn't mean that I'm broken. We may not be normal, but we aren't different either. All we really want is to belong, and isn't that what everybody wants? To fit in? To enjoy life?

"*Tate* is the one who taught me that my life shouldn't be over just because I'm Defective. He taught me that everyone's life has value, and if we have the power to save another person, we need to use it. I'm going to use it. I'm going to use all of my power to save Tate's life. I saw him last night when I went back to the Institute. He's alive, but he won't be for long if we don't do everything we can to get him out of there. I'm going to save him, even if it means hurting people, even people I love." Chad finally looks up at me when I say this. It's clear it was him I was referring to. I begin to walk out but turn at the last minute to say one last thing. "Tate is still one of your leaders. If you believe in him, you should believe in what we're doing. When this plan succeeds, we'll all be free."

Ebb and I turn to walk out as a low murmur breaks out in the crowd. Belle tries to talk rationality into the group. "By doing this, you're only hindering our progress here," she directs at me.

"Your progress?" I turn back and face the room. "All you're doing out here is hiding. We have the chance to save hundreds of lives and prevent the torture of countless others. When we take over the Institute, our fight may not be over, but we will be working towards something. I can't live out here and enjoy the freedom we have been blessed with without feeling immense guilt for the others who do not have that option."

The room falls silent. I don't know what else to say. I see movement out of the corner of my eye and watch as Nina steps forward.

"Nina," Cyrus says. "You can't."

"Yes, I can," she says, walking over to him. "I want my girls to grow up in a world where they don't have to hide." Nina caresses the side of Cyrus's face. "You're a good father, and I know you will do a great job with them if … if I don't return. I need to do this. I don't want them growing up knowing I was a coward. I have a real chance to change everything. We all do." She kisses him on the cheek lightly before making her way through the group of people who separates us.

Chad moves towards us too, but Belle grips his arm, trying to pull him back. "Remember what we talked about," she says in a threatening tone.

"You know what, Mum?" Chad responds. "Give the council

spot to someone else. I don't want it, not like this. Tate's still alive, it's rightfully his."

Well, that certainly explains a lot.

Chad walks over to Ebbodine and me. I smile up at him as he towers over me. "Are you sure?" I ask.

"What good is being on the council of a group who won't need to exist in a few hours, right?" he says, still sounding a little unsure.

"I don't want you to make the same mistake twice. You know, the whole defying your mother, chasing a girl, and following her to the Institute."

"The only mistake I made was not doing it sooner," he says, smiling back at me. For a moment, I lose myself in his eyes. I barely notice the grimace on Belle's face, but I do, and it makes me smile wider.

Ebb sticks her head in between us. "That's great and all, but we really should be going. They could be coming for us any time now. We need to get back."

I look to the crowd of people, uncertainty on a lot of their faces. "Anyone else coming?"

CHAPTER EIGHTEEN

I'm shocked when twelve more people step forwards to join us. It's almost as if they wanted to join us all along but just needed someone to push them over the edge, just like Paxton said they would. I finally start calming down—maybe this plan hasn't gone to shit like I first suspected. Ebb and I teleport back to the town hall with Chad, and now we just have to wait for everyone else to arrive. I'm really hoping they get back here before the Institute comes, we need them to, or we really will be screwed. They've had to take three cars from the safe house to fit everyone in. Ebb suggested that we could try to teleport them back instead of drive, but we agreed it would take a lot out of us, even going one at a time, and we need our energy for later. I understand now what she meant earlier about it being difficult.

Even though we should be helping prepare everything for the

takeover, Chad and I find ourselves sitting against the shed wall, not talking to one another. He reaches over and takes my hand in his, but the silence still drags. We can't even look at each other. It's one thing to turn your back on everything you've been raised to believe in, but what comes next? What happens *after* your boyfriend makes the grand gesture? Awkwardness. That's what happens. In our case, at least.

"So you really got to see Tate?" Chad finally breaks the silence.

"I did." I half-smile. "As angry as he was to see me, I think he is really glad we're doing this."

"Is he okay?"

I take in a deep breath, contemplating how to answer that. "He will be. When this is all over."

"What have they done to him?"

"You know. The usual stuff for the Institute," I reply vaguely. The disappointment on Chad's face lets me know he's not happy with my answer. "He's okay," I say, trying to reassure him. "He's got a few bruises and hasn't been fed for a while, but he's okay."

Chad sighs. "I guess I was naïve to think Brookfield would just let us walk away without any form of retaliation." He runs his hands through his hair. "How did everything get so messed up? Between Tate and me, you and me … I screwed everything up. And for what? A seat on a council that even Tate felt uncomfortable being in."

"He did?" I ask, surprised.

"He always used to tell me that he felt like a kid sitting at the grown-up table. He took over his mother's position, but it felt like they gave it to him not because he deserved it, but because they could bend him to their will."

"To have another vote on their side," I say.

Chad nods. "I want you to know that I wasn't against you doing this because of the council position. I meant it when I said you're more important than taking over the Institute. You're everything to me. I thought that if I could get Tate's position on the council, I could use it to get what *we* wanted without putting you in danger." He shakes his head. "But Mum manipulated me without me even knowing it. Already I was making sacrifices I wasn't willing to make."

"You were doing what you thought was best for everyone here," I say reassuringly. "You didn't want to see me get hurt, and I understand that. I don't know what I would do if I lost you. Leaving you last night was the hardest thing I've ever had to do, but I also knew that if I didn't, I would've regretted it. I need to do this."

"We all need to do this," he says, bringing me closer to him, my head nuzzling into his shoulder. "Did you mean what you said? Back at the safe house?" he asks.

"I meant every word." I don't know exactly which part he is referring to, whether it's the reasons I'm doing this or that I love him. I have a feeling it's the latter, but my answer sums it up anyway. I meant all of it. It's funny how I basically poured my heart out in front of everyone in that room, and yet here I am alone with Chad, and I struggle to say the words.

He kisses the side of my forehead and holds me tighter. I sit there in his arms, not wanting to get up. I don't want to leave him again.

But it's time. He stands and pulls me off the ground. He wraps his arms around me, and I breathe in his sweet scent. I pull back from his embrace just enough that our faces are almost touching. My breath catches in my throat, and I try to squash the desire I have to start crying.

"Just think—if we're successful—"

"*When*. When we're successful," he interrupts. "I can't go into this thinking there's a chance you won't make it. We have to pull this off."

"We will. And then it will be you, me, living wherever we want, doing whatever we want."

"As long as it's together, I don't care where we go." He leans in and kisses me, gentle and sweet. "Be careful out there."

"You too."

My feet refuse to cooperate, stumbling as we go our separate ways, but I force myself to keep going. We'll meet up again later, after this is all done.

* * *

It takes close to an hour for the others from the safe house to arrive. My nerves are shot. It feels as if I've had six cups of coffee, I'm shaking that bad. But now that they're here, we're ready. Everything is set. Nina, Licia, Ebb, and I watch from afar as the cars start rolling in. Licia somehow convinced me to take her back with us. I'd much rather know she was safe in the desert or at least back in the dorm at the Institute, but she's stubborn and we don't have time to argue.

We're watching from one of the upper cliffs, looking down where the plateau sits. Adrenaline floods my body, my heart beating against my chest, trying to find an escape. All we can do is watch as agents and guards from the Institute file out of their cars. Four-wheel drives, hatchbacks, and sedans overrun the streets of our little town. They have everyone working on this. I can't make out which one Drew is, but I assume he's the one in front, leading the group of uniformed guards into the town hall. They're all wearing protective vests and helmets and all are armed.

I grab Ebb's arm to steady myself as I begin to wobble from the sick feeling in the pit of my stomach. What if they don't arrest them as planned? What if they start shooting? My whole family is in there.

"It will be okay," she says, trying to reassure me. "Come on, let's get to work."

We've stockpiled an arsenal—guns, ammo, and knives—into two oversized bags to take with us. We gave the thirty-four people in the shed twelve guns between them, but that's only for show. They plan to surrender them as soon as the agents go in there. As dangerous as it is arming them—if the agents see the guns, they may get trigger happy—it wouldn't have made sense for them to be totally unarmed. We can't make it too easy for them to be arrested, but we don't want to make it too hard either. Too hard will result in the need for body bags.

Ebb starts dragging me away from the view of the street. "Wait," I say. "I just want to see them being led out, to make sure they're okay."

Chad and Shilah are the first two to be brought out, no doubt because they're ex-agents and viewed as the most dangerous. I can't be sure, but I swear Chad looks up in our direction, flashing me a knowing smile. It's enough to reassure me.

"Okay. We can go now," I say.

"Where to first?" Ebb asks.

"Paxton's office. I've never been there before, but he explained where it is, and I think I can get us there."

"You think?" Ebb says a little uneasy. "You're going to have to do better than 'think' if we're going to make it."

"That's why Nina is here." I gesture to her with a smile. "I'm confident we can get close enough and lead the way from there. No one will see us."

Ebb starts to turn a shade of green. "Okay," she almost whispers.

"Are you okay? Are you going to be able to do this?" I ask, pulling her away from Licia and Nina so they can't hear.

"Yes. I can do it," she replies confidently and a little angrily.

We turn to face Nina and Licia. "Nina can you cloak us all,

for the entire time?"

"I can try, but I've never had to hold my ability for that long."

"Okay, you stick with me and I can amplify it."

All four of us link hands in a line. I focus on amplifying both Ebb's and Nina's abilities while thinking of the hallway near Lynch's office at the Institute. Paxton said his office is at the end of that hallway.

I nod to Nina to do her thing, and I see the others vanish. Looking down at my body, I'm invisible too.

"Okay, stick together," I instruct. "Don't let go or we won't be able to find you again. We're obviously invisible, even to each other."

Breathing deeply, I close my eyes. The more I teleport, the less motion sickness I'm feeling each time, and when my eyes open again, we're just outside Lynch's office at the Institute.

Someone is coming towards us from the opposite direction. I flatten myself against the wall and pull on Nina's hand, indicating for her and the others to do the same. My heart starts to pick up the pace as the adrenaline starts pumping through it again. Does one have an adrenaline limit? I have a feeling I will go through my stores today. I can feel myself going red from holding my breath. I slowly let some air out of my lungs and casually, ever so quietly, breathe in again. I'm starting to think this plan was the stupidest thing I've ever done. I hold my breath again as the woman walks by. She stops a few feet past us, like she can smell something. She lifts her nose in the air, and I'm worried she can smell the fear coming out of me. Or maybe I'm sweating from the nerves of being caught.

That's it. We're caught. We're done for.

After what seems like an eternity, she shakes her head and keeps walking.

I let out a small sigh of relief. Why on earth did I agree to do this?

We continue down the hall, passing offices on our left, each door with a different name. I begin to lose hope that we've actually come to the right place, when we reach the very last door that reads: "Paxton James" with "Trainee supervisor" underneath. We found it. I try not to let out a celebratory "Yes!"

I knock.

"Really? You're knocking?" I hear Nina whisper.

"We need to make sure he's alone before just randomly opening the door like some poltergeist," I whisper back.

Paxton comes to the door, giving a confused look when he sees no one is actually there. I quickly glance around him and notice his office is empty before pushing him back into his office and following him in.

"What the—" he says before I reappear in front of him, and he immediately takes me in his arms for a hug. It takes me a little off guard.

Nina appears next to me, then Licia, and then Ebbodine. "Hey, Paxton," Nina says casually.

"It's actually happening," he says with a smile. He picks up the phone and presses one of the buttons on the receiver. "Hey … yeah, it's me. It's on … yes, now. Get everyone ready." He hangs up the phone and looks back at us. "Let's do this."

CHAPTER NINETEEN

We leave Paxton's office and start heading to the training orientation room to meet up with the people who will help, all of us invisible again except for Paxton. As we enter the room, Nina lets go of her ability, and we all reappear, taking a few people by surprise. Paxton shakes his head at us, closing the door and shutting the blinds over the window. Perhaps we should've waited for him to do that before exposing ourselves.

A few more people arrive as we take out seats, and it's almost a full classroom.

"As you may all be aware, a mass arrest is currently taking place on the outside," Paxton starts. "The only thing I can tell you about these people is that they were all informed and prepared for this arrest. They, along with our help, are going to take over the Institute. The plan is to overthrow Brookfield, who we all know cowered out of going on the arrest himself. Fortunately, he's so predictable." He pauses for a moment to smile. "With all of his goons and the best people out there on the job, we now have minimal security to deal with."

One of the guards stands up. I recognise him as Ty, the guard who exposed my ability and treated me like a prisoner ... which I guess technically I was. I don't judge him for how he treated me, but I'm surprised that he is with us. He seemed to enjoy tormenting me.

"Whoa. No one ever said anything to me about taking on the boss." His voice is deep and authoritative. I'm reminded of the times he stood behind me during my meal breaks on interrogation days, towering over me, making me flinch with every word he said.

"When you were told we were going to fight, what did you think it entailed?" Paxton asks in a condescending tone.

Ty shrugs. "I don't know. Escaping, fleeing, getting the hell out of this place."

"And you think we could accomplish that *without* taking on Brookfield?" Paxton looks annoyed at the simpleness of Ty. No wonder he wasn't chosen for the mass arrest.

Ty thinks about it for a moment before shaking his head. "I guess not," he says, sitting back down.

"Now, two of his personal guards have stayed behind, and they are up in Brookfield's office while the arrest has gone on. We don't have much time left. We need to get Brookfield neutralised before the arrest team comes back. Agent Daniels and I will be running that. We need you to start containing everyone who isn't on the arrest. We need this place locked down by the time they get here—that's your job. Explain a lockdown has been put in place for the imminent arrival of the arrestees. Once Brookfield is out, the takeover should be a lot smoother as everyone else will be looking for someone to lead them."

"Won't his second in charge be responsible for that?" a female voice from the front of the room says.

Paxton smiles. "Are you aware of whom that is?"

Someone else says, "Lynch."

"No. It's Zac," another person adds.

Paxton shakes his head. "Try again," he says, smiling.

I narrow my eyes. "It's you. Isn't it?"

Paxton just smiles wider, and I find it to be contagious. *This is going to work.* I didn't have all-round certainty until just now.

But that queasy, unsettled feeling appears in the pit of my stomach again, telling me something isn't quite right. With Brookfield out of the way, Paxton will have full reign over the Institute. I'm not saying Paxton will do a bad job, I think he would be great, but I'm suddenly aware of the political gain he will get from taking Brookfield out, and I begin to wonder what his true motives are for this plan. He's already admitted to me that the reason he's here is for political advancement, but I assumed that it was just a side benefit for helping his daughter, Nuka. I don't want to think it, but there's a nagging part of me that feels as though I've been manipulated into this position.

"I wanted you all to know what was going to happen today. Just remember to tie these to your arms when everything starts to go down." He passes around pieces of red material, just big enough to tie around your biceps. "Anyone in uniform wearing these is on our side, and the rebels will be able to see who of you could be helpful. It will also avoid you getting shot or hurt."

The certainty I was just feeling moments ago dissipates as he says the words "shot or hurt." I know that this is a big possibility, but hearing the words puts me on edge. This could go down numerous ways, and there are very few possible outcomes where no one goes unscathed.

"Don't forget to let the others know. Understandably not everyone could make this meeting, so we need to get word out that the takeover has been moved up. So if you're ready, let's do this," Paxton says.

Everyone leaves, except Paxton, Licia, Nina, Ebb, and me. Nina and Ebb look as nervous as I feel. Licia and Paxton look raring to go, which is helping me remain confident ... on the outside at least. The inside is another story.

"So we ready?" Paxton asks.

"As ready as I'll ever be," I say. I look to Ebb though who looks almost as white as a sheet. "Are you okay?" I ask her.

"Yeah," she stutters back. "I'm fine." I give Paxton a look. Ebb is not fine. "No, no. I can do this, really," Ebb says unconvincingly.

"You don't have to though," I say, putting one arm on her shoulder. "We're not going to force you to do anything you don't want to, and if I'm completely honest, we need someone who's going to be one hundred percent ready for this."

I see colour come back to her face already as she hangs her head and nods. "I really do want to help," she says. "But I just can't seem to get myself under control. My nerves are shot, I don't know what's wrong with me." I've never seen Ebb in such a vulnerable state either.

"How about you go back to my office and wait up there until this part is over? We can come get you when we really need you. The four of us can handle this bit," Paxton says reassuringly. Ebb nods, avoiding eye contact with us all as she disappears.

Arming ourselves with guns, we make our way up to Brookfield's office. Nina cloaks herself and Licia, while I borrow her ability to cloak myself. Paxton approaches the guards standing outside Brookfield's office.

"I need a word with the man," Paxton says confidently. I jump at the sound of his voice. Maybe my nerves are a bit shot, too. Brookfield's personal guards stand at the door with unpleased looks on their faces.

"Can't. He's busy," one guard replies.

"Oh, he'll want to hear this."

"Let him in," Brookfield yells from inside his office.

We follow Paxton and the guards into the room, and I narrowly miss getting the door shut on me. Paxton moved painfully slowly into the office to help us out. I just hope the other two made it in here. I also didn't realise how hard it is to make footsteps silent. It's damn near impossible. But the carpeting helps—I'm sure if Brookfield had hardwood floors, we'd have been caught already.

"Got time for a chat?" Paxton asks.

I tell myself to breathe normally, but every time I remind myself, I find myself breathing deeper, causing more air to move in and out of my lungs and more noise to come out of me as I exhale.

"Not really," Brookfield replies, "But what's up?"

"How's the arrest going? Any word yet?"

"Is that what you came to discuss?" Brookfield asks with a tone of annoyance.

"Actually, no. Are we able to have this conversation in private?" Paxton gestures to the guards.

Paxton begins to sweat, a sure sign the nerves are starting to get to him too. But instead of being suspicious, Brookfield seems intrigued. He dismisses his guards with a wave of his hand and a half-smile on his face. I'm almost getting the impression that he knows what Paxton is about to say. He looks right into Paxton's eyes, almost challengingly.

"So you've come to admit you're the mole then?" Brookfield asks.

"The mole?" Paxton asks, surprised.

"I had a suspicion it could have been you. You've been calling in sick a lot recently, haven't you? I didn't know for sure until just now. Why else would you be here now—while the biggest arrest of my career is taking place—looking so nervous?" he raises an eyebrow.

Paxton wipes sweat off his brow. I reveal myself and step forward. "He's nervous because of me," I say confidently, putting a hand on Paxton's shoulder, causing him to flinch. He's better at this acting thing than I expected him to be.

Brookfield's face drops, the colour draining from it rapidly. "How did you ... what are you doing?" His hand drops below his desk, I assume to press the panic button that Paxton warned me is there.

I raise my gun, pointing it at someone for the first time ever. My arm starts to shake a little, and I take my hand off Paxton to steady myself and the gun.

"I wouldn't do that if I were you," I say threateningly.

"Why not?" Brookfield asks. "Are you going to take on all of my guards by yourself? Should I be scared?"

"You mean your two guards? Where's everyone else right now, Mr. Brookfield?"

Realisation and fear wash over his face before he tries putting on a brave façade. "Two on one—I still like those odds," he says, making a movement with his arm letting me know he's pushed the silent alarm.

Brookfield's guards come rushing in, guns aimed at me—I'm assuming anyway since I haven't taken my eyes off Brookfield.

"Actually," I say, hoping Licia and Nina are in position. "It's three on two." I smile as Brookfield's face drops once again.

That's enough confirmation for me that Licia and Nina have my back. "You might want to order them to drop their weapons," I instruct. Brookfield nods at them to do so. "Now both of you go stand over there next to Brookfield," I order, and they obey. "And keep your hands where I can see them."

As they step around his desk, I can't help but match their smiles. They're both wearing red armbands. "Looks like my odds just got better," I boast.

Brookfield fixes his eyes on mine. "So what are you going to do now, Miss Daniels?" he asks. "No matter what you threaten to do, you're not going to make me do what you want. You're going to have to kill me. And if you kill me, then you'll have Paxton to deal with, then Lynch after him, the list is endless. You really think I'm your sole enemy—that if you get rid of me, your problems will be over?"

"The public need to know how we are treated here," I say.

"And how are you going to go about letting them know?" he asks casually. If I couldn't see his face right now, I wouldn't even think he was scared. His tone is downright composed.

"That's easy. You're going to tell them," I say, smiling.

Brookfield scoffs. "With a gun to my head?" he asks. "That will just cement the public's view of Defectives. Won't that show them that I am, in fact, doing the right thing here?"

"Oh, I think you'll do it all on your own," I say confidently, even though I don't believe what I'm actually saying. We'll have Hayden to help us with that.

"And why is that?"

"What will our leading politicians do if they found out what exactly goes on here? They are technically your bosses, right? What would that do to your career? I'm having visions of possible jail time, no job, no money; your wife would leave for sure."

"Exactly. So why would I want to let everyone know?"

"Because we are giving you an out. You are going to organise a press conference—coincidently I know of one already happening this afternoon regarding this mass arrest." I smile. No, it's more like a cocky smirk. "You are going to resign as director of the Institute. You're burnt out, you need a break, you're not providing the high level care as required, and that needs to change for the welfare of the human beings that are in your care. You will still be admitting guilt, but the extent of it will save you from ruining your life. I'm going to give you what you once gave me. I'm offering you the chance to go back out into the real world, a free man. Will you have to find another job? Yes. Will your political career be over? Yes. But that sounds like a pretty good option to me over jail time."

He shakes his head. "That's not going to happen."

"Are you sure you don't want to think about it?" I ask. He just stares at me, blankly. I nod, feeling disappointed. "That's fine by us. The alternative is getting rid of you and putting Paxton in your place. He seems to be a lot more cooperative." I cock my gun, poised to shoot.

"Wait!" Paxton exclaims, standing up from his chair. "At least give him a while to think it over," he says.

"Okay." I shrug, lowering my gun, putting the safety back on, and placing it in the waist band of my jeans, sitting it in the small of my back. Brookfield lets out an enormous breath. I think I actually convinced him I was going to do it. I had no intention of actually shooting him. "Let's take him to where he belongs," I say.

Considering Brookfield's brave front, it's relatively easy to get him moving. But I guess six on one has something to do with that. The hallways leading us down are empty. I can only assume that the others have finished with the lockdown process. As we walk Brookfield and his two guards down to The Crypt and past the cells of inmates, cheers and whooping sounds surround us. I assume no one down here actually knows what's going on—they're just excited about the look of Brookfield, restrained and overpowered. I give a crooked smile.

We lead them to the last cell, the one leading down to the hidden cellblock.

"What's the code?" I ask no one in particular. No one answers. I get my gun again, placing the barrel to the back of Brookfield's head. "Code?" I ask again.

"One, two, three, four," Brookfield answers solemnly.

"Wow. That's secure," I reply sarcastically. When the door opens, I push Brookfield in between his shoulder blades with my gun. "Move," I demand, and he starts climbing down the stairs.

We reach the bottom, and out of the corner of my eye, I see Tate stand up. He's weak, steadying himself on the bars to keep balance.

It's okay, Tate. We're here.

'What's going on, Allira?' he asks me telepathically, in a very worried tone. *'It's really you this time?'*

Yes. It's really me.

"Open his cell," I demand.

"I've got it," one of the guards says. He walks over and opens Tate's cell. He helps Tate walk when he realises just how much he's struggling. Nina rushes over and takes Tate from the guard. I signal to her to take him upstairs.

"Your cell awaits," I say to Brookfield.

"No. No way. I'm not going in there," he says, backing up, involuntarily jabbing himself with the barrel of my gun again.

"Going to do the press conference?" I ask.

"No," he replies confidently.

"Then I beg to differ. You *are* going to go in there."

"Then you're going to have to shoot me," Brookfield says.

"Really? That's interesting. You can dish out this kind of treatment but will not subject yourself to it? You think you're better than us because you're normal?" Brookfield doesn't answer, but thanks to Tate—who's still within range—I can hear that it's exactly what Mr. Brookfield thinks.

I nod to the two guards who move forward and force Brookfield into the cell.

"I'm not worried," he says as his cell door is locked shut.

"Oh?"

"You're not going to win. This will fail and I will finish you when I get out."

I just nod before turning to go back upstairs. I don't have anything to say to that because if I'm completely honest with myself, what he's saying is probably true.

The first thing I do when we reach The Crypt floor is attack Tate in a huge hug. He's taken aback, and because he's so weak, he nearly stumbles.

'You're an idiot. A careless, stupid ... brave idiot.'

"I missed you too," I say, hugging him just that little tighter. "Now that that's out of the way," I say, turning to look at my fellow conspirators. "What the hell was that?" I'm met with three confused faces. "How in the world did I end up leading that ... that ... whatever the hell that was?" The plan was for Paxton to take over.

Paxton laughs but I'm not finding it funny at all. In fact, now that I've had time to process it all, I'm floored. I even begin to panic. I place my hands on my knees and bend over to catch my breath. *What did I just do?*

"I didn't intervene because you were doing so well," Paxton says, pulling me up and holding my shoulders in place. "You seriously keep amazing me with everything that you do." He hugs me and I welcome it. I need something to lean on.

I think my body is just catching up as I begin shaking. Paxton pulls back and I look at him. He puts both his hands on my cheeks and tries to soothe me with hushing sounds.

'Calm down, baby girl. Calm down,' I hear him think.

'Baby girl?' Tate asks in an overprotective, almost aggressive way.

I pull away from Paxton and turn to Tate. *It's not like that.*

'Uh-huh,' he thinks unconvincingly.

Seriously. I don't know where that came from. I—

We're interrupted by Ty, from atop the stairs that lead to The Crypt. "Lockdown secured. ETA fifteen minutes on the arrest."

CHAPTER TWENTY

Paxton and I take Tate to safety, dropping him off in the hospital wing, which is eerily empty.

"Lockdown," Paxton explains.

We place Tate in a bed and tell him to rest. I find a food cart out in the hallway and take him two trays of food.

"Eat up. I'll be back when this is all over."

Heading back down the hallways, we pass two staffers wearing the red armbands. We nod in their direction and keep going until we arrive at Paxton's office. Once we have the weapons and Ebb, we teleport back to The Crypt where Licia and Nina are waiting for us. Ebb still seems really freaked out.

"It's okay. No one will be able to see you," I reassure her. She nods, numbly. I lean down, opening one of the bags full of our supplies. I grab out a knife for each of us and hand them out. "Cut their restraints with this, hand them a weapon. Nina's ability will be cloaking us and the weapons, but we have to move quickly. We don't know how long she can hold it. I can help, but we don't know how much by. It's just best if we get it done, okay?" Now I'm the one starting to panic, even I can hear it in my voice. Not to mention, I'm repeating what we've already gone over numerous times.

Ebb leans over to me. "It's okay. We can do this."

How did the tables turn so quickly?

I close my eyes, inhale deeply, and tell myself that this is what I was meant to do. I've risked everything for this. Now's not the time to be chickening out.

We divide up the weapons, putting as many as we can in our pockets and strapped to our bodies so we don't have to keep going back to the bags that are stashed by the stairs. Nina does her thing and cloaks herself and the other two. I borrow her ability and cloak myself plus the bags of weapons on the floor.

We wait on the main floor of The Crypt, Licia and Nina on the left side of the stairs and Ebb and me on the right. Paxton is in the wings until it's his time to make an appearance. They start to file in, and Lynch comes down first with Shilah in tow. I stifle my involuntary nervous gasp. He's the only one who's being escorted, and I wonder where the rest of the arrest team and extra guards are. I look up at the top of the stairs and see that they have spread themselves out on the upper level of The Crypt. That doesn't exactly work in our favour; they have the advantage of shooting from above. I have to hope it doesn't come to that. Some of the people up there are on our side too. I just don't know which ones. I look for the red armbands but can't see any from down here—perhaps they haven't put them on yet.

I wait until a few more people come down the stairs before I make my move. They're separated in two single lines which we were expecting them to do to fit everyone in here. We need to be quick, but it's more important to be silent. Ebb said she will start from the back of the line and move forwards, I start from the front of the line, and we will eventually meet in the middle, hopefully not bumping into each other.

I move swiftly and cut the restraints off Shilah. Even though he was expecting it, he is taken off guard a little, stepping forwards and turning his head to me—even though he can't see me. It only takes him a second to realise what's happening, and he grasps the gun I put in his hand.

I move down the line, going back to the bag when I need to restock weapons. I haven't seen Chad yet; he should've been one of the first ones to come in if he was taken the same time as Shilah. I cut free and arm ten people, mainly people I have only ever made small talk with. I don't even remember most of their names. There's still no sign of my mother or Chad. I see Dad though, on the other side with Licia's and Nina's line.

Lynch takes it upon herself to go stand on one of the dinner tables that are cemented to the ground at the end of the room where the mess hall is. I continue my work of un-restraining everyone from the Resistance as she starts talking.

"Okay," she says, waiting to get everyone's attention. "This is what's going to happen while you're here ..." Wow, she's actually taking the time to explain things? I was awarded no such luxury on my arrest. "You will be housed down here for now. It's not ideal, we know, we apologise for that. It should only be for a little while. The more cooperative you are, the sooner you get out of here and given more accommodating residences. We will be taking our time to question each and every one of you, so you will need to bear with us until we can talk to each of you separately. We thank you in advance for your cooperation and understanding." *Someone is on a recruitment campaign by the sounds of it.* I'm guessing whoever cooperates with them will be asked to join their side.

I take a deep breath. It's up to me to instigate the beginning of the takeover, but looking up at the guards above us, I see we're still outnumbered and disadvantaged with positioning. While I'm thinking it over, guards start descending the stairs, I assume to start escorting the prisoners to their cells. Before they can reach the floor, I need to make my move. This is it. This is our only opportunity, and I can't let it go by.

"Now!" I yell as loud as I can, revealing myself and drawing my weapon—aiming it at Lynch still on top of the table. Everyone follows suit, drawing their weapons and aiming at someone, anyone on the opposite side. *Don't start shooting, please don't start shooting.* Lynch looks directly at me and cocks her head in confusion. She jumps down off the table and starts walking towards me.

"Don't," I warn. "Don't come any closer."

Lynch sighs. "What is this about, Allira?"

"This is about you ordering your agents to stand down."

"And why would I do that?"

Paxton makes his appearance from behind her. "Because I tell you to."

Lynch turns to see Paxton approaching. "Last I checked, I don't take orders from you," she says.

Considering the amount of weaponry in this room right now, the amount of people, I'm surprised how quiet it is. No one is even moving let alone talking.

"Yes, that's true—last time you checked," Paxton says arrogantly.

"Where's Brookfield?" she asks, her voice shaking.

"How shall I put this … he has been forcefully removed from his position."

Lynch looks around. She looks at the guards up top and all of the arrestees.

"Doing the math?" I ask. "You know this isn't going to end well if you don't do as we ask."

She deliberates. I can almost see her mind working overtime to come up with some plan of attack. "It's worth the chance," she says, drawing her gun.

Then suddenly, everything turns to shit. I hear a loud popping sound from above, and I don't know exactly where it came from, but all-out gunfire erupts. I hit the ground with a hard thud. It's unclear who fired first, but everyone is in on it now. I start panicking—it wasn't meant to happen like this. No one was supposed to shoot.

My first instinct is to run, but where? People are getting shot,

I need to do something! As soon as I realise what needs to be done, I'm army crawling my way along the ground, and then I'm up and running. I run through the shower of bullets, the shouts, and the collapsing bodies around me. Searching and calling for Nina—even though I doubt she can hear me over the gunfire—I finally find her near the stairs, grabbing the bag of weapons, trying to arm more of us. I run to her, exposed as I am. If I get to her, we can stop this.

I reach her, bend down, and touch her shoulder, concentrating on everyone on the main floor. I focus but no one seems to be disappearing. I'm too worked up, and it's not working.

"A little help?" I ask, yelling in her ear. She realises what I'm trying to do, and suddenly everyone on The Crypt floor disappears.

The gunfire dies down and is replaced with stunned silence. Or maybe I'm just deaf after having guns going off next to my ears. I stay where I am, holding on to Nina and amplifying her ability to keep everyone hidden. Now that a few moments have passed, I can hear painful groans and sobs coming from the floor. Most of the guards up top are still standing, but I count three bodies lying up there, one surrounded by so much blood I don't expect him to get up again. I'm thankful that the mess on the floor beside us is hidden. I'm too scared to see who's left.

I need to do something. No one is saying anything, and the guards up top are looking around in confusion, unsure of what just happened.

"You need to drop your weapons," I yell. The guards all take a step back in shock, poising their guns to shoot once again.

"No! Do as I say or more of you will die. Drew? Are you up there?"

"Right here," he replies, stepping forwards from the back of the group of agents.

"Everyone pass your weapons to Jacobs," I order. No one moves. "Now!" I yell.

"Do it," I hear Lynch say from somewhere on the other side of the room. She's down here with us too, so she's also being cloaked. They obey her and once the guns have been handed over to Drew and another person wearing a red armband, I let go of Nina and people on the floor start to reappear.

So many faces are looking at me, but none of them are the ones I'm looking for. A few Resistance members are still pointing their guns at the now unarmed guards up top, so I concentrate on finding my family without the worry of the guards starting a riot in here.

I stand and start to walk through the mess. I see now that Lynch has been shot in the leg. She's far away from the group, sitting, leaning up against one of the cells on the left. My foot hits something, a body. I don't want to look down but I do. I find Hayden, lying there, eyes wide open but glassed over, no life left in him. Hayden. *Hayden's gone.* My heart stops for a beat. I know I didn't know him well but … he's my age. He has a younger brother, Brayden. I took him away from his family. The tears start rolling down my cheeks, guilt making me feel the repercussions of my actions.

Strong arms wrap around me, lips kissing the back of my head and neck. I turn into Chad's arms and he holds on tight. The relief that washes over me only makes the guilt of what happened to Hayden intensify.

"I've got you," he says. "I've got you, you're okay," he soothes. I don't know if he's reassuring me or himself.

"It's my fault," I whisper. "He's dead because of me."

"No, he's not. He's dead because he was fighting for what he believes in. I don't want you to ever think any of this was your fault. You want to blame someone? Blame Brookfield, blame this government. They killed him. You did nothing but try to save him. You tried to save all of us." He pulls away, cupping my face with his hand.

His words make me feel better, but I'm still too upset over the loss of Hayden to gain any sort of composure. I suddenly start looking at the other bodies on the ground, my heart not wanting to see any more, but I need to. I fear my eyes will land on my family, but I'm relieved when I hear my mother's voice cutting through the crowd of stunned guards and Resistance members.

"What do you need us to do, Paxton?" she asks loudly, letting everyone know that he is now in charge. I smile when I turn and see her, unharmed, walking up and standing next to Paxton in a display of unity. Paxton doesn't seem to be injured either. My father and brother go to join them. Dad is hobbling, I think he has been hit, but he looks right at me and assures me that he is fine with a simple nod and dismissive wave.

"There's going to be a few changes around here," Paxton announces loud enough for everyone to hear.

While he starts rambling about where to go from here,

ordering the Resistance to start containing the guards upstairs, I let out a sigh of relief for my family and look back to Chad. He's studying me with a concerned expression, as if he's looking for signs that I'm about to crack. And if I'm completely honest with myself, I wouldn't be surprised if I did lose it.

"I'm okay," I say through broken tears. "It's just … it wasn't meant to happen this way." I knew it was a possibility. Paxton drilled it into us numerous times, but I guess I just wanted to believe that no one would get hurt. Naïve as that may have been.

"I know," he says embracing me again.

I look around at the people left standing and those on the ground. The guilt only worsens when I don't recognise anyone else on the ground, and I find myself happy about that. Not knowing them or their history, their families … it makes it that tiny bit easier, but they were still human, and it doesn't change the fact that I did this to them.

There are a few who are injured—I see Ebb holding up an injured Hall near the stairs—there are a few on the ground who are going to make it, but the important thing for me is that my family is safe. Chad is safe. And we're almost at the finish line.

"It's over," Chad assures me, pulling me close and breathing me in. "We did it—"

A loud pop blasts in my right ear. I hear another and feel a burning in my right shoulder. The pain comes fast and hard. My arm feels as if it's on fire. Something hot and thick runs down my arm. Chad loses his balance, slumping into me.

Another bout of pain rushes my shoulder under his weight. I don't quite know what's happening, but I do know I've been shot. Which means ...

Oh my God, no. "No, no, no, no, no, no," I say as I lower Chad to the ground, his head in my lap. More gunfire erupts but it's brief and over with within a couple of shots. I fear I've been hit again, but I don't feel any more pain, only the pain of my shoulder and the pinch in my chest as I see the colour drain from Chad's face. "Stay with me. You can't leave me. No," I whisper to him.

The blood pooling out from the side of his chest makes me want to gag, but his ragged breathing as he struggles is more concerning to me right now.

"Help!" I yell. Ebbodine runs to our side. She places her hands over Chad's wound on his chest, trying to stop the blood.

"There's too much," she mutters to herself, but I still hear it.

Chad grips onto my shirt, "Not your fault." He speaks quietly but forcefully. "I love you."

"No. Do not say goodbye. You can't leave me. You can't. Because, I love you." I start to rock back and forth. I can't do this. I can't lose him. "I can't do this without you. I can't live—"

"Yes. You can." He's slipping away, his words raspy and gargled. This is all happening too fast. He's losing too much blood, too quickly. Only seconds have passed, but it feels like minutes. "This isn't your fault. I should have shielded us." He's whispering now, struggling to even talk.

Even in his death, he's still trying to reassure me, telling me that I'm doing the right thing even though that thing is killing him right in front of my eyes.

"No. You're going to be okay. You have to be. You *have* to. I need you. I *need* you to be with me."

"I always will be." He closes his eyes, and his hand releases my shirt. He's letting go.

"No! Don't let go." I grasp him tighter. I don't want to believe this is the end. "You're going to make it. You're going to be okay." My vision blurs as the tears spill over my cheeks.

"He's gone," Ebb says to me.

I shake my head. "No."

"Allira, you need help. You've been shot. You're losing a lot of blood."

"No" is all I can say.

Shilah comes over to me and tries to pick me up.

"No!" I yell, gripping onto Chad tighter. My body heaves with sobs.

"Allira, you need to go to Aunt Kenna. Now," Shilah says forcefully.

"No. I need to be with Chad."

"He's gone, Allira. I'm sorry, but he's gone."

I swallow, hard. I look down at Chad's lifeless body, the sticky mess on my arm and body. Some of it's my blood, but most of it is Chad's. This time when Shilah tries to pick me up, I don't fight him. I want to, but I'm too numb to try—mentally and physically—I can't feel my right arm at all.

As Shilah turns to start walking me up the stairs to The Crypt to take me to the hospital wing, I see it. I see what happened. We disarmed everyone from the upper level of The Crypt, but there, slumped in a heap on the left-hand side of the cells, is Lynch. She has a gun in her hand but is no longer moving. She shot me, she killed Chad, and then our side killed her. Justice was served quickly and without hesitation, but it doesn't feel like it's enough.

Suddenly angry, the fury builds inside of me to the point that I feel I need to do something about it. I struggle in Shilah's arms to get free, to do something, *anything*. I need to run back to Chad, shoot Lynch again even though it would be pointless. I need to do something. But instead of breaking free, I surrender to the darkness as red and black spots fill my vision.

CHAPTER
TWENTY-ONE

Distraction. It's amazing how a ten-second slip of concentration means the difference between winning and losing, living and dying. I want to wake up from this nightmare. I want to go back to a world where I'm in Chad's arms, in his bed, by his side. I want him to come back to me.

I open my eyes and see the bright white lights of the hospital room and Drew leaning over me. "Hey," he whispers and smiles. "You had me worried for a moment there."

I look around the room. I'm hooked up to a machine that's monitoring my heartbeat, and it's beeping at an alarmingly fast pace.

"Chad," I manage to choke out, sounding hoarse and gravelly. Drew just looks down and shakes his head. "I was hoping I dreamt it," I say as tears start falling. "What happened?" My memory is hazy. I just remember everything happening so fast. Too fast. One minute he was with me, and the next he was gone.

"Lynch," Drew replies, taking a seat next to my bed. I have a flash of memory, seeing her dead on The Crypt floor. So I was right about it happening that way. "I guess after all the commotion, someone neglected to check her for her weapon." He looks down at his fidgeting hands, trying to hold back tears. "I shot Lynch when I saw her shooting at you. I was so scared I was going to lose you."

Drew saved me? I'm too taken aback by his words to focus on that though—I was never his to lose. I go to open my mouth to say just that, but he puts his hand up to stop me.

"I don't mean that the way you're thinking. You may not have done it intentionally, but you've been the closest thing to a friend I've had in years, maybe even since I first came to this place. If I were to have lost you, I … I don't want to even contemplate that. I have every intention of making sure I become a better person. Everything that I am is because of you, and I'll be forever grateful." He sighs as he leans forwards and takes my hand in his. "I'm really sorry I wasn't quick enough to save Chad too. I wish I could go back, I wish I could bring him back, because … you deserve to be happy."

No, I don't. It's my fault he's dead. I don't say this aloud, even though I know it's the truth. I just nod to Drew and thank him, which I'm pretty sure doesn't even make sense at this point.

'It's not your fault.'

Tate?

The curtain beside my bed is pulled back, and I find Tate in the bed next to mine.

"Sorry. I didn't realise I had a roommate," I say quietly. Is he angry at me? Does he blame me like I blame myself?

'No, I don't blame you, and while I understand your need for self-pity and loathing right now, you're going to have to stop that. None of it was your fault. You did something amazing. You need to remember that.'

I got my boyfriend killed, is what I did. By my count, I got at least eight people killed.

'You paid a price that needed to be paid.'

How can you say that? It's too high a cost to pay. My freedom is not worth that.

'Your freedom might not be, but the freedom of the lives around you? I know it hurts. I've lost Chad twice now—once when Shilah told me he was dead, and then again after being told he was actually alive all this time. I know it's hard, but we're all here for you.'

"Are you guys doing it right now? Talking in your heads?" Drew interrupts. I turn to look at him, a guilty smile plastered on my face. "Shilah was right. That *is* annoying."

"You're awake." Paxton's voice carries from the doorway. He walks in and shakes Drew's hand as he gets up.

"I'll let you guys talk," Drew says, preparing to walk out.

"Come see me later. There are things to discuss," Paxton tells him. Drew leaves and Paxton comes closer, leaning down to kiss my forehead before taking the seat Drew was in.

"Lia!" I hear a little voice yell. A young voice? Only Mum and Aunt Kenna call me that.

I sit up to see a cute, young blonde girl running in and jumping on my bed. "Nuka," I say, smiling, happy to see she's okay and didn't get caught up in the mess.

"Careful, baby girl, don't hurt Allira," Paxton says as Nuka tries to climb higher on the bed. "She's been through a lot." It's at that moment that I realise the "baby girl" he called me earlier in his mind wasn't a form of affection like Tate assumed. If Paxton is so comfortable calling me what he calls his daughter, we have absolutely no issue whatsoever.

"Is it true you got shot?" Nuka asks.

"Nuka!" Paxton exclaims. "I told you not to mention that." He looks at me. "Sorry."

I give a little laugh. "No. It's okay. It's true. I did get shot, right here," I say pointing to my shoulder.

"Did it hurt?" she asks, running her finger over my bandage.

"Nah. I'm strong," I say, flexing my muscles on my good arm. She smiles and I can't help but smile back. I didn't want to tell her the truth that getting shot was the second most painful thing that's ever happened to me.

'Losing Chad is the most painful thing that's ever happened to me, too.' I look over, giving Tate a sympathetic stare.

Shilah comes in at that moment, his eyes full of happiness and tears. He sits on the other side of my bed from Nuka, and suddenly my bed seems to be shrinking by the minute. Shilah leans in and hugs me. I try not to wince from the pain, but I let out an involuntary grunt.

Shilah pulls back but stays sitting on my bed. "Sorry. Does it really hurt?"

"How about I shoot you so you can see for yourself?" I almost get the whole sentence out before I crack a smile. I shake my head. "It's not so bad." *Totally lying.* I hear Tate chuckle in his mind. "Where's Mum and Dad?" I ask Shilah.

"They'll be here soon. You've been out of it for a while," Shilah replies.

"I have? How long?" No one answers me. I try to concentrate on their thoughts. Tate is giving me nothing but static, Nuka has no idea what is going on, Shilah's inner voice is debating whether or not to tell me, but it's Paxton who gives me an answer.

'Three days. Three long, terrifying days.'

"Three days?" I exclaim.

"Paxton!" Tate scolds.

"I'm sorry, I'm not used to having to keep my thoughts to myself like all of you are," he replies.

Aunt Kenna rushes into the room. "What are you all yelling about?" She looks at me and smiles. "Oh good, you're awake," she says relieved. "How are you feeling?"

"A little confused," I reply.

"You lost a lot of blood. It goes with the territory," Aunt Kenna says as she starts fiddling with the machines I'm hooked up to. She grabs a blood pressure cuff from beside the bed and starts to check my stats. "Shilah, can you give me a bit of room here, please?"

"Sure." Shilah gets up from my bed and walks over to Tate, kissing him on the cheek. *'Sorry. I didn't say hello to you yet,'* he tells Tate telepathically.

Tate smiles. "You're forgiven." Shilah brings a chair over to the middle of our beds and sits between us.

Paxton is about to ask who's forgiven for what, before he realises and bites his tongue. *'It's going to be a pain in the ass learning to be around Tate again.'*

"Ha. Welcome to my world," I say to Paxton.

He rolls his eyes and sighs. "Not you, too."

Now it's Mum and Dad's turn to rush in to see me. "You're awake," Dad says, relieved and excited. Mum's eyes fill with tears. "Drew came to tell us, but we didn't believe him."

"Yes, I'm awake. Why does that seem to be a big deal to everyone? I got shot in the shoulder. It's not like I got shot ..." *in the chest like Chad.* I don't finish the end of that sentence out loud.

'Maybe because you've been out of it for three days,' Shilah answers me telepathically.

Oh, right. That, I answer him before remembering he can't

hear me.

A weird silence falls over the room. Everyone's staring at me, all of their thoughts jumbled. They all seem to be worried about telling me something, I just don't know what it is and they're not letting themselves think it either.

"Okay. Someone is going to have to tell me what is going on. What are you all so worried about? What aren't you telling me?"

Aunt Kenna stops taking my stats and goes to join Mum and Dad who are standing at the end of my bed. Shilah and Tate are on my left, holding hands and completely shutting me out of their thoughts. I look to Paxton with hope that he might give it away again. He doesn't. In fact, all he is thinking is that he needs to get Nuka out of here before they tell me anything. Whatever it is, it must be bad.

"Come on, Nuka, we'll leave and let Allira get some rest, okay?" he tells her.

"Okay, Daddy," she replies, jumping off the bed.

"I'll come by and see you later," Paxton says before leaving, Nuka in tow.

"There's something you need to see, Allira," Mum says once they've gone.

Shilah reaches for the remote and turns on the television that's hanging in our room. "What channel should we be on?" he asks.

"It has been playing on repeat on all the news stations," Dad replies.

I'm not used to having a television. We had one in our house when I was an agent with Drew, but I never watched it. We didn't have one in Eminent Falls. We didn't have many luxuries at all, but I liked it that way.

I'm suddenly looking at Paxton looking strikingly handsome and charming sitting behind Brookfield's desk.

"When did this happen?" I ask.

"Two days ago," Shilah replies. "We postponed the press conference by a day to get everything and everyone sorted and organised after …" He doesn't finish his sentence.

On the television, Paxton starts talking. "I address the entire country tonight. My name is Paxton James, and there have been some developments here at the Institute. Developments that not only affect those of us here but every member of society.

"I have worked for the Institute for four years. In my time here, I have seen the level of care of the Defective population go from minimal to downright appalling." The screen flashes to images of The Crypt, of some of the interrogation rooms, even a photo of Tate, almost starved and rotting in his jail cell.

"When was that taken?" I ask.

"I have no idea," Tate replies. "I haven't had a chance to ask Paxton about it yet. He's been too … busy."

"Imprisonment, torture, unmentionable acts against fellow human beings, all at the orders of one Bartholomew Brookfield," Paxton continues.

The screen goes back to Paxton, behind Brookfield's desk. "As of today, Mr. Brookfield will no longer be serving as director of the Institute. I have been his second in command for almost two years, and I've tried endlessly to change the ways of the Institute. That change will start today, in full force.

"The time has now come for the nation to turn a new page by righting the wrongs of the past and moving forward with confidence to the future. A future where we embrace the possibility of new solutions to enduring problems where old approaches have failed. A future based on mutual respect, mutual resolve, and mutual responsibility. A future where everyone and anyone, whatever their origins, are truly equal partners, with equal opportunities and with an equal stake in shaping the next chapter in the history of this great country."

I have a feeling I know this speech. I'm pretty sure he's basically taken an old political speech from years ago and reworded it to fit our situation. It was given by one of our prime ministers back when we were still part of the Commonwealth and not an independent country. It pisses me off that this speech is even useable. How have we not learnt from our past mistakes? Why do we keep doing the same things over and over again?

I focus back on Paxton and his words. "Our law currently dictates that anyone who discovers they are Defective must be brought into the Institute for ongoing treatment. For years this has meant taking away the rights of those born with this defect. We have taken away their homes, their families, and their lives. This practice is going to stop."

My heart starts rapidly beating at his words. I keep my eyes glued to the screen in a surreal euphoric state. It's actually happening.

"Nowhere in the law does it state that Defectives are to be locked away, kept hidden, and taken out of society, even though essentially that is what has happened. This practice began with the founding director of the Institute and was carried on by all of his successors. But it ends with Mr. Brookfield.

As of today, we are implementing a new program. One where Defectives are given their basic human rights back. One where they will not have to live in fear of being caught, and one of equality between the normal and the Defective.

"Defectives will re-join society, they will get jobs, they will live like any other citizen. They will return to the Institute quarterly. They will have their check-ups, their regular counselling treatments, and their safety levels monitored. There is no reason why we cannot live in a society where we are together as one."

"Does that mean what I think it means?" I ask no one in particular. "We're free?"

Everyone smiles and my eyes begin to water. *We did it.* But then their faces drop. There's something else they aren't telling me.

Another news article begins, and as I see the headline and hear the anchor's words, my heart starts racing uncontrollably, the beeping from my monitoring machine reaching a high level of annoying as it beeps faster and faster. "Wanted fugitive Bartholomew Brookfield, still at large."

"Allira, you need to breathe. Calm down," Aunt Kenna instructs, rushing over to me.

"How did this happen?" I ask in a rush.

"When the authorities came to take Brookfield into custody. They went down to the cells where we were keeping him, but when they got there, the door was open. Brookfield was gone," Mum explains.

I look back to the television and catch the news anchor as she gives an update. "If you are contacted by Bartholomew Brookfield, or if you believe you have sighted him, please call the number on your screen. We ask that you not approach him, that he may be armed and dangerous. We will continue to give you updates on this man hunt as it progresses."

"He's gone? But how?" I ask, trembling.

"We don't know," Mum says. "We're thinking at least one, if not more, of those who sided with us might have not been as loyal to us as we first thought."

"Someone let him out?"

* * *

I don't know what happened next. I know there was a lot of uncontrollable crying about Chad, about Brookfield, about everything. Then I remember a hazy, floating feeling as I slipped into unconsciousness.

I come to in an empty room. Well, relatively empty compared to what it was when I fell asleep. Shilah is asleep in the chair between Tate's and my bed. Tate sleeps on his side, facing Shilah. They're still holding hands. I push down the stabbing pain of jealousy at the sight. I really am happy for them but sad that I will never have that again.

I try to regain some composure. What do I know? I know that we took over the Institute. I know that Chad is dead. I was shot and have been unconscious for days. Paxton is now the director of the Institute. We are all free. *We're free*. My brief elation at the thought is ripped away when I remember the other bit. Someone let Brookfield escape. He's out there, somewhere.

"They're going to find him," Tate says reassuringly.

"Sorry. I didn't mean to wake you," I say, startled.

"It's okay. I haven't been sleeping all that well anyway," he says.

"So where do we go from here?"

Paxton's voice comes from the doorway. "You go home. You live your life. You move on," he says.

"I don't even know where home is," I remark, more to myself than anyone else.

Paxton comes to the side of my bed and sits next to me. "Then you make one." He reaches for my hand, and that's when I see it—a confusing blur of a vision.

I'm sitting on a white, modern, *expensive* couch in a lush apartment, overlooking the city. I'm in an amazing emerald green evening dress, my hair curled and styled over one shoulder and … I'm being proposed to … by Paxton. The vision fades before I see my answer.

I end up with Paxton? I unintentionally screw up my face. What the hell?

'What the hell, indeed.'

"You saw that?" I ask Tate.

"I saw what you were thinking."

"Saw what?" Shilah asks.

I didn't even realise he'd woken up. "Have you got your ability back? When?" I ask him. Last I knew, he couldn't see anything.

"I got it back after everything went down. I think you were right—I was too worked up and nervous to concentrate. I was forcing it and it's not something that can be forced. Did you have a vision?"

"I did, but I don't see it coming true anytime soon, if at all. It has to be wrong." I shake my head.

"What did you see?" Shilah asks.

"It's not important," I reply, looking at Tate. *Please let this go. I can't deal with it—not right now.* Even in my thoughts,

I'm pleading. The vision has to be wrong.

Tate just nods. *'Okay.'*

"What's going on?" Paxton asks, still holding my hand.

"Nothing," I say, trying to tell the warmth of my cheeks to go away.

"So any news on Brookfield?" Tate asks Paxton, and I'm relieved for the subject change.

"Not yet. We'll get him, I promise you. I won't let him hurt you," he says to me.

"Me? Why would he be after me?" I ask, confused. "Do you really think he would try something?"

'He already has,' Paxton thinks.

"What?"

"Damn it, Paxton. Get out. You need to leave right now," Tate says. "Shilah, you too. I need to speak with Allira, alone."

"Sorry," Paxton says as Shilah starts dragging him away.

Tate gets out of his bed and comes and lies down next to me in mine.

"The reason you were out of it for three days and the reason I'm your roommate in a practically empty hospital wing is ... well ... we don't know how or who, if it was Brookfield himself or someone working for him, but they slipped you something in your central line. Your aunt is the one who picked up on it, but she was worried she caught it too late. We didn't know if you were ever going to wake up."

"Brookfield tried to … kill me? Why me?"

"We don't think he's only after you. Paxton and Drew aren't safe either. Word has gotten out about you three. Everyone knows it was you who made this happen."

I don't know what to say to that.

"You don't have to say anything."

"So he's just out there, waiting for another chance to kill me?" I ask.

"We'll find him. It will be okay."

"Easy for you to say. You don't have a target on your back."

"You need to look at the bigger picture here, Allira. Brookfield may be gone by now. He may have tried to kill you, but that doesn't mean he'll try again. In fact, he'd be stupid to try. Everyone is looking for him now. Until we see a real threat, I think it's safe to say we have bigger issues to worry about."

"We do?"

"We deserve to revel in the fact that we can walk out of here. We can go into the world and live the life we deserve. I'm not saying it will be all smooth sailing though. We will have to face everyone out there who still thinks we don't deserve this. But Allira, we're free."

ABOUT THE AUTHOR

As a writer, I lead an extremely exciting life. When I'm not base jumping, playing my guitar and singing for a sold-out crowd, or having tea with the queen ... Okay, all of these things are lies.

The truth is, I live on the Gold Coast in Queensland, Australia, with my husband and son and you'll most likely find me with my laptop on my lap and a coffee in my hand.

www.kaylahowarth.com

OTHER WORKS BY KAYLA HOWARTH

RESISTANCE

(Book 2 of The Institute Series)

DEFECTIVE

(Book 3 of The Institute Series)

THROUGH HIS EYES: An Institute Novella

(Book 4 of The Institute Series) EBOOK

EXCLUSIVE

THE LITMUS SERIES

(An Institute Spin off)

LOSING NUKA—Available Now

PROTECTING WILLIAM—Available Now

SAVING ILLYANA—Coming 2017